"Please don't fire us."

Jack pinched the bridge of his nose. They couldn't pretend to like each other for longer than two minutes, even when both of their jobs were at stake. What was this? Kindergarten?

"Fire you?" Colette's brow furrowed. "I'm not following."

"Clearly there's been some confusion. What is it, precisely, that Daphne and I need to make work?"

"Your engagement," Colette said, as if that made a lick of sense.

"Our w-what?" Daphne sputtered. She'd gone deathly pale, those luminous, blue-green eyes of hers huge in her delicate face.

Jack's chest went so fiercely tight that he couldn't breathe. Maybe they'd both heard Colette wrong. Maybe he'd just had some sort of stress-induced auditory hallucination. Maybe he needed to pack up his stapler and his desk blotter and find a new job.

"I beg your pardon?" he manage

Dear Reader,

Welcome back to the glittering world of *Veil*, Manhattan's premier high-fashion bridal magazine! *Faking a Fairy Tale* is book two of the Love, Unveiled series, which follows the romantic entanglements of a group of family members and friends who make up the editorial staff of the magazine. Each book can also be read as a standalone, but if you missed the first— *Her Man of Honor*—you can still pick that one up at any online retailer!

Faking a Fairy Tale is the story of beauty editor Daphne Ballantyne and her work nemesis, fact-checker Jack King. These two have been butting heads since Jack started working at *Veil* five months ago. People are starting to talk...and what they're saying isn't remotely flattering. But when Daphne and Jack are called upon to go undercover and pose as an engaged couple for a series of articles about a bridal etiquette class for Manhattan's elite, they do their best to put their differences aside and get the job done. Things get complicated when Jack's cover is blown, though. Suddenly their private lives get dragged into the charade and playing pretend begins to feel all too real.

Thanks so much for choosing this book. I hope you enjoy Daphne and Jack's love story. Please look out for Love, Unveiled book three, coming this Christmas!

Happy reading,

Teri

Faking a Fairy Tale

———

TERI WILSON

HARLEQUIN

SPECIAL
EDITION

Recycling programs
for this product may
not exist in your area.

ISBN-13: 978-1-335-59421-1

Faking a Fairy Tale

Copyright © 2023 by Teri Wilson

For questions and comments about the quality of this book, please contact us at CustomerService@Harlequin.com.

Harlequin Enterprises ULC
22 Adelaide St. West, 41st Floor
Toronto, Ontario M5H 4E3, Canada
www.Harlequin.com

Printed in U.S.A.

USA TODAY bestselling author **Teri Wilson** writes heartwarming romance for Harlequin Special Edition. Three of Teri's books have been adapted into Hallmark Channel Original Movies, most notably *Unleashing Mr. Darcy*. She is also a recipient of the prestigious RITA® Award for excellence in romantic fiction and a recent inductee into the San Antonio Women's Hall of Fame.

Teri has a special fondness for cute dogs and pretty dresses, and she loves following the British royal family. Visit her at www.teriwilson.net.

Books by Teri Wilson

Harlequin Special Edition

Lovestruck, Vermont

Baby Lessons
Firehouse Christmas Baby
The Trouble with Picket Fences

Furever Yours

How to Rescue a Family
A Double Dose of Happiness

Montana Mavericks: Six Brides for Six Brothers

The Maverick's Secret Baby

Love, Unveiled

Her Man of Honor

Visit the Author Profile page
at Harlequin.com for more titles.

For my Jubilee girls, Kristin, Sharon and Julie.

I can't wait to go back to London and do it again for the coronation!

Chapter One

Fashion closet. Now!

Daphne Ballantyne's glitter-manicured fingertips tapped out the frantic group text as she rushed past a rolling rack full of designer wedding gowns. With her head bent over her phone, a wisp of gossamer-thin, embellished fabric hit her in the face—just another occupational hazard of working at *Veil*, Manhattan's premier bridal magazine.

Daphne brushed the organza aside, stilettos clicking on the smooth marble floor as she rushed toward the fashion closet in a whirl of furious, sparkling indignation. Jack King had done it again, and this time, he'd really gone too far. Daphne was going to lose it, albeit in exquisitely groomed fashion.

As the magazine's beauty editor, it was Daphne's job to keep up with the latest trends in cosmetics, skin care and body care, and Daphne did so with unbridled enthusiasm. Just this morning, she'd added fresh sparkles to her hair with the bedazzling tool that had gone semi-viral online after she'd featured the device in the June issue of *Veil.* She had an appointment after work to get new eyelash extensions. Daphne was in the middle of writing a feature on various lash options for brides and had been offered a trial run from a popular salon in Chelsea that had styles ranging from the demure, understated Blushing Bride all the way to the dramatic Bridezilla. Daphne fully intended to take the Bridezilla lashes for a spin. Go big or go home.

First, though, she had a war to wage right here at *Veil.*

"What happened? Is everything okay?" Addison England, the magazine's deputy editor and one-third of the trio of best friends who called themselves *the* Veil *crew,* was ready and waiting when Daphne stormed into the fashion closet.

Everly England Aston—Addison's younger sister, who'd recently been promoted to features editor—breezed in right on Daphne's heels.

"Of course the pregnant lady is the last one to get here. What did I miss?" Everly asked, gaze swiveling back and forth between Daphne and Addison as she rested a gentle hand on her ever-expanding belly.

"Nothing—" Addison said with a shrug "—*yet.* We just got here too."

The sisters both turned curious eyes on Daphne.

"Spill," they said in unison.

Daphne hadn't expressly stated that she was currently in crisis mode when she'd fired off the group text message. The urgency of her situation had been a given because the words *fashion closet* said it all.

The *Veil* closet was an enormous space within the magazine's sleek, Upper East Side headquarters where articles of clothing that had either been gifted or loaned to *Veil* were stored with meticulous care. Couture wedding gowns and bridesmaid dresses hung from the maze of rolling racks crisscrossing the closet. The walls were lined with shelves upon shelves of designer shoes and custom drawers containing wedding veils stitched from fine organza, illusion tulle and exquisitely crafted Burano lace. Somewhere among the miles of bridal white fluff was a small collection of bespoke men's tuxedos...supposedly. None of the *Veil* crew had actually set eyes on it, but rumors of its existence abounded.

Daphne couldn't remember exactly when or how the fashion closet had become a place of refuge for her, Addison and Everly. But whenever one of them needed a shoulder to cry on or just a place to vent, they gathered on the closet's enormous white silk damask tufted ottoman. It was hard to be upset surrounded by all of those exquisite gowns. Being in the closet always made Daphne feel just a little bit like a princess—even today when she was royally ticked off.

"It's *him*." Daphne fumed. "Again."

"Oh, boy. This is going to take a while, isn't it?" Everly kicked off her Audrey Hepburn-esque ballerina flats and lowered herself onto the ottoman. For a woman who was expecting twins in less than two months, she still moved with an impressive amount of grace.

"What did Jack do this time?" Addison said as she picked an invisible speck of lint from her ivory and black tweed skirt suit.

Was it Daphne's imagination or was her girl gang acting unusually blasé about her state of unease?

Daphne crossed her arms and shot an indignant glance at her friends. "Neither of you seems to be taking this very seriously."

"We are." Everly nodded with a yawn. "*So* seriously."

"I'm going to overlook the yawn because you're with child and all, but you—" Daphne's gaze swiveled toward Addison, who was now inspecting her perfectly polished nails. The color looked like Essie's Ballet Slippers, a favorite of brides the world over. Daphne would've bet her entire paycheck on it. "—Where's your sense of outrage on my behalf?"

"First of all—" Addison raised a single Ballet Slipper-tipped finger "—you haven't even told us what he did yet. And second…"

Everly finished for her. "Jack isn't such a bad person. He sent me a really nice text when my first feature article went live. Everyone in the office seems to like him."

Daphne arched an irate brow. "With one very notable exception."

"Everly is just trying to explain that we don't quite understand why you two can't seem to get along," Addison said.

"This." Daphne slapped the yellow Post-it note she'd been clenching in her fist down onto the ottoman. "*This* is why."

Addison and Everly leaned over the offending square of paper and peered down at it.

Daphne smoothed the creases out of the Post-it until Jack's annoyingly perfect penmanship was clearly legible. Then there they were, his four favorite words in all of the English language.

We can't print this.

Everly frowned. "Did he shoot down another of your articles?"

"Yes, he most definitely did. And this time, he didn't even have the decency to e-mail me an explanation. He just stuck a Post-it on my pages and left them on my chair for me to find first thing this morning." Daphne's head hurt. She couldn't deal with this before her morning cup of coffee.

Although, Addison always joked that Daphne put so much flavored creamer in her brew that it no longer resembled actual coffee. Whatever. All Daphne knew was that there was a cookies-and-cream flavored caffeinated beverage sitting in her cubicle, waiting to be consumed. She just needed to eviscerate Jack King first.

Metaphorically speaking, of course.

"This is the third time he's pulled one of my articles," Daphne said.

"That's really not so bad, Daph." Everly shrugged. "He's been at *Veil* for at least five months by now."

"The third time *this week*," Daphne clarified.

"Ouch." Everly winced. "Point taken."

At long last, Addison cast Daphne a properly sympathetic look. "I can see why that would be frustrating."

She had no idea.

Daphne sighed and glanced from Addison to Everly and back again as she collapsed into a dejected heap on the ottoman. "How many times has he done this to you two?"

"Actually, he's never pulled one of my articles," Addison said.

Everly shrugged. "Me either."

Daphne wanted to scream into one of the white satin ring pillows stacked on the shelf immediately to her right. "You've *got* to be kidding me."

And just like that, she was on her feet again, pacing around the cramped space. For some reason, all the bridal white taffeta, airy organza and shiny little beads were doing nothing to calm her nerves this morning. When couture fashion and a bit of sparkle failed to make

Daphne feel better, she knew there was something seriously wrong.

"He's making me crazy." She threw her arms in the air, narrowly missing a Monique Lhuillier mesh tulle dress with blue floral appliqué.

Daphne paused for a beat to admire it. She *refused* to let Jack steal her appreciation for a wedding dress with a touch of color. If Daphne ever got married, she wanted her gown to look like a designer puff of pastel cotton candy.

Not that she had any intention of walking down the aisle in the foreseeable future. Maybe not ever. Dating was usually a prerequisite to getting married, and Daphne hadn't been on a real date since high school. Plenty of men had expressed interest in the years since, but she had no desire whatsoever to go down that humiliating road again.

"Daph, you know I adore you, but fact-checking is Jack's job," Addison, ever the voice of reason, said. "It's right there in his title—fact-checker. If every word of an article can't be verified, he has no choice but to intervene."

Daphne knew this, of course. She'd been working at *Veil* for a decade already, straight out of high school. She'd started off working the night shift with the cleaning crew while she attended community college classes during the day in Queens, where she'd still lived at home with her dad. The moment she'd set foot in the glamorous office, Daphne knew she wanted to work on the staff someday. She spun stories in her head about the beautiful gowns she spied hanging in the fashion closet while she emptied the trash bins and dusted cubicles. To her father's bemusement, she started reading the Vows section of *The New York Times,* learning everything she could about weddings and bridal fashion. And when the time came to choose a major at school, Daphne selected journalism without the slightest hesitation.

When a receptionist job at *Veil* became available during her junior year, she spent every spare dime she had on a knockoff Chanel suit and all but begged Colette Winter, *Veil*'s editor in chief, for the position during her interview. It paid even less than her cleaning job, but the first time she took a seat behind the magazine's glossy white reception desk, Daphne cried actual tears of joy. She'd done it—she was a *Veil* girl.

She finished her degree by switching to night classes. Three years after taking the receptionist job, she got promoted to an assistant position and she'd been working her way further up the glittery, glamorous ladder at *Veil* ever since. Sometimes she had to pinch herself to believe how far she'd come. Other days, all it took was a simple Post-it note to remind her that, unlike the rest of the staff, she hadn't gone to a fancy Ivy League university or grown up on the Upper West Side.

Perhaps she was reading too much into her ongoing battle with Jack King. Then again, maybe she wasn't.

"I knew it." Daphne felt like crying. Either that or strangling a certain fact-checker. "He's targeting me."

"I really doubt that. Fact-checking is a touchy business. Also—" Addison pulled a face "—you two might want to at least *try* and get along. People are starting to talk."

Daphne blinked. Seriously? Everyone at the magazine loved her. Almost everyone, anyway. "What people?"

"Literally everyone in the building," Everly oh-so-helpfully added. "We've all heard you and Jack arguing about your copy."

"It's only a matter of time until Colette notices, and

you know how she feels about staff members not getting along." Addison bit her lip.

As much as Daphne loathed to admit it, Addison was right. Their editor in chief ran a tight ship, and Colette was fundamentally opposed to anything that disrupted the workplace.

Everly nodded. "If there's one thing Colette hates, it's drama."

"And sensible shoes," Addison said.

"And casual Fridays," Everly added.

Addison arched a knowing eyebrow. "And white after Labor Day."

They were getting way off track. Daphne didn't need help writing a listicle about Colette's likes and dislikes. She needed Jack to leave her alone. Or, preferably, to leave altogether and take a job someplace else—like *Robot Monthly*, maybe, since he had about as much personality as a washing machine.

Daphne had never once seen the man smile. Nor had he ever taken a single bite of the wedding cake samples that popped up from time to time in the break room. What kind of monster didn't like *cake*?

Daphne groaned. "What am I going to do?"

"For right now, I think it's best to just lay low and do whatever it takes to get along with the guy. I know you think he's impossible, but Colette loves him, and the last thing you want is to get on her bad side for any reason whatsoever." Everly shot her a meaningful look. "Trust me on this."

"I hear you," Daphne said. She had, after all, witnessed every painful moment of Everly's recent struggles at work. Colette had even demoted Everly for a while, but Everly had risen to the top, just like cream. Because she loved her job.

Just like Daphne loved hers. She couldn't let Jack ruin things at *Veil* for her. She wouldn't.

"Okay, the new game plan is to smother Jack with sweetness," she said. She couldn't keep bickering with him if everyone in the office was chattering about their feud. It wasn't as if all the quarreling was doing any good, anyway.

Addison's eyes narrowed. "You don't mean smother him in the literal sense, do you?"

"No, of course not." Although the idea wasn't without its appeal.

"Good, just checking," Addison said.

"You should also avoid Colette at all costs until things settle down between you and Jack." Everly folded her arms over her pregnant belly. "Just saying."

Daphne took in a deep breath. "Done."

Then the door to the fashion closet swung open, and Colette's assistant rushed inside. When her gaze landed on Daphne, the assistant's slim shoulders sagged in relief. "Oh, good. Here you are."

"Me?" Daphne's hand fluttered to her heart. She swallowed, fervently hoping there was some invisible person standing behind her.

Alas, there wasn't.

"Yes. You, Daphne." The assistant waved her toward the door. "I've been looking everywhere for you. Colette wants to see you in her office right away."

"Oh, she does? Great." *So, so great.* This couldn't be good. Daphne's legs went wobbly as she stood and smoothed down the front of her retro-inspired dress. The bubblegum pink fabric was decorated with tubes of lipstick and bright red kiss marks. Her career might be on the brink of going down in flames, but at least she'd look cute as it burned.

She shot a parting wave at Addison and Everly, who'd both gone slightly wide-eyed.

Text us, Everly mouthed.

Daphne nodded. *Will do.*

As she followed Colette's assistant toward the editor in chief's office, Daphne concentrated on breathing in and out, just like she'd advised nervous brides to do in the article she'd written last month called "Say I Do to Pre-Wedding Yoga." Jack had made her omit two full paragraphs from that piece, because of course he had.

Stop thinking about him, her subconscious screamed. *He's utterly unimportant to your life or your career.*

That last part wasn't quite true, though. If she wasn't careful, Jack and his irritating pad of Post-it notes could fully torpedo her standing at *Veil*…

But only if Daphne let him.

She took in a ragged, non-yoga-like breath as she passed the cubicle area of the office. A few curious faces swiveled in her direction, and she forced herself to hold her head high. Whatever Colette wanted probably had nothing whatsoever to do with their ongoing feud. The last time Daphne had been unexpectedly summoned to her boss's office, she'd been offered a promotion. *And* a raise. This was probably a good thing. She really needed to stop letting Jack get inside her head.

Except the second she stepped through the doorway of Colette's office, she realized all her efforts to forget about Jack would be futile. He wasn't just in her head…he was right there, sitting across the cream-colored lacquer desk from their boss with his annoying backside planted in one of Colette's white faux fur chairs.

Daphne wished she hadn't noticed that his backside, while every bit as annoying as the rest of him, also looked quite nice in a tailored suit. Unfortunately, she'd come to that realization on his very first day at the magazine. His chiseled face wasn't any less appealing, even though the set of his jaw was typically so hard that it looked as if his pearly white molars could cut coal into diamonds with minimal effort.

Stop thinking about him, she repeated to herself. *And* definitely *stop thinking about his backside.*

What was wrong with her?

Daphne stood rooted to the spot. One thing was clear: this meeting wasn't about a promotion. Quite possibly, it was about the opposite. Colette had certainly demoted people before. If ever there was a time to smother Jack King with kindness, it was right here and now, while the editor in chief was watching.

Jack swiveled in his chair, glittering gray eyes settling on Daphne with a perfectly inscrutable expression. The man was dead inside. She managed to paste a smile on her face, but it felt more like a snarl. Then the corner of his mouth twitched into a reluctant looking half grin. Super. Stony-faced Jack King, lover of obscure facts and hater of cake was *laughing* at her.

Daphne smiled so hard that her head hurt.

What was *he* doing here?

What was *she* doing here?

Jack King blinked against the assault of glitter sparkling at him from Daphne Ballantyne's hair. As per usual, the beauty editor looked like she'd had a run-in with a chandelier on her way to work. Also as per usual, she was glaring at him as if he'd just kicked a puppy.

Jack hadn't kicked a puppy, obviously. Never had and never would. Not that Daphne cared, as she seemed to have somewhat of a loose relationship with actual facts.

"Jack," she said as she took the seat beside him. For

some reason, she appeared to be trying her best to smile at him. Clearly it pained her.

Jack couldn't help feeling the slightest bit amused. Was that an immature reaction? Probably. Then again, Daphne herself hadn't exactly been a beacon of professionalism yesterday when she'd barged into his office, accused him of being a control freak and purposely rearranged his carefully organized office supplies in an attempt to rattle him.

Jack had definitely been rattled. Fine, he could admit it: he liked things orderly and predictable. Was that really such a bad thing? The last time he checked, neatness was a positive trait in the workplace. Daphne might want to try it sometime. Earlier this morning, when Jack tried to stick a Post-it note to her desk, there hadn't been a square inch of available space to affix it to. Her cubicle was filled to overflowing with makeup brushes, cosmetics, hair products and more bottles of hand lotion than he could count. And glitter! Glitter *everywhere.*

Jack had very carefully pressed the Post-it note to her pages and left them on the seat of Daphne's chair. Even so, he'd somehow found himself plucking specks of glitter from his necktie half an hour later.

"Daphne," Jack said to her in return. He stood while she took her seat, because in addition to liking things neat and orderly, Jack also had manners.

"Oh, were you just leaving?" Daphne asked as he towered over her. Her smile suddenly seemed more genuine.

"No." Jack sat back down, spine ramrod straight. "I was simply being polite."

She snorted and then tried to cover it with a cough.

Jack's jaw involuntarily clenched. The woman was a bewitching, bedazzled, thorn in his side. He truly didn't know why he let her get to him the way that she did.

He swiveled to face forward, focusing all of his attention on Colette. Still, Daphne shimmered in his periphery, about as easy to ignore as a disco ball.

"Good morning," Colette said. She folded her hands on the surface of her pristine, cream-colored desk. There wasn't a laptop or even a pen in sight—only a tasteful bouquet of white roses in a vase on the desk's far right-hand corner. Minimalism at its finest. With any luck, Daphne was taking notes.

"Morning, Colette," Daphne gushed beside him.

Jack cleared his throat. "Good day."

A trickle of unease snaked its way up his spine as Colette's gaze flicked back and forth between them. What was the purpose of this meeting, exactly?

"Thank you for coming in. There's something very important I need to discuss with both of you," Colette said.

"Yes, of course," Daphne said.

Jack remained silent. He was beginning to get a bad feeling about where this conversation could possibly be headed.

"How would you say the two of you get along?" Colette asked.

And there it was.

He and Daphne had been hauled into the editor in chief's office like two schoolchildren who'd been ordered to see the principal. Jack didn't know whether to be mortified or furious.

Both.

Definitely both.

This wasn't him. Jack took his job seriously. He didn't engage in petty work squabbles. In prep school, he'd been voted "most likely to become a workaholic," and he'd been the top-ranking student in his class at Yale. His work ethic was legendary.

He was a model employee, damn it. Or he had been…

Until his world had been turned upside down six months ago.

Jack was getting back on track, though. He really was. The only visible cracks in his composure came about when Daphne Ballantyne was in the immediate vicinity.

"We get along great." Daphne beamed at him. "Jack is wonderful. *So* fastidious."

He narrowed his gaze at her, ever so slightly. "Yes, we work very well together. Daphne is undeniably…colorful."

They sat staring at each other for a beat, gazes locked in silent warfare. Then Daphne licked her lips, and Jack's attention strayed toward her mouth—accidentally, of course. But for a strange, nonsensical moment, he couldn't bring himself to look away.

"Good, I'm glad to hear it," Colette said.

Focus, Jack's subconscious ordered. He snapped his head back toward his boss, tugging slightly at his shirt collar.

"Because I have to say, I've sensed a bit of animosity between you a time or two, and this is never going to work if that's the case." Colette held up her hands.

"What?" Daphne sputtered out a laugh. "Animosity? No, absolutely not. Honestly, Colette, I'm not sure where this is coming from. Right, Jack?"

"Correct." He gave a wooden nod. Jack had always been a terrible liar—again, something he'd always considered to be a positive attribute.

Not so, if the momentary spark of fury in Daphne's aquamarine eyes was any indication.

She sighed and turned her gaze back to Colette. "Please don't fire us."

Jack pinched the bridge of his nose. They couldn't

pretend to like each other for longer than two minutes, even when both of their jobs were at stake. What was this? Kindergarten?

"Fire you?" Colette's brow furrowed. "I'm not following."

"You just said this is never going to work if Jack and I don't get along." There was an unmistakable tremor in Daphne's voice that made Jack's body feel leaden all of a sudden. Or maybe that was simply a by-product of his pending unemployment.

"We can make it work," he said, tongue tripping only slightly on the word *we*. As if the very thought of being part of a collective with Daphne was so inconceivable that his mouth refused to cooperate.

"Still not following." Colette shook her head. "At all. Regardless, I have no intention of firing either of you. You both do excellent work."

Daphne's knee, just out of Colette's sight, gave Jack's thigh a sharp nudge. He could practically hear her internal squeal of triumph. *Did you hear that, Jack? I do excellent work.*

He sighed mightily. What was it going to take to get Colette to cut to the chase so he could get out of here? He longed for the solitude of his office, where his stapler was always situated precisely one inch to the left of his leather desk blotter, and he knew exactly what was expected of him from one minute to the next. Fact-checking suited him. Verifying information was black and white, with no room for gray. No room for confusion. No room for surprises or chaos.

Which had a lot to do with why he excelled at it.

"Colette, if I may…" Jack said, ignoring Daphne's invisible eye roll in response to his formality. "Clearly there's been some confusion. What is it, precisely, that Daphne and I need to make work?"

"Your engagement," Colette said, as if that made a lick of sense.

"Our w-what?" Daphne sputtered. She'd gone deathly pale, those luminous, blue-green eyes of hers huge in her delicate face.

Jack's chest went so fiercely tight that he couldn't breathe. Maybe they'd both heard Colette wrong. Maybe he'd just had some sort of stress-induced auditory hallucination. Maybe he needed to pack up his stapler and his desk blotter and find a new job.

"I beg your pardon?" he managed to utter.

"Your engagement," Colette repeated, this time with a sense of finality that settled like a rock in the pit of Jack's gut.

He didn't dare look at Daphne. In fact, he preferred to pretend she didn't exist altogether. Whatever this was couldn't be real. In no universe could Daphne Ballantyne be his fiancée.

"I've chosen the two of you to go undercover for a *Veil* special assignment," Colette said, as if they'd both just won the lottery. Then, oblivious to their mutual suffering, she flashed Jack and Daphne a wink. "Congratulations! You're betrothed."

Chapter Two

"Betrothed," Daphne echoed. She couldn't make sense of the word all of a sudden, as if it was something she'd heard on *Bridgerton* but had no bearing on her very contemporary, very independent-city-girl life. Then with a horrible rush, it came into crystal clear focus.

Betrothed, as in *engaged to be married*.

She gaped in horror at Jack, still sitting beside her in all of his classically handsome glory. He'd always reminded her of old photos of JFK Jr., complete with the amazing hair, smoldering gaze and classic New England vibe. Daphne just knew there was a burgundy sweatshirt with the word "Harvard" emblazoned across it hanging in his closet.

Not that Daphne had the first clue whether or not Jack had ever set foot in Cambridge, Massachusetts. That was just a technicality, as far as Daphne was concerned. She'd bet her yellow patent leather Kate Spade taxicab flats on the fact that there was a trust fund and an Ivy League diploma somewhere with his name on them. Jack just had that affluent, well-bred vibe about him—minus every single drop of JFK Jr.'s legendary charm.

"To *him*?" Daphne blurted before she could stop herself. She felt like she might be sick.

I'm willing to do a lot of things for this job but marrying my work enemy isn't one of them.

"That's what I had in mind," Colette said, glancing back and forth between them. "Honestly, I expected you two to be thrilled about this. Didn't you hear the part about going undercover?"

"Yes, but…" Daphne said.

Jack talked over her, because of course he did. "I really don't think…"

Colette held up a hand, silencing them both. "Let's go over the details, shall we? And then you can thank me."

Thank her? Daphne fought the urge to laugh out loud. The struggle was real.

"The Plaza Hotel has started a new etiquette class for engaged couples called Elegantly Engaged. It began with very little fanfare, almost as if the hotel was trying to keep it a secret. For the past few months, the news has been spreading like wildfire, solely through word of mouth, among upper-crust Manhattan," Colette said.

Daphne tried to tell herself she was simply imagining things when her boss's gaze flitted toward Jack as her mouth formed the words *upper-crust*, but there was no denying it. She was staring straight at the buttoned-up fact-checker. It was suddenly as if Daphne was no longer part of the conversation.

"Perhaps you've heard of it?" Colette said, raising her brows as her attention homed in on Jack's cuff links. They were silver with interlocking *C*s, just like the Cartier logo.

Daphne had never darkened the door of the famous

jewelry store, but the company purchased ad space regularly in *Veil*. One didn't need to be born with a silver spoon in one's mouth to recognize a pair of cuff links that probably cost more than Daphne's rent.

She cleared her throat, desperate to once again be an active member of the discussion.

Why? You don't want to have anything to do with this, remember?

Oh, she remembered. But if she was going be cut out of the conversation, she wanted it to be on her own terms. Not because the other participants thought she didn't have something valuable to contribute simply because the term *upper-crust* usually made her think of a loaf of bread instead of the social register.

"I've heard of the Elegantly Engaged class. In fact, I know someone who attended it," Daphne said.

Jack turned dubious eyes on her. Seriously? Was it really so hard to believe that Daphne knew people who ran in posh, well-mannered circles?

She glared at him as Colette asked her to elaborate.

"Perfect. Do tell," her boss said.

"One of the regulars at the blowout bar I frequent took the class with her fiancé," Daphne said.

Okay, so maybe she didn't actually know the woman personally. That shouldn't have mattered, though, since she'd talked about the class in great detail for the duration of her hair appointment in a voice loud enough to be heard over a dozen high-powered blow-dryers.

Jack's expression went from dubious to full-on disbelief.

"Why are you looking at me like that?" Daphne asked through a tight smile. "Do you think I'm making this up?"

His gaze flitted to the sparkles in her hair. "Not at all. I was just under the assumption that you did all that—"

he waved a hand, encompassing her entire head "—yourself."

Daphne's cheeks burned with the heat of a thousand high-end curling wands. This was never going to work. She and Jack would *never* pass as an engaged couple.

"I think we're getting off track again," Colette said. Her left eye was beginning to twitch like it had the time when her favorite bridal fashion designer decided to show an entire collection of black gowns during Bridal Fashion Week.

Daphne winced. "Sorry."

Why was *she* apologizing when Jack had been the one to bring up her hair? *He* should be the one groveling, not her.

She snuck a sideways glance at him only to find that he didn't look sorry in the slightest. In fact, he appeared to be bored out of his mind. Daphne wondered what he could possibly be thinking about—something riveting like his beloved office supplies, no doubt—and then she wondered why on earth she cared.

In true Colette form, she dispensed with the chitchat and got down to the nitty-gritty. "I've arranged for you to attend Elegantly Engaged as a couple. The class is on Friday evenings from seven to nine o'clock. The program lasts for four weeks. The two of you will attend, undercover of course, and cowrite a feature article every week describing the experience. The articles will run just under the masthead on the *Veil* digital site first thing on each subsequent Monday morning."

Daphne raised her hand. "This sounds like an amazing opportunity, but why us?"

Jack was a fact-checker. He didn't do any actual writing. And while Daphne was undeniably flattered to be offered such a major assignment—despite the involvement of the most annoying man she'd ever encountered—she didn't write serious pieces like this. Case in point: she was currently halfway through an article on flavored lip gloss as bachelorette party favors.

"Because the two of you are perfect for this. Daphne, you're one of the most talented writers on staff with the added benefit of being a total chameleon. You're constantly changing your look," Colette said.

True, but she was the beauty editor. She played with eyelash extensions and colored her hair for fun, not subterfuge.

"All of our other lead writers and editors are too recognizable. They'd never get away with going undercover." Colette waved a finely-manicured hand toward Daphne's mortal enemy. "Jack's previous experience as a features writer at *Sports World* will be immensely helpful. And with his current position as a fact-checker, he's virtually anonymous. I doubt anyone even knows he's on staff at *Veil*."

Daphne blinked. *Sports World?* She didn't realize Jack had ever worked there. What kind of reporter decided to go from writing features to working as a fact-checker?

She slid her gaze toward Jack just in time to see him shake his head. A fascinating knot was beginning to form in his finely sculpted, all-American jaw. "Evenings aren't good for me."

"Excuse me?" Colette tilted her head. Her signature chin-length bob hairstyle didn't budge.

"I have a…" Jack paused for a beat. "…dog."

"Is it a golden retriever?" Daphne asked before she could stop herself. She could see it now: Jack frolicking with a pedigreed golden on the emerald green lawn of Sheep Meadow in Central Park. They'd look like they walked right off the pages of a J. Crew catalogue. So predictable. "It is, isn't it?"

Jack ignored her question, but the way the knot in his jaw flexed told her that he'd definitely heard it.

"And what do you do with this dog during business hours?" Colette said. Her bob quivered in indignation.

Had Jack lost his mind? No one said no to Colette. It just wasn't done. Daphne realized he was relatively new to *Veil*, but five months was definitely enough time to realize how things worked around here.

"She has a nanny," Jack said without even flinching. He had guts. Daphne would give him that.

Still, she stifled a laugh. *A nanny?* She hadn't pegged him as the type to have an overly pampered pooch that required a dog nanny, of all things. She tried to picture him with a small fluff-ball of a dog or a Frenchie, perhaps.

Nope. Daphne's money was still on the golden.

"A nanny," Colette repeated slowly, eyes narrowing into slits.

Daphne gave Jack's leg another bump with her knee under the desk—hard enough that he emitted a muffled *oof* sound. Good. He needed to get a hold of himself. As much as she loathed the idea of pretending to be his fiancée, she *refused* to let him ruin this opportunity for her.

"I meant a sitter," Jack corrected. "A dog sitter."

No one said a word for long, awkward moment. Under any other circumstance, Daphne would have relished the chance to witness her nemesis in the hot seat. But clearly Colette already saw them as a team, and Daphne wasn't about to let him drag her down with him.

"I'm sure Jack would be happy to ask his sitter to work a little overtime on Friday nights," Daphne said brightly. She turned what she hoped was a dazzling-yet-sinister smile on Jack. "Wouldn't you?"

His eyes met hers, and for some ridiculous reason, Daphne's heart leaped straight to her throat. She told herself that the only reason for the goose bumps that skittered over her flesh was because—as crazy as it seemed—Jack suddenly held her professional future in his hands. Coauthoring an important series like this could mean a promotion and maybe even a bonus. But she wasn't altogether sure that the truth was really so simple, especially when his gaze hardened and he looked away again.

"Apologies," he said to Colette. "But as...*interesting*... as this opportunity sounds, I'm going to have to decline."

"He said *what*?" Addison gaped at Daphne over the top of her martini class later that evening as Daphne gave her *Veil* girls the debrief of her meeting with Colette and Jack.

Since today was Thursday, there was only one place in Manhattan where Daphne, Addison and Everly would possibly be. Martini Night at Bloom, a chic bar tucked into a posh residential area just around the corner from the *Veil* offices, had been their private little tradition for several years now. Daphne loved the neighborhood. With their intricate iron fretwork and decorative molding, the rows of beaux-arts-style townhomes reminded her of a fancy, three-tiered layer cake piled high with swags of frosting. Bloom was the perfect spot on the perfect street for their weekly girls' night, made even more perfect by the specialty cocktail that the bar's owner had created just for them—the wedding cake martini.

Daphne closed her eyes and took a sip of hers. How whipped-cream-flavored vodka, pineapple juice and vanilla vodka could combine to taste exactly like a slice of bridal-white wedding cake was a mystery she couldn't begin to fathom, but she was certainly a fan.

Jack would probably despise this, she thought as she took another decadent swallow. *Hater of baked goods that he is*.

"Earth to Daphne." Addison's voice dragged Daphne's eyes open. "I just asked you a question."

"Oh, right." Daphne set her glass down. She almost wished she hadn't brought up the meeting. She was tired of thinking about her nemesis. Tired of picturing him at home with his pampered dog. Tired of wondering what would possess him to turn down the opportunity to cowrite an entire series of feature articles instead of combing through pages and pages of print looking for factual inaccuracies.

You, her subconscious screamed. *He turned it down because it meant he'd have to spend time outside the office with* you.

"He said—and I quote—'evenings aren't good for me. I have a dog.'" Daphne's face burned with humiliation every time she revisited those nonsensical words. Honestly, if he couldn't come up with a better excuse, he probably wouldn't be able to write his way out of a paper bag. She was better off without him.

As if she hadn't known as much before she'd ever set foot in Colette's office.

"I don't get it." Addison shook her head. "That doesn't make sense. Even Everly wouldn't turn down a plum assignment like that to stay home with her dog, and the last time I was over at her and Henry's apartment, she had Holly watching an animated squirrel video on an iPad."

"Hey, I'm sitting right here," Everly said, pouting into her virgin wedding cake martini. "And Holly Golightly has separation anxiety. Her iPad soothes her when I'm away."

Daphne bit back a smile. "*Her* iPad? Are you telling

us that your Cavalier King Charles spaniel has her own smart tablet?"

"Maybe." Everly lifted her chin and then let out a sigh. "Yes, actually. She does. Don't judge me."

Daphne held up her hands. "You do you, girl. We all love Holly. No judgment."

Except for the part where they would be judging Jack King. The flimsy dog excuse was a total lie. Daphne just knew it.

"Why him, anyway? I don't get it." Addison's forehead puckered. "Colette hasn't breathed a word to me about any of this."

"It's supposed to be top secret, so maybe don't mention it to her." Daphne pulled her phone out of her handbag and typed Jack's name into the Google search bar. "And speaking of why him, I just remembered something Colette said earlier. She casually mentioned that Jack used to be a features writer for *Sports World*."

If she hadn't been worried about Jack catching her googling him at her cubicle, Daphne would've left the meeting and gone straight to her desk to conduct a thorough internet deep dive into this matter. She'd rather die than let him know she was curious about his background, though—especially now that she knew what lengths he'd go to just to get out of having to spend time with her outside the office.

"Oh, wow," she said as a whole string of links to high-profile feature articles flashed onto the screen. "Look at this."

She slid the phone across the table toward Addison and Everly. They both bent over it, eyes wide.

"Wait a minute. Jack is a sportswriter? Did this just slip my mind because I have pregnancy brain, or are you two as surprised by this as I am?" Everly asked.

"Stunned," Daphne said.

Addison nodded. "Utterly shocked."

"Then what's he doing working as a fact-checker?" Everly twirled the stem of her glass. Her nails were painted Tiffany blue, her favorite color. "At a bridal fashion magazine of all places?"

Daphne arched a brow. "That's the million-dollar question, isn't it?"

Who *was* Jack? Who was he, really?

"Maybe he quit because his high-pressure job interfered with his relationship with his dog," Addison said with a snort. "It looks like he traveled a lot to cover away games."

"Did you say evenings weren't good for him?" Everly slid the phone back toward Daphne. "Because there are dozens of photos of him sitting front row at Madison Square Garden covering the Knicks games, and I'm pretty sure they play in the evenings."

They most certainly did. Daphne's dad was always glued to television whenever the Knicks played.

"So he lied. I *knew* it." She glared at the images lighting up her phone screen and drained her martini glass. Like magic, Ron the bartender appeared and placed another one in front of her.

Daphne thanked him, and once he was out of earshot, she gestured to her friends with her drink. "Why can't more men be like Ron?"

Addison raised a brow. "You want Jack to serve you wedding cake martinis at your desk?"

"No. I simply want him to be kind," Daphne said. Although a martini every now and then wouldn't hurt. Anything cake-flavored, really. "He made up a whole story about a needy dog just so he wouldn't have to work with me."

Everly held up a hand. "Now, hold on. We don't know that for sure."

"He hasn't worked for *Sports World* in months. There could be any number of reasons he said no." Addison said.

"Right, because people tell Colette no all the time." Daphne gestured to the world at large. No one said no to their boss. She was a legend in publishing, and when Colette said jump, people normally asked how high.

Everly bit her lip and swiveled her gaze toward Addison. "Daphne has a point."

"I suppose you kind of do, Daph." Addison sighed. "Although, anyone who can stand up to Colette definitely has a mind of his own. It's actually sort of…"

"Do *not* say hot." Daphne shook her head so hard that one of the rhinestones in her hair flew off and landed in her drink with a tiny splash.

"Fine. I won't." A smile danced on Addison's lips. "But you can't stop me from thinking it."

Daphne dropped her head in her hands. It was official: everything about this day was a complete and total disaster—except for the Bridezilla lash extensions. They were *perfection*. She'd made a beeline to the salon in Chelsea the instant she'd finished her lip gloss article and she'd arrived at Bloom earlier with eyelashes so long and lush that she felt a breeze coming off of them every time she blinked.

"You can't possibly be serious," Daphne said when she finally looked up and met Addison's gaze again.

Addison never commented on the attractiveness of men at the office. Or at any function that was remotely connected to *Veil*. It was like she had blinders on when it came to the magazine. Work first, everything else a distant second—especially when it came to romance.

"I'm a professional. I'd never even think about dating him. But come on, Daphne." Addison's gaze narrowed. "Surely you've noticed that the man is attractive."

"Oh, she's noticed," Everly said.

Daphne wanted to disappear beneath their high-top table, eyelashes and all. "I have no idea what you're talking about."

"Please." Everly licked the sugared rim of her mocktail. "I've seen you staring at him. A lot."

"You're mistaking fury for attraction," Daphne said. She reached for her glass, but it was empty again already. Funny how that had happened so quickly.

"Too bad you can't find out if he does, in fact, have a dog. Then you'd know precisely how furious you should be," Everly said.

Daphne sat up a little straighter. "I like that idea."

She liked it a lot. At that precise moment, with two wedding cake martinis sloshing around her otherwise empty stomach, Daphne could think of nothing more important than finding out if Jack was telling the truth about his supposedly needy dog.

"What idea?" Everly's forehead puckered. "All I said was that it was too bad you didn't know if he actually has a dog."

"Exactly." Daphne slid off her bar stool and reached for her purse. "Let's go."

Addison and Everly exchanged a glance that seemed somewhere between amused and horrified.

"Put the Chanel bag down," Addison said slowly, as if talking to a spooked horse. "We're *not* about to go stalk one of our coworkers."

Daphne's bag wasn't actually Chanel. It was a knock-off, just like all of her other handbags. Addison only thought it was real because Colette had gifted all of the editors on staff genuine, quilted Chanel bags for Christmas last year. Daphne's had been the softest, supplest pink leather that she'd ever felt. It had nearly killed her to list the bag on a resale site the following day, but she'd had no choice. Her dad had needed shoulder surgery last winter, and the cost of that bag had covered every bit of his co-pay, plus a new recliner for him to enjoy during his recovery. She'd nearly been able to spring for a new flat-screen for him as well.

Daphne couldn't tell her friends that, though. She knew them well enough to know that they'd never judge her, but old habits die hard. Daphne had been struggling to fit in for her entire life. If her *Veil* girls had noticed that she'd replaced the gift from Colette with a knockoff she'd picked up on Canal Street, they'd been kind enough to pretend otherwise.

Daphne's heart swelled with affection for her *Veil* crew. This job was the best thing that had ever happened to her. Then she remembered Jack King's fancy Cartier cuff links and got mad all over again.

"Don't think of it as stalking. We're simply going to do a little…" Daphne weighed her next words carefully "…*fact-checking.*"

She grinned triumphantly. Who could argue with that logic?

"Good one." Everly laughed.

"It will be easy as pie. We'll just go over to his building and sneakily wait around outside to see if he walks his alleged dog." Daphne shifted her weight from one stiletto-toed foot to the other. Why weren't her friends getting up?

"I hate to tell you this, but that is the literal definition of stalking," Addison said.

Everly let out a laugh. "And don't take this the wrong way, but it also sounds a little crazypants."

Daphne cast her a pointed look. "Says the woman with a subscription to *DOGTV*."

Everly's mouth turned down into a pout. "I thought you said no judgment."

"That was before you two started judging *me* for simply wanting to check Jack's pitiful dog excuse for factual accuracy." Daphne jammed her bag under her arm with a tad too much force.

Addison's brows raised. "Aren't you forgetting something? You don't even know where Jack lives."

"I do." Everly sat up a little straighter. "Sort of, anyway. I almost forgot—I've bumped into him a few mornings right around the brownstone and every time, he was all dressed up for work. He must live close by. If he's got a dog, he's sure to go to the same dog park where I take Holly. Everyone in the neighborhood walks their dogs there."

"Perfect." Daphne flashed a triumphant grin.

Addison's brow furrowed. "Then why haven't you seen him there when you've visited the dog park with Holly?"

Daphne's point, éxactly.

"Because *there is no dog*," she said.

"I can't have any part of this whatsoever if I expect Colette to promote me to editor in chief one day. You two have fun." Addison bit her bottom lip and frowned down at her empty martini glass. "Christmas will mark her thirty-fifth anniversary as head of the magazine. That's longer than Anna Wintour has been editor in chief at *Vogue*. She *is* going to retire at some point, isn't she?"

"Of course she is," Everly said.

Daphne wasn't so sure. Colette lived for the magazine. But if she ever did make the decision to step down from her position and entrust *Veil* to someone else, that person would certainly be Addison. No question.

"You're right. When Colette promoted me to assistant editor in chief, she told me she planned on retiring once she hit her thirty-five-year milestone. If she changed her mind since then, she would've mentioned it to me by now. The three of us are going to be running that place some-day—someday *soon*." Addison narrowed her gaze at the two of them. "So please don't do anything too crazy to-night, okay?"

"You worry too much. It's a dog park. Trust me, literally nothing exciting happens there. It's not like we're going to be spying on the man through his apartment windows." Everly gave Daphne a little nudge. "Right?"

Daphne nodded. "Of course not."

Although as the saying went, all was fair in love and war.

Chapter Three

"This might have been a bad idea." Daphne crossed her legs as she sat on a park bench beside Everly.

Correction—a *bark* bench, as it was cheekily labeled by a gold plaque with engraved lettering. The Upper West Side didn't mess around when it came to their pampered pooches. Everly's dog park was nicer than any children's playground Daphne had seen in the neighborhood where she'd grown up in Queens. Posh surroundings notwithstanding, Holly Golightly the Cavalier King Charles spaniel sat perched on Everly's lap instead of setting paw on the neatly manicured ground.

Everly stroked the dog's furry back with one hand while the other rested on her baby bump. "A bad idea? Why do you say that?"

"Because we've been here an hour, and Jack and his imaginary dog are nowhere to be seen." Daphne peered into the horizon.

Antique lampposts dotted the small park, casting an

elegant glow over the area. In the span of time since she and Everly had stopped by Everly's brownstone to pick up Holly and commenced with their stakeout, they'd spied two toy poodles, half a dozen Frenchies and one medium-sized shaggy dog of dubious heritage. That was it—not a golden retriever or a stupidly handsome fact-checker in sight.

"Maybe that means you're right and there is no dog." Everly yawned. It only took a millisecond for Holly to do the same, emitting a cute little squeak as she did so.

"This doesn't actually prove he was lying, though," Daphne said. She hadn't thought through the logistics of this ill-fated effort. She hadn't been thinking at all, actually. This entire escapade had been fueled by wedding cake martinis and rage. "It's official—I'm a terrible stalker. The worst ever."

"Who, exactly, are you stalking?"

The voice came from behind, and it nearly made Daphne fall off the bark bench. It was also annoyingly familiar, although the shiver that coursed through her at the sound of it was undoubtedly the most annoying thing of all.

She flew to her feet, wobbling a bit on her stilettos. High heels at a dog park—yet another bad decision. "Jack."

Daphne's nemesis stood just behind the bench, close enough to have heard every word she'd just uttered. Clearly.

"Oh, hi, Jack. Fancy meeting you here." Everly stood and placed Holly on the ground. The Cavalier immediately scrambled to greet the dog sitting stoically at Jack's loafered feet—a golden retriever, just as Daphne had predicted.

"Really? Because we run into each other quite often

in the mornings. I can only assume you knew I lived in the neighborhood." Jack tilted his head as he spoke to Everly, but his gaze never left Daphne's. It burned into her, all-seeing, all-knowing.

Daphne's heart hammered in her chest. She longed for the ground to open up and swallow her whole. Or better yet, a fairy godmother to come along, wave a magic wand and make all of this go away, starting with the smug expression on Jack King's face.

He knew exactly what she was doing there. His dog probably did too.

Daphne swallowed hard.

Busted.

You are so busted. Jack bit back a smile. He'd never seen Daphne Ballantyne squirm like this before. It was rather amusing.

"Um." Everly's eyes flitted from him to Daphne and back again.

Daphne appeared to pull herself together and managed to turn a glittering smile on her friend. "Everly, why don't you go ahead and take Holly home? I know you're both exhausted."

Everly cast a wary glance at Jack. "Are you sure?"

"Seriously?" Jack arched a brow. "I'm the stalk*ee* in this scenario, not the stalk*er.* How could that possibly make me the dangerous party?"

"Point taken. See you both tomorrow." Everly gave them a wave and then headed toward the dog park's gate with Holly prancing merrily alongside her.

Daphne watched her friend go, and when she once again focused on Jack, her shoulders were squared, ready for battle. Ah, there she was. The Daphne Ballantyne he knew and loved—ironically speaking, obviously.

"I knew it would be a golden retriever," she said, and her lips pursed just enough to draw Jack's attention straight to her mouth.

Crushed strawberries. His pulse kicked up a notch. He really wished she hadn't written that article about flavored lip gloss that he'd had to fact-check at the end of the day. Now he knew exactly what that obstinate mouth of hers would taste like.

He cleared his throat. "What are you doing here, Daphne?"

"What's your dog's name?" she asked, ignoring his question altogether. It was just as well. They both knew exactly why she was there.

"Buttercup," Jack said flatly.

At the sound of her name, the dog's thick tail swished back and forth against the trimmed grass and her big pink tongue lolled out of the side of her mouth.

Those strawberry lips of Daphne's twitched, like she was doing her level best not to smile. "Cute. I would've guessed something more along the lines of Chilton or Choate or Rory."

Jack snorted. "She's a dog, not a character on *Gilmore Girls.*"

"Is that what you do all those evenings you insist on spending at home—watch *Gilmore Girls* reruns?" she asked, and this time there was a definite bite to her tone.

Jack's annoyance flared. Was it not enough that he had to deal with this woman each and every workday? Finding her here was like having a glitter bomb dropped right in the middle of his personal life. "If you have something to say, just come out and say it, Daphne. I don't have time to sort through all of this fluff in search of the point."

He needed to get back upstairs to his apartment. *Now*—not ten minutes from now, not five minutes from now, but immediately. Unfortunately, Buttercup hadn't even done her business yet.

Daphne's mouth dropped open as he bent to unclip his dog's leash from her collar. "Was that a dig at my writing?"

Buttercup trotted toward her favorite leafy corner of the park, oblivious to Jack's suffering. *Man's best friend, my foot.* "I didn't say a word about your writing. You clearly came here looking for me, so you've got to have some sort of agenda. Let's hear it."

She crossed her slender arms and blinked at him with eyelashes that looked as though they'd somehow tripled in size since he'd last seen her just a few hours ago.

He took a step closer to her, his body going rigid as the lush scent of strawberries and cream washed over him. "Cat got your tongue?"

Her cheeks flushed a lovely shade of pink, but she held her ground and lifted her chin to fully meet his gaze. "Tell me why you won't work with me."

He shot her a look. *Aside from the obvious?* She didn't like the idea of working together any more than he did.

"I know there's something you're not telling me. I came here to prove that your ridiculous dog excuse was a lie," she said.

Jack cast a pointed glance at Buttercup, writhing around on her back in the grass a mere three feet away. "And yet all you've discovered is that I do, in fact, own a dog."

"Buttercup seems very well-adjusted. I'm sure she'd survive for a few hours on her own." Daphne shrugged one shoulder. "You could always get her an iPad and a subscription to *DOGTV.*"

"Have you been drinking?" Who on earth bought smart devices for their dog?

"What? No." Somehow, beneath the heft of those lashes, Daphne managed to roll her eyes.

"Now who's lying?" Jack said. He knew all about Daphne and her friends and their weekly Martini Night. Everyone in the office did.

"I had one teensy wedding cake martini." She held up one finger, then added another. "Okay, maybe it was two, but that was hours ago."

Jack shuddered to think what a cocktail with that name tasted like. "That's not a real drink."

"And what do you consider a real cocktail? Wait…" Her eyes danced. He was getting used to the dramatic eyelashes. Heaven help him, he actually sort of liked them. "Let me guess. You prefer an old-fashioned."

Jack's jaw clenched. First the dog, now his drink. Was he that obvious?

"Did it ever occur to you that you might not know me as well as you think you do?"

"So it's not an old-fashioned then?" She tilted her head and long blond curls cascaded over her shoulders, rhinestones twinkling in the darkness.

Jack blew out a tense breath. He refused to be blinded by Daphne's dazzling light. She'd just admitted to *stalking* him, and somehow, he'd become the one on trial for everything from his choice of dog to his preferred happy hour beverage.

"Nice try, but you're veering way off course again. I could report this little visit to HR, you know," he said. Just like he could've reported the various temper tantrums involving the rearrangement of the items on his desk.

Come to think of it, why hadn't he?

"Fine." Daphne crossed her arms. At the mention of HR, a bit of the fight had gone out of her, and a nonsensical stab of disappointment hit Jack square in the chest. "Look, I really want that undercover assignment. It's important to me, and since I apparently can't do it without you…"

She looked him up and down, and her flush deepened ever so slightly. The ache in Jack's chest burrowed deeper, changing into something else entirely—something that felt far too much like attraction.

Nope. Not going there.

He averted his gaze and focused on Buttercup, who'd begun chasing after the colorful autumn leaves that fell from the trees overhead.

But then Daphne spoke again, and this time, there was a tenderness in her tone that made it impossible to look away. "I'm asking you to please, *please*, reconsider."

Their eyes met, and Jack sensed that at long last, he was getting a glimpse of the real Daphne Ballantyne— the woman beneath the glitz and sparkle. Passionate. Determined. And perhaps a bit more vulnerable than Jack had realized.

It was that hint of vulnerability that did him in. He'd figured that somewhere underneath all the glitter, there was more to Daphne than the Disney princess she appeared to be on the outside. No one was that talented… that confident…that *perfect*. Which was precisely why Jack kept engaging in their twisted little office games. As crazy as it seemed, a part him liked knowing that he got under her skin as much as she got under his.

This was different, though. This wasn't a game.

This was real.

Jack didn't have room for anything else real in his life. He'd had about as much reality as he could take lately, and he had no business signing on for anything that would take up his Friday nights for the next four weeks.

Free time didn't exist anymore. If it had—or if he still had any semblance of a personal life—he'd still be working for *Sports World*. He didn't even have time to be standing here in the park having this bonkers conversation.

"Please," Daphne said again, and her teeth sank into her plush, strawberry-flavored bottom lip. Jack was a dead man. "Do this for me, and I'll never rearrange your desk again. I'll never push back on any of your fact-checking at all. I'll even let you take the lead on the pieces we cowrite about the etiquette class. Whatever you say, goes."

Jack didn't believe her for a hot second. Still, he couldn't force himself to say no. Not quite.

"I'll think about it."

Chapter Four

Early the following morning, Jack returned to the scene of the crime—the crime being stalking, and Daphne being the perpetrator.

Buttercup tugged on her leash all the way to the dog park, panting up a storm. Jack broke into a jog in an effort to keep up, inspecting every shrub, tree and hedge along the way, half expecting Daphne to pop out from behind one of them. Even after he'd closed the dog park's iron gate behind him and let Buttercup off her lead to romp around the dewy grass, Jack kept an eye out for her glossy strawberry lips and mammoth-sized eyelashes. Thankfully, it appeared as though he and Buttercup had the place to themselves.

Jack squinted at the sunrise as light poured between the surrounding skyscrapers like liquid gold. It was barely 7:00 a.m. The nanny had arrived just moments ago and was busy making breakfast for her charge. It was no wonder Daphne wasn't here. She didn't strike Jack as an early riser. It probably took hours every morning just for her to choose an outfit and bedazzle her hair.

Jack blew out a breath as Buttercup pounced into a pile of red and orange maple leaves. Regret nagged at him, despite the early morning calm. He should've never told Daphne he'd reconsider the undercover assignment. When he'd told her he'd think about it, she'd taken his answer as a yes. He'd seen it in the way her blue-green eyes had glittered at him and in her beaming, princess-like smile. She'd probably gone straight home and written an outline for their first article.

A pledge to think about it wasn't the same thing as an unqualified yes, though. Not in this case, anyway.

Jack *had* thought about it, as promised. And his answer was the same as it had been when Colette first suggested the ridiculous arrangement. He'd just gotten his new life somewhat on track. There was no reason whatsoever to toss a fake engagement into the mix. For a moment or two, standing opposite Daphne Ballantyne in the moonlight, he'd thought maybe…just maybe…

But Jack had come back to his senses in the cold light of day. There was no way he was going to parade around the Plaza and pretend he was engaged to Daphne. Word would get around. In the social circles Jack's family ran in, it always did. A charade like that could have real-life consequences. He'd tell Daphne to count him out the minute he got to the office. If she wasn't at her desk when he got in, he'd scrawl it on a Post-it. That should put an effective end to the discussion if past history was any indication.

"Buttercup, let's go." Jack let out a whistle, and the golden promptly ignored him, transfixed by a squirrel flicking its tail at her from a nearby tree branch.

Jack sighed and walked toward the rambunctious dog,

leash in hand. He'd taken no more than three strides when
the cell phone in the pocket of his suit jacket rang. His
footsteps paused and he sighed again.

Only one person called him this early in the morning.

Jack briefly considered letting the call roll to voice
mail, but then thought better of it. His mother was relentless. If he didn't answer now, she'd keep calling until
he picked up.

He pulled the phone from his pocket and held it up to
his ear. "Good morning, Mother."

"Good morning, darling," his mom said in a singsong
voice.

Eleanor King sounded unusually chipper—always a
bad sign. Jack braced himself for whatever was coming.

"I haven't interrupted anything important, have I?
You're just so busy these days," she said.

It's called working for a living...among other things.

"I'm at the dog park with Buttercup," he said tersely.

Bored with the squirrel, the dog trotted toward Jack
and dropped a filthy tennis ball at his feet. It smelled
horrendous. There was no telling where she'd found it.

"You still have that dog?" His mother tut-tutted on the
other end of the phone. "She's going to wreak havoc on
your interior decorating. You know that, right?"

They'd been over this before, and Jack's leather sectional sofa was indeed sporting a brand-new hole in one of
its cushions. But that was Jack's problem, not his mother's.
Every time he looked at that hole, every time he stepped
on a jagged, half-gnawed rawhide bone with his bare feet
and every time Buttercup knocked something over with
her thick, bushy tail, Jack reminded himself of all the
times he'd begged his parents for a dog when he was a kid.
Some things were more important than what his apartment looked like from the outside looking in.

"Buttercup is here to stay," he said simply. Then he bent and picked up the disgusting tennis ball with two fingers. He tossed it toward the other side of the park and the golden scampered after it.

God help him, he was going to have to brush the dog's teeth again, wasn't he?

"Was there something you wanted, Mother? I need to get to the office," Jack said.

"Nothing major. I just wondered if you were bringing a guest this evening."

Jack felt himself frown. "I have no idea what you're talking about."

"The symphony benefit. You know I'm the gala chairperson this year," Eleanor said, placing so much emphasis on her title that she may as well have just been elected president of a small country.

"Weren't you the chairperson last year too? And the year before that?" Jack asked. He thought so, but he couldn't be certain. Trying to keep up with his parents' social calendar was next to impossible.

"Of course, but that doesn't make this year any less important now. Does it?"

Buttercup returned with the tennis ball, which was now coated in slobber in addition to whatever had caused the original stench. Jack gave it another toss.

"Well, congratulations," he said and hoped that would suffice.

"Thank you," she said, and Jack could sense her beaming all the way from his parents' sprawling penthouse on Central Park South. "But I need to know how many seats to reserve in your name. You haven't answered a single one of my text messages about the gala."

He should've known he wouldn't be able to get off

with a simple congratulatory comment. "Because I'm not going. I told you that already."

Jack was done with those sorts of social obligations. He'd made himself clear on this subject on numerous occasions.

"Don't be silly. Of course you are." Eleanor let out a huff.

"Mother," he countered.

"It's *one evening*. The world won't stop turning if you step out for a simple little gala."

There was nothing simple about it, though. Jack's life hadn't been anywhere close to simple for quite some time. Plus, he knew his mother. If he gave in once, she'd expect him to do so again and again. Jack couldn't even keep track of all the galas his parents attended. For as long as he could remember, his mother had spent more time at board meetings than your average Wall Street CEO.

"I won't be there. Feel free to do whatever you like with my seat." Jack scrubbed the back of his neck with his free hand. Buttercup must have picked up on his irritation because she'd abandoned the filthy tennis ball to stare intently at him with her furry head cocked in concern.

"Honestly, Jack. There's no reason whatsoever why you can't attend. You think I don't know what you're doing, but I'm quite aware. Whatever grand statement you're trying to make is absurd. You had a perfectly lovely upbringing," Eleanor said loudly enough for Buttercup's ears to prick forward.

Jack needed to get off the phone before she turned on the crocodile tears. If that happened, he was going to lose it. He and his parents maintained a cordial relationship, despite Jack's insistence on forging his own path. Jack had the feeling his mom and dad were simply waiting things out, certain of his eventual return to the fold.

If so, they were in for a rude awakening. But now wasn't the time to disrupt the King family's delicate equilibrium.

"Mother, I really do need to get to the office." Jack rested his palm on Buttercup's head and the dog nestled against his legs.

"If you worked for your father, you wouldn't need to be in such a rush," Eleanor said.

"We've talked about this, Mother. I'm not going to work for King Investments." Not ever, if Jack could help it.

"I understand. But that doesn't mean you can't attend a social gathering with your family, does it?" His mother sniffed.

She wasn't going to let this thing go, was she?

Jack closed his eyes, took a deep breath and said the first thing that sprang into his head—the *only* thing that might put an end to the conversation. "Even if I wanted to come, I can't. I have a work obligation this evening."

The second the words left his mouth, he wanted to reel them back in. But for reasons he couldn't explain—not even to himself—he didn't. Spending a few hours a week with Daphne couldn't be as bad as making the rounds of the autumn gala circuit.

Could it?

Her promise from the night before floated to the forefront of his consciousness.

Do this for me, and I'll never rearrange your desk again. I'll never push back on any of your fact-checking at all. I'll even let you take the lead on the pieces we cowrite about the etiquette class. Whatever you say, goes.

"Yes. It's a weekly thing, so I'm afraid I'll be tied up for the next few Friday nights as well," he heard himself say.

"But that means you'll miss the ballet gala. And the party for the natural history museum." His mother gasped. "And the black-tie fundraiser for the Conservatory Garden!"

Not the black-tie fundraiser! Jack bit back a smile. It looked like being fake-engaged to Daphne might not be the worst idea in the world after all. The second worst, maybe, but not the absolute worst.

Keep telling yourself that, idiot. You just traded one set of troubles for another.

Too late, though. Jack was in—for richer or poorer, in sickness or health, to love and to cherish.

For better or worse.

Daphne spotted the Post-it from clear across the editorial department as she walked into the *Veil* offices on Friday morning. There it was—stuck to her chair, just like the last one.

Her stomach dropped as she squinted at the little yellow square from a safe ten feet away. Maybe if she didn't get any closer, she could somehow avoid being infuriated by whatever Jack had written on it. Like a bomb waiting to explode in her face, if she stayed far enough back, she could avoid triggering the detonator.

He said he'd think about it, she reminded herself.

Last night, that had seemed like good news. Daphne had practically floated home from the dog park, convinced the undercover series was a go. She'd gone to sleep with visions of her name moving up the masthead. Maybe once Addison took over as editor in chief, Daphne and Everly could be codeputy editors. Daphne wasn't sure if that was even a thing, but she didn't care. So long as she was dreaming, she was going to dream big.

Then, this morning, she'd woken up with a weight the

size of the Empire State Building pressing down on her chest. She hadn't simply been doing a little fact-checking last night. She'd been spying on Jack. Okay, fine… she'd been stalking him. And he'd *known*. There was no way he was going to pretend to be her fiancé. He'd probably only promised to think about it so she'd go away and leave him alone. What's worse, she wasn't even sure she blamed him.

But a Post-it? Again? *Really?*

The man was impossible. She'd basically begged him to reconsider, and he was going to reject her on a Post-it. Maybe it was a good thing she wouldn't be waltzing into the Plaza tonight and pretending to be in love with him. What had she been thinking? The two of them never would've been able to pull it off.

Daphne squared her shoulders, marched to her desk and snatched the Post-it off the back of her chair.

See me when you get in.

Jack King

She blinked. What did that even mean? And who signed a Post-it with their first and last name?

Daphne balled the square of paper in her fist and stormed toward Jack's office. She was tempted to make a leisurely stop at the espresso machine, because honestly, who did he think he was, ordering her around like that? But as much as she would've liked to put him in his place and make him wait, she wanted to go ahead and get the rejection over with. Onward and upward.

As fate would have it, Jack was already bent over his desk, attacking an article with a red pen when she reached his office. Daphne immediately recognized the typewritten page as the lip gloss piece she'd just written the day before. While she lingered quietly in the doorway, he drew a big red *X* over one of her middle paragraphs. Just like that—two aggressive slashes.

Daphne winced with each stroke of his felt tip marker— little arrows to her heart. He was murdering her article right before her eyes. First the bossy little Post-it, now this.

Her face burned with indignation, and before she could think better of it, she drew back her arm and threw the balled up Post-it note directly at Jack. It hit him smack in the center of his forehead and then fell onto the pages spread out in front of him. If Daphne hadn't been wearing the very tallest stilettos she owned—the ones coated entirely in silver glitter with giant, sparkly bows on the backs of the heels—she would've done a little victory dance.

She did a fist pump instead.

Jack lifted his gaze and regarded her through narrowed eyes. "What, may I ask, was that?"

"A fist pump. Surely you recognized it. From what I hear, it's a sports thing." Daphne crossed her arms and tilted her head.

That's right. I know all about your previous life as a sportswriter, Mr. Secretive.

He looked at her long and hard, until a forbidden chill made its way up and down Daphne's spine.

"Stalking me again, sweetheart?" The endearment dripped with sarcasm, but her heartbeat kicked up a notch all the same. Damn him, and damn that penetrating stare of his.

"I'm not your sweetheart," she said.

A muscle in his jaw flexed—at long last, a human reaction. So he wasn't a cyborg after all.

He rose from his chair, plucked the balled-up Post-it note from his desk and dropped it into the trash. Then he strode past her to close the office door, shutting them inside together.

Daphne's breath caught in her throat when he came to stand just opposite her. She drew herself up to her full height, but even in her sky-high glitter heels, Jack still towered over her. Why did the room feel so small all of a sudden? And why couldn't she remember how to breathe?

"My mistake." Jack sat down on the very edge of his desk and arched a single eyebrow. "I thought you *wanted* to be my sweetheart."

"You're hilarious," she said, but neither of them laughed.

Wait… What was happening? Were they arguing or flirting? Daphne could have sworn it was the former, but it was beginning to feel like something else entirely.

"When I asked what you were doing, I wasn't referring to the fist pump. I meant the wadded up Post-it to the forehead." He searched her gaze, and she felt as diaphanous and transparent as a wedding veil. "I thought we weren't doing that sort of thing anymore."

We. As if they were a team. A unit. A couple.

Daphne's head spun. She really should've had a proper breakfast this morning. All she'd eaten were the macaroons she'd swiped from the elegant tower that Ladurée had sent over yesterday in anticipation of the special feature Everly was writing on alternatives to traditional wedding cakes. No wonder she was feeling so weak in the knees. This light-headed sensation *couldn't* be because of Jack. No way.

"I only promised a truce if you agreed to go undercover with me," she said and then paused when the full meaning of their back-and-forth sank in. "Wait… You don't mean…"

"I spoke to Colette this morning and told her I'd had a change of heart." Jack's forehead creased as if he was trying to make sense of his own decision. Daphne knew better that to question his reasoning. It was happening. That's all that mattered. "So if you're still up for it…"

"Yes!" Daphne blurted, and then she had some sort of crazy out-of-body experience. All of a sudden, it was like she was watching the scene transpire from high above, and a woman who looked exactly like her had just launched herself at Jack, wrapped her arms around his neck and pressed herself against him as if he'd just proposed marriage to her for real.

"Thank you, thank you, thank you," her identical twin gushed.

"Um," Jack said, and Daphne felt the hum of his voice rumble through her body, warm and delicious. His heartbeat crashed against hers as fast as a jackrabbit's.

Oh, no. Daphne blinked as she returned to her body and realized with no small amount of horror that there was no identical twin. There was only her—and she was clinging to the man she loathed like a barnacle. *No, no, no.*

She sprang backward so fast that Jack had to reach out and grab hold of her shoulders to steady her.

"Are you okay?" He tilted his head, eyes boring into hers. His pupils were dilated, leaving just a sliver of steely gray visible in his irises.

Daphne swallowed hard as she pulled out of his grasp and righted herself. "Fine."

She was decidedly *not* fine. What had just happened? *You threw yourself at Jack King. That's what happened.*

And for a nonsensical moment, being in his arms had felt good. Very, *very* good.

"You sure?" Jack said. Was it her imagination, or did he seem a bit jittery? He ran a hand through his hair, leaving it charmingly rumpled. As if he'd just climbed out of bed.

Daphne's mouth went dry. She needed to get out of this office immediately. "Yes. Of course. Completely and totally fine. Why wouldn't I be?

A hint of a smile danced on his lips. "You tell me."

The man was far too handsome when he wasn't scowling. Daphne dropped her gaze to the knot in his tie and did her best to focus on the smooth silk. "There's nothing to tell. I'm fine."

"So you said." Jack's voice dropped so low that it seemed to scrape her insides, leaving her breathless.

"I should go. I have loads of work to do before the class tonight." She looked past him toward her article that was bleeding red comments all over his desk. "Including rewriting the lip gloss piece, apparently."

"Daphne." There was a reprimand in his tone this time, laced with just a touch of amusement.

She held up her hands. "Not that I'm complaining."

She'd made a promise, and she intended to keep it, no matter how impossible it now seemed.

It's just four weeks, she told herself. *Only one month out of your life.* She could do anything for four short weeks.

Couldn't she?

Chapter Five

Six hours later, after spending the majority of her workday rewriting the lip gloss article, Daphne sat across from Jack at her favorite high-top table at Bloom.

"Hi there, Daphne." Ron flashed her a wide smile. "What a treat seeing you here on a Friday. Is this a special occasion?"

He slid a curious gaze toward Jack.

Why yes, I'm fake engaged! Meet my pretend fiancé!

"Just a business meeting. We're work colleagues," Jack said before she could utter a word, because apparently, he wanted to make sure no one thought they were on an actual date.

"Right. Strictly business," Daphne said through gritted teeth.

"Okay then," Ron said, suddenly looking like he wanted to flee lest he get caught up in the awkwardness. "Shall I get your usual, Daphne?"

"Yes, please. And an old-fashioned for my *work colleague*." She batted her lashes at Jack.

"Coming right up," Ron said and disappeared before Jack could interject.

"Still think you have me all figured out?" Jack narrowed his gaze at her once they were alone.

"Isn't that what this business meeting is all about?" she shot back.

They had less than two hours until their first Elegantly Engaged class, and they were under strict orders from Colette to make sure they knew enough about one another to pose as a believable couple. Bloom seemed like as good a place as any for an emergency cramming session, with the added benefit of giving Daphne the home court advantage.

She still felt a little rattled by the electric sparks that had been zinging around his office earlier. The last thing she needed was to feel in any way attracted to Jack. That would just mess everything up, in addition to being flat-out absurd. She needed to keep her wits about her if they were going to pull this thing off.

Unfortunately, if Daphne thought he'd seem in any way less attractive out in the wild instead of tucked away in his freakishly neat office, she'd been mistaken. Dang it.

"Drink of choice?" she asked. "You should probably tell me. For the article and all."

"Fine, you got me. Old-fashioned," he said with no small amount of reluctance.

She grinned. "Nailed it."

His dark eyes glittered in the dim light of the bar. "Pleased with yourself?"

She held her thumb and pointer finger just a smidge apart. "A little bit, yes."

Ron returned, drinks in hand. "Here you go. Just let me know if you two need anything else."

Daphne gave the sugared rim of her glass a little lick, and Jack shook his head in disapproval.

She glared at him. "What?"

"As I've said before, a wedding cake martini isn't a real drink. And didn't you have cake for lunch today?"

Daphne squared her shoulders. Yes, there'd been wedding cake in the break room again today, and yes, she might have had a slice or two. But that had been an afternoon snack, not lunch. She'd skipped lunch today because she'd been buried in rewrites, thank you very much.

"The cake was just a midafternoon pick me up," she said.

"In other words, lunch." Jack smiled into his drink. "Nailed it."

"I'm mentally adding freakishly competitive to your list of personality quirks in case that comes up at class tonight. Just so you know," she said.

He snorted. "Like you're not?"

"Maybe that's what initially attracted us to one another." Daphne's face went warm as Jack's glass paused halfway to his mouth. "In the land of make-believe, I mean."

He regarded her over the rim of his glass but said nothing.

She took a generous swallow of her martini. "This is never going to work if you keep doing that."

"I'm not doing anything," he said flatly.

"Exactly. You're shutting me out, as per usual. The whole reason we're here is to learn enough about each other to pass as—" Daphne swallowed, stomach twisting in knots at the very thought of saying *lovers*, and she cleared her throat "—significant others. Isn't there anything you want to know about me?"

He studied her for a moment, and her face went warm under his scrutiny.

"I think I know quite a bit about you already," he said.

She crossed her arms and leaned back in her chair. "Oh, really?"

"Your favorite food is cake. Favorite color—pink. Your desk is an outright disaster area, which tells me that you thrive best in chaos. You probably adore spontaneity and things like midnight pizza..." He paused. Daphne did, in fact, love getting pizza at midnight—almost as much as she loved cake. Jack winked. "Or going straight from happy hour to the dog park to spy on your charming coworker."

"Charming?" A laugh burst out of her. "You wish."

He smoothed down his tie, completely unbothered. Probably because he knew she didn't fully mean it, since he could apparently read her like a book. On the surface, anyway.

"So that's it? I'm basically a pink cupcake covered in glitter. That's how you see me?" she asked.

"That's how you *want* me to see you. All of this—" he waved a hand, encompassing her general appearance "—is a type of armor. Beautiful armor, to be sure. But I suspect that underneath it all is a tender heart and undoubtedly the most wildly creative writer I've ever worked with before."

Daphne's breath clogged in her throat as she stared at him in utter disbelief. Everything he'd just said sounded suspiciously like a compliment. Office nemeses didn't talk about each other like that, especially face-to-face.

"Cat got your tongue?" he asked, then sipped his drink as if he hadn't just turned her knees to water.

She took a deep breath and forced herself to say something. "I don't understand. How can you think I'm wildly creative? You rip all my articles to shreds."

"Precisely. You write like a novelist, not a journalist. And before you think about tossing that monstrosity of a martini in my face, I mean that in a good way. Creativity is something you're born with, and you have it in spades. The reason I have to cut so much from your pieces is because all your witty commentary isn't fact-based. That doesn't mean it's not brilliant writing."

Brilliant writing. Was he drunk?

Daphne's gaze flitted to his glass. It was still nearly full.

"Thank you." She swallowed hard. A strange lump was beginning to form in her throat. He thought she was a tender, beautiful, creative mess. Why on earth did that make her feel like crying? "It's your turn now. Tell me something about yourself."

"What would you like to know?" Jack tugged gently at the knot in his tie, loosening it an infinitesimal amount. To the naked eye, that Windsor knot looked exactly the same as it had two seconds ago.

Way to relax, Mr. Secretive.

"Where did you grow up?" Goodness, getting information out of this man was like pulling teeth.

"Central Park South."

It figured. Daphne forced a smile. "Where did you go to school?"

"Yale," he said. So, she'd been wrong about Harvard, but not by much. "Before that, I attended private school here in Manhattan."

Daphne's grip tightened around the stem of her glass. "Where, exactly? What private school?"

"You seriously think that might come up while we're

learning how to fold napkins into swans? It's ancient history." He took a swallow of his drink.

"Humor me," she said as a ball of dread settled in the pit of her stomach.

Jack shrugged. "Emerson Academy."

Daphne promptly choked on a mouthful of wedding cake martini.

"Are you all right?" Jack leaned toward her from across the table. "Daphne?"

"F-fine," she sputtered before erupting into a coughing fit.

Of all the hoity-toity schools in New York City, Jack King had gone to Emerson Academy. She should probably just let herself choke to death. It would be easier than dealing with this little surprise nugget of information.

"You're clearly not fine."

"My drink went down the wrong pipe, that's all," she lied.

He arched a brow in that maddening way that he always did—just shy enough of cocky to be attractive. "You've heard of Emerson then?"

"Yes." She did her best to sound as bored as possible, hoping he wouldn't notice the way she could no longer look him in the eyes. "My father works there, actually."

Jack shot her a crooked smile, as if they truly had something in common besides their choice of workplace. "Really? What does he teach?"

People always went there. The minute they heard her dad worked at a fancy prep school, they assumed he was a teacher. It had been happening Daphne's entire life.

She took a deep breath, but before she could answer, Jack's cell phone rang.

Saved by the bell.

Daphne glanced down at his iPhone, lying face-up on

the table. The words *Nanny Marie* lit up the tiny screen. "Uh-oh. Looks like you might have some sort of canine crisis on your hands."

Jack frowned as he reached for the phone. "Sorry. I need to take this."

"Understood," Daphne said, more than happy for the interruption.

She fully expected him to get up and leave the table, but he stayed put while he answered the call.

"Is anything wrong?" he asked once the initial pleasantries were over.

Daphne pretended not to listen. The struggle was very, very real.

"I see." The relief in his eyes was palpable. "It's Friday, so if she wants to stay up until I get home, it's fine. Maybe let her camp out on the sofa and watch some television. I shouldn't be too late."

Good grief, his dog was more spoiled than Everly's was.

"Sorry," he said again as he hung up. "Where were we?"

They'd been talking about Daphne's dad and Emerson Academy, but she wasn't about to remind him. She loved her father with her whole heart, but someone who'd been born with a silver spoon in his mouth and had the kind of resources to employ a dog nanny, of all things, would never understand what it was like to grow up the way Daphne had. There was no way she was telling him. If she did and he looked at her with even an ounce of pity in his gaze, she'd lose it.

Since when does Jack King's opinion matter so much?

Daphne swallowed around the lump in her throat, which seemed to be growing bigger by the second.

"You did it, didn't you? You got that subscription to *DOGTV* I mentioned." She shot him a knowing look as she sipped her drink.

Jack's brow furrowed. "Pardon?"

"You just told your dog nanny to let Buttercup stay up late and watch television," Daphne said.

"Right. Yeah, no." His lips tugged into a half grin, and rebellious little butterflies took flight in Daphne's belly. "She prefers sports, actually."

Daphne laughed, even as the butterflies swooped and dived. "I think you might be projecting your own personal tastes onto Buttercup."

He shook his head. "Nope, she likes anything that involves a ball. Trust me."

Daphne swallowed. *Trust me.* She knew he was only teasing, but Jack had just cut straight to the heart of her biggest insecurity. Trust didn't come easy. Years ago it might have, but not anymore. Daphne could hardly remember what it felt like to live with her heart open wide.

The more she found out about Jack, the less reason she had to believe she could ever be vulnerable with him. Especially now that she knew he'd gone to Emerson Academy. She felt sick just thinking about it.

Daphne couldn't trust this man if she tried...

No matter how tempting the thought might be.

Jack placed his hand on the small of Daphne's back as he escorted her up the red-carpeted steps of the entrance to the Plaza. Her eyes widened slightly at the contact, but she kept her gaze glued forward on some invisible point on the horizon.

They were going to have to work on the PDA thing. Engaged couples touched. Held hands. *Kissed*, for crying out loud. If Daphne up and kissed him without warning, like the tackle-hug she'd given him in his office this morning, he'd probably self-combust on the spot.

Jack was a master at controlling his emotions, but

there were limits to what a person could handle—especially when paired with a partner in crime like Daphne. She was anything but predictable, and if the way his entire body had gone on high alert when she'd thrown herself into his arms earlier was any indication, Daphne's particular brand of surprise was growing on him.

This is work. *Just get the whole ordeal over with so you can go home.*

Elegantly Engaged held its classes in the Palm Court, the Plaza destination famous for its iconic afternoon tea—one of Eleanor King's favorite outings. Thankfully, Jack didn't need to worry about running into his mother, busy as she was with her gala. He should be safe from bumping into her friends too. It had been a while since he'd set foot on the room's plush carpeting, but the surroundings still looked exactly the same, from the domed decorative glass ceiling to the latticed, oval bar that anchored the center of the room beneath the shade of four towering palm trees.

"Are you ready for this?" he whispered against Daphne's ear, sliding his hand to the curve of her waist.

"Not in the slightest," she said with a tremble in her voice that gave him the distinct impression she was worried about more than trying to convince people they were an actual couple.

They'd made very little headway at the bar. After the phone call, pretty much all they'd managed to discuss was Daphne's name. Colette had registered her for the class as Daphne Grace, her first and middle names. She'd had to drop *Ballantyne* since that name appeared on the *Veil* masthead, for all the world to see. Since Jack's position wasn't public facing, his name wasn't a problem.

"Hey, look at me." He stopped at the periphery of the glittering crowd and waited for her to meet his gaze.

When she did, he spied a reticence in her eyes that burrowed under his skin and made him want to protect her—this frustrating, enigmatic woman who was fully capable of taking care of herself. Ah, at last: a glimpse of that tender heart. "We can do this, Daphne. The people here are far more concerned about themselves than anyone else."

Her eyes were huge in her face. Luminous, like fine emeralds. "You think so?"

"I know so," Jack said, and before he could stop himself, he pressed a gentle kiss to her forehead.

Her lips curved into a smile. "You're really trying to sell this, aren't you?"

He wasn't trying to sell a thing. The innocent kiss had been a natural, albeit inappropriate, instinct. But Daphne definitely didn't need to know that. "That's why I'm here, aren't I?"

"Absolutely." She nodded and held his gaze for what felt like a beat too long before redirecting her attention back toward the group.

A woman dressed in a white feathered gown approached them with an outstretched hand. "Good evening. Thank you so much for joining us. I'm Melanie Miller, the instructor and creator of Elegantly Engaged. And you are?"

Daphne beamed and shook the woman's hand. A diamond solitaire glittered on Daphne's ring finger—her supposed engagement ring, which had come straight from the fashion closet at *Veil*. "It's lovely to meet you. I'm Daphne Grace and this is my honey, Jack King."

My honey. Jack had expected to be introduced simply as her fiancé, but the endearment was a nice touch. It felt sweet…intimate. Real.

"It's a pleasure to be here," he said with a nod.

"Tonight we'll be going over champagne etiquette—

from your engagement party all the way to the toasts at your wedding reception." Melanie Miller smiled at them like they were the prince and princess in an animated fairy tale.

"How wonderful," Daphne gushed as she slipped her arm through his.

"Yes, wonderful," Jack echoed.

Was it really necessary to devote an entire two hours to learning how to drink champagne?

A waiter holding a tray of slender flutes filled with fizzy liquid stopped and offered them each a drink as Melanie floated toward another couple standing nearby.

"Darling," Jack said, prompting Daphne to choose her glass first.

She plucked a champagne flute from the tray. "Your turn, snuggle bug."

The endearments were getting nuttier by the second. Jack cut his gaze toward her and gritted his teeth in an effort not to laugh.

Once the server had moved on, Jack took a generous gulp and then narrowed his gaze at Daphne over the top of his glass. "It seems you've gotten over your brief case of stage fright."

She shrugged. "I've decided to just pretend I'm someone else altogether. Works like a charm."

"Someone with a penchant for silly nicknames?"

She flashed him a conspiratorial grin. "You don't like 'snuggle bug'? Perhaps you'd prefer honey bun? Tater tot?" She blinked wide eyes at him in mock innocence. Where on earth was she getting these names? "Captain Hottie Pants?"

Jack nearly spewed a mouthful of champagne at her.

"Captain Hottie Pants, it is." She lifted her glass in their own, private toast.

He laughed—a deep belly laugh the likes of which he hadn't experienced in a long, long time. Maybe this undercover operation wouldn't be so bad. There were certainly worse ways to spend a Friday evening.

"Have you been like this with all your boyfriends, darling?" Jack winked at her. "Or am I special?"

He'd intended it as a joke—just a tongue-in-cheek comment meant to be no more serious than the words *Captain Hottie Pants*. But the instant he said it, Daphne's smile froze in place.

"Um." She swallowed so hard that Jack was able to trace the movement up and down the slender column of her throat.

"Did I say something wrong?" Clearly, he had. He just had no idea what, exactly.

"Of course you didn't," she said stiffly, but Jack wasn't buying it.

He sighed. It had been a mistake to let down his guard around her. He and Daphne weren't here as a couple. They weren't even friends. For a few minutes there, he'd let himself relax. Believe it or not, he'd even been having a bona fide good time.

He studied her, but her expression gave away nothing. The dazzling armor was fully in place.

Jack told himself to let the moment pass, to just focus on the job at hand. He hadn't exactly been an open book earlier at the bar, so why should he expect Daphne to share any details about her personal life or romantic past?

This was business, not personal. His job at *Veil* was the only reason he'd agreed to this crazy scheme....with the added benefit of having a polite excuse to miss his mother's various charity galas. Daphne Ballantyne didn't have a thing to do with it.

Jack's gut churned. *Liar.*

"Daphne, I want us to be..." he said, choking a little on the rest of the sentence. *I want us to be able to talk to each other.* Could he be a bigger hypocrite?

"What?" she said, a challenge flashing in her eyes.

They were back to their usual office games. She was on one side, and he was on the other, even if only figuratively.

Daphne sidestepped away from him a fraction, and ice trickled down Jack's spine. His jaw clenched as he sipped his champagne.

"Good evening, ladies and gentlemen, and welcome to Elegantly Engaged." Melanie Miller stood in the center of the grand room and raised her glass. "Time for a toast, as well as our first lesson. Never tap the rim of a glass to get your guests' attention. Simply stand and say, 'time for a toast.'"

"Riveting," Jack muttered under his breath, and a ghost of a smile danced on Daphne's lips.

"People actually pay money for this?" she whispered.

More money than you can possibly imagine, Jack thought, but something stopped him from saying as much out loud. From what he knew about this crowd, he'd be willing to bet that they were here to see and be seen. Not to learn anything about etiquette.

He raised his glass, then took a swallow. When he snuck another glance at Daphne in his periphery, he found her watching him. He flashed her a conspiratorial wink, and her cheeks flushed before she looked away again.

"Think of the first half of tonight's class as preparation for your engagement party. As the bride and groom, your primary goal at the party will be to interact with every single guest," Melanie Miller said, pausing to smile at each couple.

"Our engagement party." Daphne rolled her eyes. "Thank goodness we aren't actually having one of those."

"I'll drink to that," Jack said and tapped his glass against hers.

"No, no." Melanie wagged a finger at him from her post by the oval bar, and every head in the room turned toward him. "We don't clink glasses rim to rim, Jack. The rim of a champagne glass is very fragile and can easily shatter. If you must clink glasses, touch bell to bell, the roundest part of your glass to the roundest part of your bride's. Above all, remember to be gentle."

"Busted." Daphne snickered into her champagne.

But Jack barely heard her as his gaze snagged on one of the other students watching him from across the room, and his body went rigid. Bile rose to the back of his throat as the woman stared back at him, red lips curving into a catlike smile.

Seriously? Jack sighed inwardly. What were the odds?

Busted, indeed.

Chapter Six

"Hi, I'm Daphne Grace and this is my fiancé, Jack King. We love sneaking away for weekends at Martha's Vineyard and spending time with our dog, Buttercup," Daphne rattled off as she repeated the information for the fourth time.

As per Melanie Miller's instructions, they were playing the mingle game. It was mainly an exercise of moving about the room and chatting with the other couples, making sure to share something interesting about themselves during the introductions. The idea was to give the people they met something easy to remember them by.

Daphne wasn't sure where she'd gotten the bit about Martha's Vineyard. It had just fallen out of her mouth during the first introduction and Jack had rolled with the punches, dropping little bits of info about "the Cape" into the subsequent conversations. Daphne wanted to ask him if he'd ever been there or if he was lying through his teeth just like she was, but there wasn't time. As soon as they met one couple, another one popped up in their place. She felt like she was on a high society conveyer belt.

"We simply *must* get our dogs together for a playdate," the woman across from her was saying.

"That sounds lovely," Daphne gushed.

"It was a pleasure to meet you both," Jack said as his hand, once again, found its way to the small of her back. He turned toward her and smiled, but she thought she spied a new tension around his eyes. "Sweetheart, can we have a word in private really quick?"

Daphne had managed to convince herself that she'd been imaging things when he'd gone quiet a few minutes ago. She barely knew the man, but she knew enough to understand that he was no social butterfly. It hardly seemed out of character for him to be less than enthusiastic about mixing and mingling.

Something was wrong, though. She could feel it.

"Oh, um…" Daphne glanced around in search of an escape route. Sneaking off for a huddle didn't seem like a good idea. Surely whatever he wanted to talk to her about could wait. They were supposed to be blending in.

Before she could say so, a woman moved in place of the dog-loving duo that had just departed. Daphne gave Jack a tiny shrug. *Too late.* They'd have to save the debrief for later.

"Good evening, I'm Daphne Grace." She extended her hand to the woman now standing opposite her and repeated her little spiel about the Vineyard and Buttercup.

"Oh, yes. Buttercup," the woman said, eyes moving toward Jack with a flutter of her lashes as she shook Daphne's hand. The eyelashes were definitely extensions—tasteful ones, though. They were more Blushing Bride than Bridezilla. Her glossy dark hair was twisted into a low bun which perfectly showcased her under-

stated, pearl stud earrings and the matching set of triple-strand pearls around her neck. Daphne couldn't help
feeling a little cheap by comparison, like a gaudy rhinestone next to the real deal. "I remember that dog well."

"Ashley," Jack said flatly.

Wait. What was happening?

"Oh, you two know each other?" Daphne's gaze
bounced back and forth between Jack and the stranger,
whose name was Ashley apparently.

Except she wasn't a stranger, was she? Not only did
she know Jack, but she also knew his dog. It had taken an
illicit surveillance operation for Daphne to find out that
much about her notoriously private coworker.

Something that felt an awful lot like jealousy flickered
low in Daphne's belly. She started to take another sip of
her champagne and lowered her glass when she thought
better of it. Clearly the bubbles were going to her head.

Why should she care if this well-groomed woman
knew Buttercup? Maybe she was Jack's dog groomer.
Or veterinarian. Or pet psychiatrist.

Somehow Daphne doubted it.

"Er, yes we do know each other." Jack aimed a tight
smile at Daphne.

"So sorry, we're supposed to be playing the mingle
game, aren't we?" Ashley pressed a hand to her chest. A
diamond solitaire that was approximately the size of a
golf ball glittered on her ring finger. Daphne wondered
when she'd started thinking in terms of sports ball metaphors. Probably right around the time she'd begun to feel
territorial about her pretend groom, whom she didn't even
like. "I'm Ashley Foster. My fiancé, Wesley, just dashed
to the bar to get me another drink."

Ashley's gaze narrowed as she focused on Daphne
with an intensity that made her stomach churn. This was

all starting to feel very uncomfortable—and not at all like a regular day at the office. Daphne suddenly longed for her cubicle and the simplicity of writing about something like updos or eyebrow shaping. She wasn't supposed to be feeling even a little bit jealous right now. She wasn't supposed to be feeling *anything* in relation to Jack King except thinly veiled loathing.

Who *was* this woman, exactly?

Daphne shifted from one foot to the other as she waited for someone to say something. Anything, really. Daphne had never met an awkward silence that she didn't feel the need to fill with a constant stream of babble, but she couldn't come up with a single safe thing to say. Just how well did this Ashley person know Jack?

Daphne's gaze slid toward him. He seemed tenser than she'd ever seen him before, as if she'd just announced she was going to force feed him an entire sheet cake.

"Three things," Daphne blurted as she turned to Ashley again. She couldn't take the silence for another second. "You're supposed to tell us three things about yourself, remember?"

She felt Jack stiffen beside her, and she tried to brace herself for whatever came next.

"Oh, that's right. Silly me. How could I forget?" Ashley's red lips curved into a smile. Her lipstick was perfect—velvety smooth, like a rich, satin ribbon. It was obviously high-end, probably Chanel. For some reason, this irked Daphne to no end. "I guess you could say that an interesting fact about me is that just six months ago, I was engaged to your fiancé."

"How much do you hate me right now?"

Jack's breath was warm against Daphne's neck. He was so close—*too* close—but she was stuck. Now that the mingle game had ended, the class had moved on to the second lesson of the night, which was learning how to properly execute the moment at a wedding reception when the bride and groom sipped champagne with their arms intertwined. Easier said than done, especially when the bride wanted nothing whatsoever to do with her groom.

A lot. I hate you a lot *right now, Jack King.*

Being blindsided by Ashley a few minutes ago had been so much worse than the Post-it episode, and Daphne wasn't even sure why. What did she care that Jack had been engaged? They weren't a real couple. It shouldn't matter in the slightest.

It did, though. And the mere fact that it mattered was the most unsettling thing of all.

"I don't hate you," she lied. Never in a million years would she let Jack think she was jealous of the perfectly-lipsticked Ashley. She'd rather die.

"I know you're lying," Jack said quietly as they sipped from their coupe glasses, just inches apart. "You won't even look at me."

Around them, other couples giggled as champagne sloshed out of their glasses. Daphne pasted on a smile and tried to pretend she was having the time of her life— a perfectly giddy bride-to-be.

Then she forced herself to meet Jack's gaze. "Fine, I do hate you. But only the normal amount."

That got a reluctant smile out of him. "That's my girl."

Daphne's heart melted, and she hated herself for it. "I'm not—"

"Not my girl. Duly noted." His smile went sad around the edges, which made no sense whatsoever. "I'm sorry. I should've told you about Ashley while we were at Bloom."

"Why didn't you?" Daphne asked. *Why are you asking him questions? Let it go, already.*

She'd managed to fumble her way through the rest of the conversation with Ashley and her fiancé, who seemed way more up to speed on the relationship dynamics than Daphne was. But that was to be expected, wasn't it? He was part of a real couple, and Daphne was just a phony.

"Very good, everyone." Melanie Miller's voice echoed throughout the room. "But I'm still seeing a few spills here and there. Again, please."

Daphne and Jack locked arms again, pressing their bodies a smidge closer together.

"Did Ashley break your heart? Is that why you didn't want to tell me about her?" Daphne's pulse kicked up a notch as she waited for him to answer.

"No, that's not it at all," Jack said.

Daphne tilted her head and the bubbly liquid in her glass sloshed dangerously close to the rim. "What is it then?"

"Do you really want the whole truth?" he asked, and his gray eyes suddenly seemed stormier than ever, filled with a melancholy that stole the breath from Daphne's lungs.

"You should probably tell me." Daphne nodded, heart in her throat. "For our charade, I mean."

"For our charade," Jack echoed, and the look he gave her made her wonder if they were still talking about the *Veil* assignment or some other charade…like possibly the one where she was still pretending she didn't find him just the tiniest bit attractive.

"Well, go on and spill the beans," Daphne prompted. She snuck a glance in Ashley's direction and found the woman watching her from across the crowded room. For someone who was apparently engaged to another man, she seemed awfully interested in her ex.

Daphne and Jack *really* needed to be convincing as a couple now. Fooling a room full of strangers was one thing, but this was an entirely different level of subterfuge.

She gazed up at Jack with the most adoration she could muster, and Ashley promptly averted her eyes.

Jack didn't seem to notice. He'd disappeared into himself the way he sometimes did, but at least this time he kept talking to her. "Ashley and I met in college. We dated on and off during school and after graduation, and eventually my parents began to press hard for an engagement. Both of our families did, actually. Our mothers are close, and at the time, it seemed like the right thing to do. Now, if I'm really being honest with myself, it felt like a mistake from the moment I slipped that ring on her finger. I just didn't realize it until later."

The green-eyed monster lurking inside Daphne reared its ugly head again. Of course their families pressed for an engagement. Ashley was exactly the sort of woman who men like Jack married. They'd met at Yale, for crying out loud, where they'd probably gone on *actual* weekend trips to the Vineyard while Daphne had been cleaning cubicles at *Veil* and barely scraping together enough tuition money to attend community college.

"What happened later? Did you find out she was secretly allergic to dogs or something?" Daphne asked in an effort to keep things light and breezy. But the wobble in her voice surely gave her away. "Or did she do something awful like cheat on you with your best friend? She looks like the type."

She looked like nothing of the sort. Ashley oozed country clubs, PTAs and toddler playdates. In other words: wife material—the polar opposite of Daphne, with her oversize eyelashes and sparkles in her hair.

"No, but it did involve my best friend," Jack said as they linked arms again. Now he was the one who couldn't seem to maintain eye contact. His gaze dropped to his champagne glass, and he swallowed hard. So hard that Daphne was momentarily mesmerized by the movement of his Adam's apple, given that they were practically embracing.

If someone would've told her just days ago that she'd be standing here, drinking champagne with her arm looped around Jack King's, she never would've believed it. Nearly two hours into their first fake date, it was almost starting to feel natural.

"Six months ago, my college roommate and his wife passed away in a car accident," Jack said quietly.

At first, Daphne was sure she'd misheard. His words were so incongruous with the fancy, effervescent atmosphere, she could hardly wrap her head around them. There was no mistaking the ache in his eyes, though. Pain so palpable that it took Daphne's breath away.

"Oh, Jack. I'm so sorry." Without thinking, she rested a hand on his chest. His heart pounded hard beneath her fingertips and shame spiraled through her as she remembered all the times she'd referred to him as a robot or a cyborg when complaining about him to the *Veil* crew.

"That's not the half of it." Jack's champagne glass shook ever so slightly in his grasp. He set it down on a nearby table and raked a hand through his hair. "Come here."

He took her by the hand and led her behind a towering palm tree, out of sight of the rest of the group. Once they were alone and he met her gaze full-on, Daphne was suddenly afraid of whatever was coming next.

"Brian and his wife had a six-year-old daughter, Olivia. They asked me to be her godfather when she was born, and now I'm her guardian. She lives with me. The nanny is hers, and so is the dog. I got Buttercup for her shortly after she moved in." Jack's eyes narrowed, as if searching Daphne's face for a reaction. "I guess you could say that's my big secret. Olivia is the reason I adopted Buttercup, the reason I quit my job at *Sports World*, the reason Ashley and I are no longer together. It was all too much for her—not just the fact that I suddenly became a dad, but the way it changed me. How could it not, though? My life has taken a complete one-eighty in the past few months, all because of that little girl. I want to do right by Olivia. If she can't grow up with her real parents, I want to be the next best thing."

He blew out a breath and looked around. "I can't believe I'm telling you all of this here...now."

Jack had a *child*.

Daphne felt like the world had just tilted sideways on its axis. So much made sense now—his reluctance to work in the evenings, the phone call earlier at Bloom, the nanny. And yet, she had more questions than she could count.

Now wasn't the time, though. They still had a job to do. An article to write. An entire fake engagement to think about.

"It's okay, Jack," she said. "I'm glad you told me."

"I should've told you earlier," he countered.

True, but it wasn't as if Daphne had bared her soul either. In fact, she was starting to feel like some reciprocity might be in order.

She cleared her throat. "I haven't gone a real date since high school."

Jack frowned, as if trying to make sense of the sudden

hard turn their conversation had just taken. "I'm sorry. *What?*"

"I don't date. That's why I sort of froze when you made that joke about 'all my other boyfriends.'" She made little air quotes around the words and then crossed her arms. She felt acutely naked all of a sudden. Maybe Jack had been onto something when he'd said her love for sparkle was a type of armor. "Sorry for the abrupt change of subject. You just shared something personal about yourself, and it felt right for me to do the same. I've never actually had a boyfriend. Not a real one, anyway."

He looked at her for a long moment, gray eyes glittering. "I have a very difficult time believing that statement."

Daphne's entire chest filled with warmth. She felt like she might even tell him the rest of the story… Maybe, just maybe, he'd understand. Not now, though, obviously. They'd already been away from the class too long as it was.

"Maybe I'll explain sometime," she said, wrapping her arms around her even tighter.

"I'd like that," Jack said, and his mouth curved into a smile that seemed almost secretive, like it was the sort of smile he saved for people who really knew him. "I wasn't trying to be dishonest with you, Daphne. I just feel really protective of Olivia. She's been through a lot, and especially after what happened with Ashley, I try not to introduce people into our lives who aren't going to stick around. It makes things easier all around if I compartmentalize my life."

"It's okay. I understand." Daphne nodded, but there were parts of his story that she didn't understand at all. Namely, the bits about Ashley.

What kind of person broke up with a man who'd just

lost his best friend and become a parent, all in one fell swoop? Of all the things Jack had just told her, that was the most shocking of all. It made Daphne furious, as if the woman had betrayed one of her closest friends instead of a business associate—a coworker she purported to not even like. The thing was, Jack wasn't so bad now that she was getting to know the real him. Daphne wasn't sure what to make of this new, complicated version of Jack King. All she knew for certain was that suddenly, she felt like marching right up to Ashley and dumping the contents of her champagne glass on top of the woman's perfectly coifed head.

"You look like you want to murder someone right now," Jack said. He wasn't altogether wrong, although he seemed to think she was homing in on him as her victim instead of his loathsome ex-fiancée. He held up his hands. "I fully acknowledge that from where you're standing it might seem like I'm going a tad overboard in trying to control my little makeshift family."

Did he truly think she was the type to kick a man when he was down? Probably, given his romantic history along with Daphne's penchant for torturing him at the office. She didn't really care that he hadn't told her the whole truth, though—not anymore. They could still rock this undercover assignment. Daphne was certain of it. And for reasons she didn't fully understand, she wanted them to succeed now more than ever.

"You?" She let out an exaggerated gasp. "A control freak? Get out of town."

Then she reached out and gave his necktie a gentle tug, prompting a smile out of him again. Daphne's heart turned over in her chest.

She couldn't seem to let go of his tie. Her fingers curled tighter around the smooth silk, anchoring them both to this place and time—the moment when they'd truly become a team.

"We can do this, Jack." Her gaze bore into his. "You and me? We've got this."

"Ashley being here complicates things, Daphne. Trust me when I tell you that she's going to be a problem—a big one." He shook his head and sighed. "I'm not so sure we can still pull this thing off."

"You don't have to be, Captain Hottie Pants." She rose up on tiptoe, pressed a kiss to his cheek and whispered in his ear. "I'm sure enough for the both of us."

Chapter Seven

It was two hours past Olivia's bedtime when Jack got home from the Elegantly Engaged class, even though he'd come straight back to the apartment without writing a single word. Daphne suggested that they work on their article together via text messages and video chats over the weekend since she knew he was anxious to get home. Jack had promptly agreed, relieved that she hadn't invited herself over or suggested that they meet someplace on Saturday or Sunday to work together in person.

Tonight had been surprising in a lot of ways, not the least of which was the rapport that seemed to be developing between them. Somewhere between Daphne's interrogation at the bar and the moment she'd kissed him on the cheek beneath the shade of a palm tree—out of sight from anyone and everyone they'd wanted to fool into thinking they were a real couple—Jack had come to the startling realization that he enjoyed her company. Away from office politics, the Post-it notes and the mess that she called a desk, they'd been different people. And to Jack's utter astonishment, he'd liked the man he'd become for those few short hours.

Until his gaze had landed on Ashley.

He tugged at the knot in his tie as he crossed the threshold of the apartment. Olivia immediately sat up from her blanket fort on the leather sectional, rubbing her eyes as she clutched her favorite teddy bear.

The toy had been a gift from Santa Claus last year, just two months before she lost her parents. It had come with a personalized voice message in its paw. Whenever Olivia squeezed the palm of the bear's hand, she could hear her mother saying, *Mommy and Daddy love you, Vivi.*

That bear was a godsend. Neither Jack nor Olivia would've survived the past five months without it. Her teddy was the only thing that soothed Olivia when she had nightmares or a particularly bad day. Sometimes, when Jack couldn't sleep, he could hear Olivia playing the voice message over and over again in her room. It never failed to put a lump in his throat.

"Uncle Jack, you're home!" Olivia said in a sleepy voice, and her tiny shoulders sagged with relief.

Jack's gut churned. He hated that she always seemed a little surprised when he walked through the door, as if she expected some horrible tragedy to steal him away when she wasn't looking, just like her parents. No matter how many times he told her that he wasn't going anywhere, Olivia never quite believed him. Why should she? He could promise her the world, and fate might have other ideas. At the tender age of six, she'd already lost the innocence and faith of childhood. And no matter what Jack said or did—no matter how many puppies he adopted, nights he stayed home or promises he made—he couldn't seem to give it back to her.

"I sure am, kiddo. I'm right here." Jack pressed a kiss to the top of her hair as she hugged his legs from her spot on the sofa. Buttercup's thick tail beat a happy rhythm against the soft leather, but she didn't budge from Olivia's side.

Jack had never seen such a devoted creature. Buttercup had bonded to the little girl from the start and seemed to make it her mission to lick away Olivia's tears, which came often in the beginning. The dog thwarted Jack's efforts at crate training and insisted on sleeping alongside Olivia at night with her furry head on the pillow and her big paws resting on Olivia's chest, covering her broken heart. The fact that the child stopped having nightmares on the very day that Jack adopted the dog from a local rescue group was no coincidence. He'd made plenty of mistakes in the months since becoming Olivia's guardian, but getting her a dog wasn't one of them.

No matter what his mother tried to tell him.

This, Jack thought as he held Olivia tight and inhaled a whiff of baby powder and no-tears shampoo. *This is the only thing that really matters.*

He needed to stop worrying about Ashley, Elegantly Engaged and the article that he and Daphne still needed to put together by Monday morning. Nothing was as important as taking care of Olivia. So long as she was happy and felt loved, all was right with Jack's world.

"Thank you for staying so late." Jack smiled at Nanny Marie over the top of Olivia's head.

"No problem at all." The older woman hiked her handbag onto her shoulder and tucked her coat over her arm. "Did you have a nice time tonight?"

"I did." He nodded and felt himself smile. "I mean, it was a work thing, obviously. But it wasn't too bad."

He cleared his throat, feeling oddly self-conscious all

of a sudden. Marie studied him for a beat, as if waiting for him to say more.

"It was a party, of sorts." Why was he still talking? He didn't owe anyone an explanation. "A *work* party... for my job."

"I like parties," Olivia said with a yawn.

"You also like bedtime stories, don't you, sweetheart?" He nodded toward Olivia's room, formerly a home office that had once housed a framed jersey from last year's Super Bowl, along with various autographed baseballs, basketballs and footballs from Jack's tenure at *Sports World.* All those items he'd once treasured were packed away in storage now, replaced with Olivia's army of stuffed animals, shelves crammed with storybooks and a frilly pink canopy bed that looked like something straight out of the *Princess and Pea* fairy tale. Jack hadn't given the sports memorabilia a second thought in months.

"Why don't you go pick out a book for me to read you before bed?" He ruffled Olivia's fine hair.

She tilted her head and blinked up at him with drowsy blue eyes. "And then I can go to sleep in my blanket fort here in the living room?"

"You sure can, kiddo."

"Goody," Olivia whispered. She scrambled off of the sectional and headed toward her room, still clutching her bear while Buttercup trotted after her.

"She did just fine tonight while you were gone, Mr. King," Marie said quietly once Olivia was out of earshot.

Jack nodded. "I'm glad to hear it. Thank you again for staying. I've got a cab parked just outside the building, waiting to take you home."

"I appreciate the ride. And if you don't mind my saying, it's good to see you going out and enjoying yourself for a change." The nanny grinned at him one last time before heading out. "Even if it was only for work."

"Just three more Fridays, then everything will go back to normal," Jack said, lest she get any crazy ideas.

All of this is just temporary, he reminded himself. *None of it is real.*

Then, as he stood alone in his living room with a blanket fort stretched over his sofa and the twinkling lights of the New York skyline casting a kaleidoscope of dizzying lights over the quiet apartment, his phone chimed with an incoming text. A rebellious spark of anticipation skittered through Jack's veins.

Daphne.

A smile tugged at the corners of his mouth as he slid his phone from the pocket of his suit jacket. His work wife was texting him about the article already. It figured. The woman was relentless.

But the smile died on his lips when he realized the message wasn't from his fake fiancée after all. It was from his mother.

You're ENGAGED???

Fashion closet. Twenty minutes!

The text from Addison pinged on Daphne's phone early Monday morning as she was standing in line for coffee at Magnolia Bakery on the way to the office. Full disclosure: she'd also decided to indulge in one of the bakery's famous cupcakes for breakfast. A *celebratory* cupcake. She and Jack had finished their article just before Colette's Sunday night deadline after two straight days of working on it via e-mail and text messages. The assignment had gobbled up her entire weekend, and it hadn't been easy.

The article was good, though. So, so good. A journalistic masterpiece! Much like their personalities, Daphne and Jack's writing styles were polar opposites. But joined together, they somehow made magic on the page.

It's just words, she assured herself. *There's nothing to get swoony about.*

Even so, her gaze kept straying to a four-tiered wedding cake that one of the bakers was frosting behind the counter. A ridiculous vision of shoving a slice of it into Jack's mouth, bride-and-groom-style, flitted through her thoughts and her heart skipped a beat.

Daphne blinked. Hard.

"You're holding up the line." The girl behind the counter jammed her hands on her aproned hips and glared at Daphne.

"Oh, sorry. I'll have a lavender latte and half a dozen cupcakes, please." She pointed at the display case, where little cakes decorated with frothy pink icing were lined up like neat little sugary soldiers. If she was being summoned to an emergency fashion closet meeting, she may as well bring snacks for everyone.

Daphne wondered what Addison could possibly have to be upset about first thing on a Monday morning. Then again, an emergency fashion closet meeting didn't necessarily mean bad news. Maybe she simply needed help with something at the office. Or maybe she had some sort of secret news to share. Whatever the reason, cupcakes couldn't hurt.

"You're not going to believe it," Addison said exactly twenty minutes later once the *Veil* crew had assembled.

As usual, Addison was dressed impeccably with her editor-in-chief-meets-French-girl aesthetic—a white blouse tied in a black silk bow at the collar, paired with a herringbone miniskirt decorated with a row of oversize pearl buttons. Opaque black tights and block-heeled Mary Janes completed the polished look. But when Daphne took a closer look at her friend, she realized her velvet headband sat slightly askew on her dark waves. Her ordinarily perfect winged eyeliner was smudged in the corner of her left eye.

Something was definitely wrong. Something big.

"What happened?" Daphne asked around a bite of cupcake.

"Take a deep breath. Whatever it is, it's going to be okay," Everly said, already sounding just like a mom.

Addison shook her head. "I came in early to get a jump on things this morning, and when I walked past Colette's office, there it was…just sitting there. I couldn't believe my eyes."

Daphne and Everly exchanged a glance.

"We're going to need a little more information, hon," Daphne said, then sipped her latte. There wasn't enough caffeine and sugar in the world to deal with this level of drama on a Monday morning. Addison was the most levelheaded of all of them. She was their rock.

"What could you possibly have seen in Colette's office that has you this worked up?" Everly rested one hand on her baby bump and the other on Holly Golightly's slender back. The dog had become the *Veil* office's unofficial mascot shortly after Everly adopted her, and she came to work with her mistress more often than not.

"A Peloton, you guys." Addison threw her hands in the air. "A freaking *Peloton*."

Daphne opened her mouth and then closed it, not quite sure what to say. Everly and Holly cocked their heads in unison. It was always adorable, albeit slightly weird, when they did that.

"Don't either of you have anything to say?" Addison huffed.

"Sis, I'm not sure I see what the big deal is?" Everly bit her bottom lip. "A lot of people have exercise bikes. I think they've even advertised in the magazine before."

"Are we missing something? What's so offensive about a piece of exercise equipment?" Daphne asked.

"It's not the bike that's offensive. It's the bike's *loca-tion*." Addison sighed and her shoulders sagged. "Don't you get it? People who are about to retire don't rearrange their offices to make room for things like a Peloton."

"Ah, so this is about your promotion." Everly pulled a face.

"If you mean the promotion that I'm beginning to won-der if I'm ever going to get, then yes." Addison collapsed onto the ottoman between Everly and Daphne and held out her hand. "Give me one of those cupcakes."

Daphne plucked one of the cakes from the bakery box in her lap and placed it on Addison's palm. Holly lifted her head to sniff the pink icing.

"Everything is going to turn out just fine. We've been working years for this. It's going to happen eventually. I know it will," Everly said.

Addison turned to look at her sister. "Pregnancy sure agrees with you. Not only are you glowing, but you're more content than I've ever seen you before."

"It's not just the pregnancy." Everly's expression soft-ened. "It's love."

Daphne popped the bakery box open again. If Everly was about to go on about how blissfully happy she and Henry were, Daphne was going to need another cupcake.

Daphne was happy for her friend—ecstatic, even.

Everly and Henry were the real deal. When their long-time friendship had blossomed into something more, Daphne had been right there to witness the whole thing. She knew how much Henry loved Everly. She'd seen how hard he'd fought for Everly's heart. Soon they would be a family, with two tiny babies. They'd go on long walks in Central Park with Holly Golightly prancing alongside a double stroller. If anyone deserved that kind of happiness, Everly did.

It was just that seeing them together sometimes made Daphne want things...

Dangerous things. Things like romance and butterflies and having a man place his hand on the small of her back because he wanted to—not because they were playing pretend.

"I'm glad you've found happiness with Henry. You know how much I love that you two are together." Addison squared her shoulders, as if preparing for some invisible battle. "But I'm not ready for that kind of life. I might never be ready."

"All I'm trying to say is that work isn't everything. You'll be in charge of *Veil* someday." Everly lowered her voice to a whisper. "And you'll be the best editor in chief this place has ever seen—even better than Colette."

Addison's eyes went wide and panicky, like Colette might jump out from behind a pile of tulle and fire all three of them. Daphne couldn't help but laugh.

"In the meantime, just remember to actually live your life," Everly said.

Live your life.

Daphne's gaze strayed toward her favorite blue tulle Monique Lhuillier gown hanging on a nearby rack in the closet, and for some absurd reason, she thought of Jack. She swallowed. Just when his entire world had been turned upside down, the woman he'd promised to marry had turned tail and run. He had every reason to be as wary about romance as she did. Were either one of them really, truly, living their lives?

"Daphne?" Addison waved a hand in front of her face. "Yoo-hoo. You disappeared on us for a second."

"Sorry." Daphne blinked and shook her head. "I'm just distracted. The article Jack and I cowrote over the weekend went live at six this morning."

Addison gasped. "Oh, my gosh, that's so exciting. Do you know how many hits it's gotten?"

Daphne shook her head. "No, and I'm trying not to think about it. I've never had a story appear right at the top of the home page before. So long as it's not a major flop, I'll be happy."

Everly gave her a little shoulder bump. "Look on the bright side. If it flops, you won't have to work alongside your nemesis anymore."

Addison cleared her throat. "Unless you're secretly *enjoying* going undercover with Jack…"

"It's work," Daphne said primly.

Addison twirled her hair. "Come on, you're not fooling anyone. Neither of us heard from you all weekend because you were too busy with Jack—either in person or via some miscellaneous form of technology—and you haven't complained about him at all."

"Hmm." Everly cocked her head. "Now that I think about it, it's true. You haven't uttered a disparaging word about him. Not even once."

"And is that your pretend engagement ring I see on your finger? You don't have to wear that thing to work, you know." Addison's eyes widened as she took in the faux diamond solitaire that technically still belonged to the fashion closet but was beginning to feel more and more like it belonged on Daphne's hand.

"Don't read into it. It's purely a fashion statement," she said as she toyed with the ring with the pad of her thumb.

Everly smirked. "You sure about that?"

"Be careful, you two." Daphne reached for the bakery box. "Or I'm taking my cupcakes back."

Everly gasped. "You wouldn't."

"Try me," Daphne said.

"Just admit it." Addison folded her arms. "He's not terrible."

Actually, he didn't seem terrible at all. Not anymore. Daphne wasn't sure why she was having such a hard time admitting as much out loud.

Because you like him. You like him a lot.

Ridiculous. The man texted with full punctuation and acted as if he'd never seen an emoji in his life. When they'd finished their article just under the deadline, she'd sent him a whole string of fire emojis. As in, *We're on fire! We're amazing!* Jack had responded by telling her to stop texting him and call 911, as if her apartment had been engulfed in literal flames instead of the figurative blaze of a job well done.

Daphne didn't mind his serious side so much anymore, now that she knew more about him. He was a stand-up guy. A bona fide hero to a little girl who'd lost everything. That sort of commitment was admirable. *Hot*, even. There weren't enough fire emojis in the world to describe a man like that.

And he's your fake fiancé for the next three weeks— emphasis on the fake part.

"This emergency meeting isn't supposed to be about me. For some nutty reason, it's about an exercise bike," Daphne said. A weak attempt at changing the subject.

Miraculously, it worked.

"I hate that bike." Addison pulled a face.

"I heard the editor of *Cosmo* keeps a treadmill in her office, and she walks on it *in her stilettos*," Everly said.

Not exactly helpful. That particular editor had been in her position for decades with no end in sight. Addison looked like she might burst into tears.

But before Daphne could dart to her desk for a tube of waterproof mascara, Colette's assistant burst into the closet.

"Here you guys are." She sighed. "*Again*. I've been looking everywhere. Colette wants to see you right away. The magazine's digital site is a mess."

Addison frowned. "Is it the wedding gift suggestion page? That section was a little glitchy yesterday."

The assistant shook her head. "No, I mean the entire site. It's crashed three times already. Every time the tech department gets it back up and running, it crashes again."

"That's really odd. Colette must be freaking out," Addison said, squaring her shoulders as she strode toward the fashion closet door.

"She is, but it's not you she's looking for you." The assistant's gaze flitted toward Daphne. "She wants to see you, Daphne."

Daphne's stomach tumbled. "Me? Why?"

Was this about her article? Were the readership numbers terrible or something?

Probably. If the site was down, how could anyone even click on it?

"I'm not sure. She just told me to find you and bring you to her office right away. So I suggest you come with me." The assistant gestured toward the door in an exaggerated, sweeping motion. "Bring those cupcakes with you."

"Do you think they'll help Colette's mood?" Daphne

scrambled to her feet. She couldn't believe she was getting called in to Colette's office *again*.

The assistant shrugged. "They can't hurt."

Chapter Eight

Just like the last time she'd been summoned to Colette's office, Daphne crossed the threshold of the pristine white space to find Jack seated in one of the faux fur guest chairs.

Of course he was there. In addition to being her fake fiancé, he was her cowriter now. Her partner in crime. Her work husband. Their professional fates were fully intertwined.

From this day forward. Daphne's heart beat hard as she took him in. Colette was nowhere to be seen. It was just the two of them, inches apart as he stood and buttoned the coat of his suit. His manners truly were impeccable. Daphne couldn't believe he still insisted on rising to his feet every time she entered the room, but she didn't altogether hate it. *Until death do us part.*

She reminded herself that Jack was only her ball and chain until any impending *professional* death, not a literal one. This was a business partnership, not a real one. But for some reason, her body didn't seem to get the memo. Her chest filled with warmth at the sight of him, and she went a little breathless.

Breathless! Over none other than Jack King...

Until his gaze shifted at the bakery box in her hands and he scowled in obvious disapproval.

A line etched between his brows. "Are those cupcakes?"

"Yes." She opened the box, exposing the remaining cakes, topped with generous swirls of buttercream. "Want one?"

He arched a brow. "What do you think?"

"I'm guessing no." Daphne rolled her eyes. She was feeling less swoony by the second, thank goodness.

"Cupcakes are hardly a proper breakfast," he said, still eyeing her with reproach as she plopped into the chair next to his. "Have you ever heard of an egg?"

"Calm down, S.O. I don't make this a habit."

"I beg to differ. I've never seen you eat anything besides sugar." He unbuttoned his jacket and sat down beside her. "S.O.? I suppose that stands for Significant Other?"

She shook her head. "Spinach Omelet."

His gaze narrowed, but he couldn't seem to hide the humor sparkling in his stormy gaze.

Daphne arched a brow. "It's what you had for breakfast this morning, isn't it?"

"I'm not answering that question," he said.

She flashed him a triumphant grin. "Right again."

What were they doing? The last time they'd been dragged in here, Colette had dropped a major bomb on them. They should be trying to figure out how to present a united front, not teasing each other about their respective breakfast choices.

Daphne cleared her throat and turned toward him,

fully intending on asking if he'd heard about the problems with the digital site. But her gaze snagged on a tiny dab of shaving cream near the corner of his mouth, and before she could stop herself, she reached to wipe it away with a brush of her fingertips.

"Sorry," she muttered as her hand froze in place with the pad of her thumb resting gently against his bottom lip. Perhaps the line of professionalism had begun to get a bit blurrier than she'd realized. "You had a little…"

Her words stalled as Jack caught her wrist in his grasp, turned it over and pressed a reverent kiss to the back of her hand. Their eyes locked, and for a confusing, exhilarating moment, Daphne forgot how to breathe. The bakery box slid from her lap to the floor, and neither of them made a move to pick it up.

No man had ever kissed her hand before. It made her feel like Cinderella. She wouldn't have been any less surprised if a fairy godmother had just materialized out of thin air.

"Good morning, you two." A sharp voice pierced the loaded silence, and it didn't belong to a fairy godmother at all. It belonged to their boss.

"Colette." Face burning, Daphne snatched her hand away from Jack and buried it in her lap. "Hi."

"Good day," Jack said, as robotic sounding as ever. Like he hadn't just gone full-on Prince Charming on her out of the blue.

Colette paused en route to her desk. "Why are there cupcakes all over the floor?"

Daphne looked down, where cupcakes indeed littered the white carpet. "Oh, um. Sorry."

Jack dropped down on bended knee and carefully picked them up, placing them gingerly back inside the bakery box while Daphne just sat there, reeling from everything that had transpired in the past sixty seconds. Maybe if she'd eaten a spinach omelet for breakfast, she'd be able to think straight.

Get real. Your poor eating habits have nothing to do with it.

This was Jack's doing. He'd kissed her into a stupor with a simple brush of his lips against the back of her hand. If they ever kissed for real, she'd probably melt into a puddle at his feet.

She let that idea sink in as Jack handed her the bakery box, sneaking her a wink just out of view of Colette. To her great astonishment, she realized she'd never wanted to kiss a man so badly in her life.

"The three of us need to have a chat," Colette said as the office door clicked shut.

Work.

Veil.

The article.

Daphne clutched the box of cupcakes like a child with a security blanket as she tried to get her head back in the game.

"The *Veil* digital site has been crashing since two in the morning." Colette stood at her desk, hands planted on its shiny lacquer surface as she gazed down at them. The dreaded Peloton loomed behind her. "Our IT team can barely keep up, and it's all because of you."

In a panic, Daphne glanced at Jack. His inscrutable expression betrayed nothing. How could he be so calm at a moment like this?

He smoothed down his tie and shook his head. "I don't understand."

"Was there something wrong with the file we turned in?" Daphne asked. Maybe one of their laptops had a virus and they'd unknowingly been responsible for sabotaging the magazine's online presence. Could that even happen? How on earth could all of this be their fault?

So much for that promotion she'd been hoping for. Or a raise. Or three more weeks of posing as Jack's fiancée…

Daphne's stomach clenched. Why did that last one feel like it mattered so much?

"Something wrong?" Colette's face split into a rare, toothy grin. "*Au contraire*, my lovelies. Your article is so popular that it broke the site."

"Wait." Jack tried his best to wrap his head around what his boss had just told them. "You're saying this is a good thing?"

Colette finally sat down but still managed to vibrate with enough fizzy energy to power the entire Eastern Seaboard. "It's a very good thing, Jack. Even with all the outages, your feature article has already gotten more hits than any other digital piece in *Veil*'s history."

"Oh, my gosh." Daphne clutched his bicep. Her eyes were bright and shiny, brimming with unshed tears. Tears of *joy*. He was in trouble, wasn't he? So much trouble… "Jack! We broke the internet!"

He looked down at her glittery fingernails digging into his arm, because maintaining eye contact was just too much. Seeing the sheer joy in her expression made his chest swell with pride, even as he knew that what he was about to say was going to break her heart.

"That's…" *Say it. Just say it. Tell them you can't keep up this ruse. Your cover has been blown and it's encroached into your personal life.* He swallowed. "…fantastic."

All weekend long, Jack's mother had blown up his phone with text messages and voice mails. He couldn't keep ignoring her. He was going to have to come up with some reasonable explanation for his presence at Elegantly Engaged. He'd managed to convince himself that he could come to work on Monday morning and explain to Daphne that he couldn't do it anymore. The jig was up. They'd written a great article, and that was that. He couldn't let his family think he was engaged to be married. That was taking things too far, especially where Olivia was concerned. The child had already lost so much. He couldn't possibly let her believe that Daphne would be part of their lives for good when he knew it wasn't true.

But how could he possibly tell Daphne all of those things now?

He knew he should've said something Friday night, but they'd still had the feature article to write. That had been difficult enough to do without being in the same room together, but they'd made it work. Between games of Candy Land with Olivia, trips to the dog park with Buttercup and a picnic in Central Park, Jack had banged out paragraphs and edited the snippets Daphne sent him. Somehow, they'd woven together a damn good narrative.

Too good, apparently.

"You might not have broken the *entire* internet, but you definitely brought our little corner of it to its knees. The response to your piece has been like nothing I've ever seen before," Colette said.

"I can't believe it. I mean, I had a feeling that the article was good. I just never expected this." Daphne smile grew even wider. A lone tear slipped down her cheek. "Colette, you should know that Jack took the lead on this. He did a great job."

She turned glistening eyes on him, and Jack's stomach clenched. He had an absurd desire to reach for her hand and weave his fingers through hers. They were a team, after all. Neither one of them could have done this on their own.

Colette certainly understood that much.

"It wasn't just Jack, Daphne. It was both of you. This is a fantastic partnership. I shouldn't be surprised since you both do such excellent work. I just never anticipated how your writing styles would complement each other. Daphne, your sense of whimsy is perfectly balanced by Jack's pragmatism. You're both stars in your own right, but together..." Colette glanced back and forth between the two of them. "Together, you're magic."

Magic.

No one had ever described Jack's relationship with Ashley in such glowing terms. That had been different, though. His partnership with Ashley had been personal, and this was business.

Although the heat that had gathered deep in his gut when Daphne kissed him on the cheek Friday night had been anything but businesslike. And Jack had never felt quite so comfortable teasing a coworker or sharing intimate details about his personal life. He'd certainly never kissed a colleague's hand before—in the boss's office, no less.

Jack didn't believe in magic, though. Magic belonged in fairy tales, not real life. Real life didn't end with a happy-ever-after. Not in his experience.

"As good as all this news is, I'm afraid there's a problem," Jack said.

"You mean the outages?" Colette waved a hand. "Don't worry about it. The IT department assures me that everything will be resolved no later than noon. Meanwhile, the very fact that the traffic from your article brought down the entire site is a huge publicity boost in and of itself. Your piece is going viral."

Viral. Jack's head hurt. Having an article go viral was every editor in chief's dream. There was no way Colette was going to agree to end the series prematurely. He didn't even want to think about what Daphne might have to say on the matter.

He shook his head. "I'm not worried about the outage. We ran into someone I know at the Elegantly Engaged class."

"It's really not a problem, though. Totally under control." Daphne waved a hand, then shot him a warning look out of the corner of her eye. "We talked about this, remember?"

Indeed they had. *We've got this.* Daphne's whispered assurances still echoed in the back of his mind—so tempting to believe. Jack hadn't been part of a *we* in a long time. He'd been going it alone for months, making decisions about Olivia's upbringing that went against everything his own family and their social circle believed in. If his parents and Ashley had their way, the little girl would be brought up by nannies or even shipped away to boarding school. There was no reason to turn his entire life upside down. The child wasn't really his, after all.

Besides, that's the way things were done among Manhattan's elite. It's certainly how Jack had been brought up, and for the most part, he'd accepted that way of life as normal. Until the car accident. Until Olivia.

She'd just been so sad...so utterly broken. She'd deserved better. Jack had no idea what a better life for the two of them together might look like, but he was determined to find it.

For both their sakes.

Jack blew out a breath. "My former fiancée is part of the Elegantly Engaged class. She's also a family friend. My parents now think I'm engaged to be married."

There, he'd said it. If Colette and Daphne really thought continuing with the series was in any way possible, perhaps they could figure out how. He was at a loss.

"Your parents?" Daphne blanched. Finally, she seemed to fully understand what he'd meant when he'd told her that Ashley would be a problem.

"Yes. My phone has been blowing up since Friday night," Jack said.

As if on cue, the inner pocket of his suit jacket vibrated. Jack slid the iPhone from the pocket, glanced at the text and held it up for Daphne and Colette to see.

Invitations going out later today for your engagement party. Is this Thursday okay? Will assume yes if I don't hear from you.

"Who is that message from?" Colette asked with far too much nonchalance for Jack's liking.

"My mother."

"Your mother wants to throw us an engagement party?" Daphne gaped at him. "In three days?"

"I'm sure she's trying save face after having to hear about the engagement from one of her friends. She wants to look like she's involved." Jack arched a brow. "Now do you see the problem?"

"Not really." Colette shrugged.

Daphne said nothing. She didn't have to. She'd said it all at their etiquette class on Friday night. *Our engagement party? Thank goodness we aren't actually having one of those.*

"You're not suggesting we go through with it," Jack said. It was a statement, not a question. Because she couldn't possibly be serious.

"That's exactly what I'm suggesting." Colette held up

a finger. "Actually, this is a wonderful development. Your relationship will be even more believable this way. After the success of the first installment of your series, Melanie Miller is going to be on the hunt for whoever is penning these articles. Once your engagement party hits the society pages, your cover will be bulletproof."

"Society pages?" Daphne pressed a hand to her stomach. "I think I'm going to be sick."

"You know what might have prevented that sinking feeling?" Jack aimed a pointed look at the box of cupcakes in her lap.

She narrowed her gaze at him. "Do not even utter the words *spinach omelet* to me right now."

"This is perfect. You sound just like an actual couple. Adorable." Colette clasped her hands. "So it's settled. You'll say yes to the engagement party. Then, Friday night, you'll attend class again and write the second installment of the undercover series. Great work, you two."

Their boss nodded and then waved a hand, indicating the discussion was over.

Jack waited for Daphne to argue. He knew good and well she didn't want to have an engagement party any more than he did. But as usual, she refused to be the voice of reason. She simply shot him a look of utter disdain before standing up and exiting Colette's office with the engagement ring from the fashion closet still sparkling on her graceful finger.

Chapter Nine

Three days later, Daphne arrived at work to find a surprise waiting for her in her cubicle—and that surprise was only marginally better than a passive aggressive Post-it note.

"A spinach omelet? Really?" She cocked a hip as she came to a stop in the open doorway of Jack's office, juggling the cardboard takeout container she'd found on her desk in one hand and her steaming coffee cup in the other. "What on earth made you think this was the way to my heart?"

"It worked, didn't it?" He leaned back in his chair and winked. "You're talking to me again."

Heat crept up the back of her neck. So he'd noticed she'd been avoiding him since their Monday morning meeting with Colette. Daphne was kind of hoping he'd simply think they'd gone back to business as usual. After all, they really didn't have a reason to hang out together during the workweek.

Except for the engagement party, which was scheduled to take place in exactly nine hours and fifty-six minutes. Not that Daphne was keeping track or anything.

She shrugged one shoulder. "What do you mean? I was never not speaking to you."

"I beg to differ. You've been avoiding me like the plague. I haven't had to pluck a single speck of glitter off my clothing for at least the past thirty-six hours." Jack nodded at the chair situated across the desk from him. "Come. Sit. Eat."

"Are you talking to your fake fiancée or your dog? It's kind of hard to tell right now," she said, but she obeyed all the same.

She couldn't keep ignoring him—not if they had any sort of chance of fooling his family into believing they were a real couple. They really needed to get their story straight this time. Tonight they wouldn't be playing the mingle game with a roomful of strangers. Tonight would be the real deal.

"Believe me, you and Buttercup have little in common. Your eating habits, for starters," Jack said as he stood to close the office door while Daphne got situated. "That dog loves eggs."

"She'd probably love cupcakes too, given the opportunity." Daphne opened the takeout box and took in the sight of a perfectly formed omelet sprinkled with a generous portion of parmesan cheese and neatly sliced herbed tomatoes. Her stomach let out a mortifyingly loud growl.

Jack bit back a smile as he sat back down. "Hungry, wifey?"

"I'm not your wife." And she never would be. She stabbed at the eggs with a plastic fork. "I'm your fiancée."

His gaze flitted to the diamond on her finger. Fake, just like their relationship. "About that…"

Daphne twirled the ring band with her thumb. Other than her *Veil* crew, no one in the office seemed to have noticed that she'd begun sporting a flashy rock on a rather significant finger. Probably because it was so big that it screamed *fashion closet*, and all the senior staff borrowed the *Veil* goods on occasion. Every now and then they'd have a themed dress-up day at the office—like Tiara Tuesday, when the writers and editors snagged bejeweled bridal headpieces from the closet's shelves and wore them at their desks all day. What was the fun of working at a wedding-themed fashion magazine if you couldn't indulge in a little something borrowed every now and then?

"Are you sure you're up for tonight, Daphne? It's not too late to call it off. Believe me, I'd understand." Jack eyed her from across the desk in that penetrating way he had.

She took a bite of her eggs, purely to avoid looking him the eye. Dang it, they were delicious. She nearly groaned out loud.

"Of course I'm up for it. Why would you think otherwise?" she said, taking another bite before she could stop herself.

Jack leaned forward in his chair. "Come on, Daphne. We're supposed to be a team, remember? The least we can do is be honest with each other. I thought we'd moved past this point by now."

"So had I." She pointed at him with her fork. "Until you dropped the engagement party bomb in Colette's office on Monday."

Jack sighed. At least he had the decency to look contrite. "This is why you've been mad at me the past few days?"

"Yes." She swallowed, then tried to backtrack. Being

mad at him would mean that she cared, and she wasn't supposed to care about Jack King. Not in any meaningful sense. "I mean, *if* I'd been mad at you, that would've definitely been why. You should've talked to me privately first."

He nodded. "You're right. I should have. I'm sorry."

Daphne blinked. She hadn't expected an apology. Certainly not one that sounded sincere and came with a side of spinach omelet. "Why didn't you?"

She clamped her mouth closed. She hadn't meant to ask. The question had just slipped out, but now it was out there, revealing that she had, in fact, given their most recent interaction a great deal of thought.

Jack had disappointed her, and it had been all her fault. *This* was why she didn't date. So long as she didn't let herself get invested in a relationship, she couldn't be let down. She couldn't get her heart broken. She couldn't be blindsided in her boss's office on what should've been the best day of her entire career.

He looked at her a long moment, eyes fierce and glittering, before responding. "I suppose I didn't tell you because I was enjoying the time we were spending together, and I knew that mentioning the engagement would ruin it."

Oh. Daphne's mouth went dry. *Good answer.*

She felt herself smile—a ridiculous, giddy sort of smile that she had no business bestowing on a work colleague, but she couldn't quite help it. "Since we're being so truthful right now, I feel like I should tell you that this omelet is the best thing I've ever tasted."

"That's my girl," he said, lips quirking into a grin.

Daphne's go-to response flitted immediately into her thoughts. *I'm not your girl.* But she couldn't bring herself to say it.

The air between them crackled with delicious tension. Maybe it wouldn't be so hard fooling Jack's family into believing they had feelings for each other after all. Daphne was beginning to think she just might believe it herself.

Not happening, she reminded herself. There was far too much at stake. Her entire career, for starters. And more importantly, Olivia.

"So." She sat up straighter in her chair. "About tonight."

"Yes?"

"I want you to know up front that my father isn't coming. Just because your family has been dragged into this lie doesn't mean mine needs to get involved." Daphne nodded. There would be no negotiating on this point.

"Of course," Jack said, and for a second, Daphne thought she spied a hint of disappointment in his gaze. But it vanished as quickly as it had appeared. "Understood. I suppose the fact that he teaches at Emerson Academy might complicate things further. There are bound to be Emerson alumni in attendance tonight."

"My dad doesn't teach at Emerson." Daphne lifted her chin. It was past time to set the record straight on this point. She'd never once been ashamed of her father, and she wasn't about to start now, no matter who she was fake-engaged to. "He's the head of custodial services there."

To his credit, Jack didn't even flinch. Definitely not the reaction Daphne expected, considering how she'd been treated by the students at Emerson when she'd been a teenager. "My mistake. I'm sorry."

"I love him with my whole heart. My mom died when I was just a toddler, and he's pretty much been my everything for as long as I can remember." Kind of like Jack was for Olivia now that her parents had passed away.

Which was probably why Daphne had so much respect for the way he'd rearranged his entire life around being her guardian. "You asked me why I didn't date, and Emerson Academy is a big part of the reason I've chosen not to."

A muscle in Jack's jaw ticked—the same one that always seemed to make an appearance whenever he was agitated in some way. How strange that Daphne knew him well enough now to have absorbed this information.

"Go on," he said in a voice that bordered on tenderness.

Daphne didn't want or need him to feel sorry for her. He'd told her a lot about himself recently, and she was about to meet his family, so it only seemed fair to follow up on her promise to explain.

"I went to public school and after dismissal, I used to go to Emerson and spend the late afternoons doing my homework in my dad's office until he got off work. Sometimes kids who stayed after school for lacrosse practice or debate club would talk to me. I thought I was making friends." Daphne attempted a smile to prove she no longer cared about this painful period of her life, but she couldn't quite manage it.

"What happened?" Jack said, cutting to the chase. The muscle in his jaw was working overtime.

"Senior year, one of the kids invited me to Emerson prom as his date. I was thrilled. Dad bought me a fancy dress, the whole nine yards." Daphne inhaled a shuddering breath. No matter how many times she told this story, it didn't get any easier. She'd never shared it with a man before—never *wanted* to. "On prom night, he sent a car to pick me up. We were supposed to meet at the dance, which should've been a giant red flag, but clearly, I was clueless. When I walked into the party, my date was already there…with another girl. The entire episode had been a big joke. Correction. *I* was the joke. No one in that crowd would've dreamed of dating the janitor's daughter."

She bit down hard on the inside of her cheek to keep herself from tearing up. No way would she *cry* in front of Jack King. Not even a little bit. But every time she thought about sitting in the back of that car, all by herself, so full of silly, delusional hope, she died just a little bit inside. She would never, ever give a man the chance to do that to her again. A heart that remained protected could never be broken. Period.

Jack drew in a long breath, eyes blazing. "I'm so sorry that happened to you, Daph. For what it's worth, I don't think any of my school friends would've done something so cruel. I hope not, anyway. I just…"

"It was a long time ago. It's fine," Daphne said, even though it wasn't. She just didn't need Jack to fight her battles for her, even though it was nice to have someone on her side.

"No, it's not. It's not fine at all." He fidgeted behind his desk, a knight in shining armor longing for a sword. And maybe a time machine. "You still don't trust anyone enough to date. Totally understandable, but also sad. You deserve to be happy, Daphne."

"I *am* happy," she said, a little too crisply. "I have a career most people would kill for. And thanks to our new series, the sky's the limit."

Somewhere in the back of her head, she heard Everly's words of wisdom to Addison in the fashion closet the other day.

All I'm trying to say is that work isn't everything. Remember to actually live your life.

Daphne cherished Everly, but happily married newlyweds were truly annoying sometimes. That's what she told herself, anyway, whenever her mind looped back to that particular conversation, and she wondered if perhaps her friend had made a valid point.

"Can I ask what your father thought about all of this?" Jack said.

"He doesn't know."

Jack's forehead creased. "You never told him?"

Daphne shook her head. "No, and I never will. He'd only blame himself, and what happened wasn't his fault."

"Of course it wasn't," Jack agreed. "But I'll bet he can handle the truth. He raised a passionate, independent woman all on his own. I have a feeling he's stronger than you think he is."

Daphne's chest grew tight. "You're probably right. But I'm still not bringing him to the engagement party. I just don't want to involve him in all of this mess. I hope you understand."

"I'll never force you to do anything you're not comfortable with. Please don't forget that in the midst of all of—" he circled a finger, indicating their general environment—the *Veil* offices and everything the magazine encompassed "—this."

And damned if Daphne didn't get choked up.

"My dad is a wonderful person," she said, because she wanted...*needed*...to steer the conversation away from herself again and because it was the truth. Plus she wasn't about to subject her dad to scrutiny at a high society engagement party when it wasn't necessary.

Or real, for that matter.

"If he's anything like his daughter, then I'm sure he is." Jack tilted his head. "And I want you to know that I would make sure he felt welcome at the party if you chose to invite him. You have my word on that, but I understand if you'd rather not."

Daphne shook her head. "He'd never understand why I would do something like this."

"Lie about being engaged or marry the likes of me?" Jack shrugged a single, muscular shoulder.

And just like that, a crack formed in the hard shell that Daphne had formed around her heart all those years ago. Not all the way—just enough to let a bit of light in.

She warmed from the inside out, despite every effort not to. "Would you stop, please?"

"Stop what?"

"Stop being charming when I least expect it. It's…" *Borderline irresistible.* "…unnerving. Besides, we both know half the women in Manhattan would kill to marry the likes of you."

He was a King. There were entire skyscrapers dotting the Manhattan skyline with his family's name emblazoned on them. That sort of thing was catnip to some women.

Not Daphne. Just…no.

She'd done a little research into her pretend in-laws-to-be after the meeting on Monday morning in Colette's office. Jack's father ran an investment firm that had been in the family for three generations. His mother was on the board of more than half a dozen philanthropic organizations. In light of Jack's pedigree, it was no wonder that he'd once been engaged to a woman as polished and refined as his ex-fiancée.

"Ashley certainly would," Daphne said with an eye roll.

"Ashley had her chance, remember?" Jack countered. His forehead furrowed. "Why are we talking about her right now?"

Because that's the type of woman his family was expecting to meet tonight, and Daphne wasn't that kind of girl. There was only so much pretending she was capable of.

"I guess I was wondering if she going to be at the party tonight," Daphne said.

"I haven't really thought about it." Jack shrugged. "Probably."

Oh, joy. This party was sounding worse and worse the more they discussed it.

"Great," Daphne said flatly.

"Ashley and I are finished. She's marrying someone else."

"She still has feelings for you." Daphne polished off the rest of her omelet and set the empty box on Jack's desk.

Jack harrumphed. "I highly doubt that."

"Women know these things. I can tell. She certainly didn't waste any time contacting your mother after the Elegantly Engaged class." Daphne smoothed down the skirt of her A-line dress. This one was decorated with a print featuring vintage red Vespas and it went perfectly with her dangly, rhinestone pizza-slice earrings. "What about you? Do you still have feelings for her?"

"Not in the slightest. Ashley's not the one I want. I thought you knew that by now," Jack said quietly—so quietly that Daphne barely heard him over the pounding of her heart.

Not the one I want...

Who did Jack want? Daphne didn't dare ask. At least they were talking to each other now, unlike that awkward evening at Bloom when she had to interrogate him for even the most minute details about his life.

"I have Olivia now, though, so things are different.

Please don't take this wrong way, but I can't involve her in our…" He waved his hand back and forth between them.

"Farce?" Daphne raised her eyebrows. "Go ahead and call it what it is."

"Right. Choice of words aside, I can't let Olivia think I'm getting married. It wouldn't be right to introduce her to you and let her think you'll be a permanent fixture in her life. It would break her heart."

He's a good dad, Daphne thought. *Just like mine.*

"How do you know she'd even like me?"

"Trust me, I know. She'd adore everything about you." His gaze shot to the sparkles in her hair. "I'm fairly certain she'd think you're Cinderella."

"I'm going to take that as a compliment." Daphne's heart thumped hard in her chest, which was ridiculous. This entire conversation was making her feel far more vulnerable than she liked. She squared her shoulders. "So how do we explain her absence at our engagement party? Surely everyone will expect her to be there."

Jack shook his head. "No, not at all. My mother already informed me it's an adults-only affair."

"Adults-only?" Daphne grimaced. "But you're her parent, for all practical purposes. She should be a part of things—the wedding, the engagement party, everything."

"Don't get me wrong. I fully agree, and if we were really getting married, I would insist on Olivia being there. She'd be a flower girl and the whole works."

"I bet she'd love that," Daphne said. Her mind spun with frilly, feminine dress options. Olivia would probably want something princess-y, with a full skirt built for twirling.

But there wasn't going to be a wedding, so there was no need to be thinking about flower girl gowns, was there?

"Alas, that's not how my parents and their crowd do things. My mother was adamant—no children. And since it saved me from having to explain why I didn't want to tell her about the engagement, I didn't put up a fight," Jack said.

Unbelievable.

Jack's social circle sounded like a delight. Daphne shouldn't have been surprised, given her own experience with the boys at Emerson and what Jack had told her about Ashley, but she couldn't wrap her head around it.

"I will never understand rich people," she muttered. When she realized Jack himself was likely included in that particular demographic, she pulled a face. "No offense."

"None taken. And for what it's worth, Cinderella?" Affection glowed in his eyes. After all the nicknames she'd given him, he'd finally bestowed one on her. And despite herself, she sort of loved it. "I'd be disappointed if you did."

Chapter Ten

At the end of the workday, with just two hours to go until the dreaded engagement party, Addison appeared at Daphne's cubicle holding a garment bag. Daphne was so absorbed in the article she was writing about new trends in bridal updos that she barely noticed her friend's presence.

"Hey," she said without looking up from the screen of her computer. "What's up?"

"What's up with *you*?" Addison tapped the pointy toe of her stiletto on the smooth tile floor. "That article you're working on isn't due for a week. Don't you have an important party to get ready for?"

True, but if Daphne stopped typing, everyone would see how badly her hands might be trembling. At least if she was busy working, she could keep her mind halfway occupied and off of the hot mess that lay ahead.

Addison rested a gentle hand on her shoulder. Of course she wasn't fooled by Daphne's workaholic act.

No one in the world knew her better than Addison and Everly did. "Daph, stop. Please? Look at me."

Daphne dragged her gaze away from her monitor and buried her hands in her lap. Sure enough, she was shaking like a leaf.

Her nerves didn't escape Addison's notice.

"Hon, it's only natural to be anxious about tonight. There's a lot at stake." She lowered her voice to a whisper. "Where's Jack?"

"He went home to have dinner with Olivia and read her a bedtime story. I'm meeting him later at his parents' apartment building," Daphne said.

She'd promised Jack the arrangement wasn't giving her any prom night flashbacks, but he still wanted to come pick her up in his hired car. They couldn't risk anyone from the magazine seeing them together, though. The staff had been abuzz all week trying to figure out who had penned the viral article, but as far as Daphne knew, only Colette knew the truth. Plus her *Veil* girls, obviously.

"Working like a maniac until then isn't going to help," Addison said.

She was right, of course. It wasn't.

Daphne grimaced. "What will? Any ideas?"

"I know the perfect thing. But first—" Addison's gaze flitted to the garment bag slung over her arm "—what is this? It has your name on it."

"It's my dress for the party." Daphne reached for the garment bag and Addison took a backward step, holding it just out of reach.

She shook her head. "Oh, honey, no. You can do much better than this."

Everly's head popped up from the other side of the cubicle divider. "*So* much better."

Daphne bit back a smile. "What's going on here? Are

you guys really so nosy that you peeked into that garment bag to see what I was planning on wearing tonight?"

Addison shrugged. "Isn't that what best friends do?"

"I was going for conservative and understated," Daphne said. In short, she'd searched her closet for anything that remotely resembled something Ashley might wear. That's what Jack's family would expect, right?

Lurking way in the back, stuffed behind her beloved novelty-print dresses and a preponderance of tulle and fluff, was the knockoff Chanel suit she'd worn to her initial interview for the *Veil* receptionist job back during her junior year in college. It seemed like just the thing.

"I hear what you're saying, but this suit just isn't you." Everly pulled a face.

Addison looked Daphne up and down. "Wouldn't you feel more confident walking in there as your true, authentic self?"

"My entire identity tonight is a lie," Daphne said flatly. Just like at Elegantly Engaged, she wasn't even using her last name. Nor was she planning on telling anyone that she worked at *Veil*. It just wasn't possible. She and Jack had made up a whole cover story about her working at Bloomingdale's.

"Your identity might be a lie, but your sense of style doesn't have to be," Addison said.

Everly held up a finger. "Accurate. And don't you dare deprive me of living vicariously right now. Nothing in the entire closet fits me. Hashtag 'Pregnancy Problems,'" Everly said.

Daphne glanced back and forth from one friend to the other. "What do you have in mind?"

Addison waggled her eyebrows. "Just think of us as your fairy godmothers."

Everly came around from the other side of the cubicle

and tugged Daphne out of her chair by the hand. "Come with us. We have a surprise for you."

"A surprise?" Daphne's spirits lifted ever so slightly. "I love surprises."

"We know that, silly. Come on. By the time we're finished, you're going to walk into that engagement party feeling like the icing on a cupcake," Addison said.

Daphne laughed. "Now you're really speaking my language."

Daphne knew her friends were serious about wanting to surprise her when they made her put on a blindfold before entering the fashion closet.

"It's a good thing the rest of the staff has gone home, or they'd seriously wonder what was going on." Daphne held her arms out in front of her for protection as she stumbled inside. Everly had tied a white silk scarf over her eyes, completely obscuring Daphne's vision.

The last time she'd been blindfolded had been back when the *Veil* staff had played "pin the tiara on Kate Middleton" the night before the big royal wedding. She'd been an abysmal failure at that game, pinning the crown straight onto poor Kate's forehead.

"Isn't this a tad bit dramatic?" she asked as Addison reached for her shoulders to bring her to a steady halt. "I'm fairly certain I've seen everything in here."

"Impossible," Everly said, somewhere to Daphne's right. "You could get lost in here."

True. The closet contained enough organza alone to swallow a person whole.

"We just want you to see the entire effect all at once." Addison gave her shoulders an affectionate squeeze. "Ready?"

She sighed. "As ready as I'll ever be."

Getting excited about the party was next to impossible, no matter what she wore. She and Jack weren't actually getting married, and now that their undercover personas had become intertwined with their very real lives, their engagement no longer felt like an exciting work assignment. It felt like a big fat lie.

Because that's precisely what it is.

She couldn't believe she was going to have to look his parents in the eyes and pretend they were going to be her in-laws. The conversation with Jack earlier in his office really made all of it hit home. This was a real family. Real people—people she had nothing in common with at all. Just thinking about raising a glass with them and toasting her fake engagement to their son made her stomach tie itself up in knots.

Everly started to countdown from five, her voice as bubbly as a glass of champagne. "Five…four…three…"

When she got down to one, Addison untied the blindfold and removed it from Daphne's face. "Ta-da!"

Daphne's eyes fluttered open. She blinked a few times as she took in the sight of a pair of pale blue Jimmy Choo stilettos with crystal-encrusted ankle straps. The tip of one pointy toe said "I" in rhinestone lettering, while the glittering stones on the other shoe "Do."

I do. Just like a wedding vow.

The shoes were very sparkly, very bridal, very over-the-top in a Daphne-esque sort of way.

"Which one of you found the Jimmy Choos? They're perfect," she said.

"I did." Everly raised a hand. "But, *ahem*, didn't you notice the dress? We both knew exactly which one."

Daphne's gaze darted upward. "I don't understand. Where?"

Her favorite gown—the blue Monique Lhuillier mesh

tulle dress with the delicate floral appliqué—hung in the same spot where it always did. There wasn't a cocktail dress in sight.

"Right here, silly." Everly gave the diaphanous skirt of the gown a reverent pat.

"What? No." Daphne shook her head. "No way. Have you both lost your minds? That's a *wedding gown*."

"Is it, though?" Addison tilted her head and squinted at the dress. "It looks like a light blue gown to me."

"Very Cinderella." Everly pointed a finger at Daphne. "Very *you*."

Daphne's heart fluttered. *Cinderella.* Her new nickname.

But really? Daphne was no stranger to extravagant fashion. She still had the bedazzled hair and Bridezilla eyelashes to prove it. Showing up at the engagement party in this gown seemed a step too far, even for her.

"Be honest." Addison plucked the dress's hanger from the rack and spread out the sheer fabric so the tiny mesh flowers quivered like butterfly wings. The gown was breathtaking—even prettier up close than it had been hanging on the rack where Daphne had always admired it from afar. "If you saw this dress on Emily Blunt at the Oscars, you'd never ask why she'd turned up at an award ceremony in a wedding gown."

"True." Daphne gave her friends a once-over. "But you both seem to be forgetting the fact that I'm not Emily Blunt."

"No, you're not. You're our good friend Daphne— beauty editor extraordinaire, total fashionista and cow-riter of the most read article in *Veil* history. This dress is *worthy of you*, not the other way around." Everly's eyes went misty as she looked at Daphne, affection oozing from her every pore.

Daphne's throat closed up tight. Her friends were right. What was she doing, trying to emulate Ashley? She'd never be able to pull that off.

But no one was better at being Daphne Ballantyne than she was.

She reached out to touch the dress's delicate mesh fabric. It was buttery soft, like something a ballerina might wear. "You're sure it would be appropriate to turn up at an engagement party in a full-length gown?"

Addison gave a dismissive wave of her hand. "Oh, honey, the party is on Central Park South."

"And don't forget…" Everly's grin brightened. "You're the bride!"

Jack's bride-to-be.

His fiancée.

His.

As if Daphne could forget.

Jack cursed as he climbed out of a yellow taxi at the curb outside the *Veil* office and glanced at his watch. He was late. Daphne had probably already left for the party, which was the exact scenario he'd been trying to avoid.

He jammed a hand through his hair and searched the surroundings. She was nowhere to be seen. He'd thought he had plenty of time to slip into his tuxedo and head back to the office after dinner and story time with Olivia, but the traffic had been horrendous. He should've known better than to try to get here by car. This was why he usually walked to work.

"Can you wait, please?" Hands braced on the open window of the cab, he implored the driver, "Just a few more minutes?"

The driver shrugged. "It's your money, pal."

"Thanks," Jack said.

He stood to his full height and blew out a breath. Daphne had been so insistent about meeting him at his parents' building and logistically, it made perfect sense. The office was in the opposite direction of the King family's penthouse. They'd drive straight past his apartment on the way. But after the story she'd told him about prom night at Emerson Academy, there was no way he was going to let her get all dressed up and ride over there by herself.

What those kids had done to her back then made his blood boil. Teenagers could be cruel, but that had been beyond the pale. After work, Jack had gone through his old yearbook and found a photograph of Daphne's father. He recognized the older man instantly from his private school days. Daphne's dad was practically an institution at Emerson. He'd been at the school for decades. Jack remembered him as kind and supportive—a comforting presence in a high-pressure world, both socially and academically.

He just couldn't believe those boys had played such a cruel prank on Daphne. She was five years or so younger than he was, so Jack had already been away at Yale when the prom incident took place. He wished he'd been there. He would've fixed things.

He wanted to fix it now. Still.

But Jack knew good and well that he couldn't change the past. He tried to do that exact thing nearly every day where Olivia was concerned. Painful memories left scars, and the invisible kind sometimes seemed even harder to heal than the ones that left a mark for all the world to see.

All he knew was that Daphne deserved to be happy. She deserved to be loved. She deserved a man who would treat her with gentleness and respect. With reverence.

Jack was not that man. Of this, he was certain. He

hardly had the time and space in his life to be fake-engaged, much less be involved in a genuine relationship. He was still trying to figure out how to be a family man. A father. His life had spun completely off the rails six months ago, and he was still trying his best to wrestle it back under control. Every day seemed to be a reminder that he couldn't. The control that he craved so much was elusive. The more he tried to hold on tight, the further it slipped through his fingers.

The very fact that he was standing here, looking for his work-nemesis-turned-fake-fiancée to accompany him to a party his parents were throwing for their nonexistent engagement was a prime example of how far he'd let himself get dragged away from reality. He wasn't even sure what was real anymore and what wasn't.

Except for the ache in his chest that he got when he thought about Daphne riding alone in a cab to her own engagement party. Fake or not, he wasn't going to let that happen.

Unless he was already too late…which appeared to be the case.

"Jack?"

Relief washed over him at the sound of her voice—a relief so palpable it was almost alarming. He told himself he was simply trying to be kind, to do what little he could to right a wrong. After all, wasn't that what the ring in his pocket was also about? But then he turned in the direction of the sound of his name and caught his first glimpse of Daphne, and he wasn't sure of anything anymore.

Wow.

He drank in the sight of her bare shoulders, her upswept hair and a dress that looked like it was straight out of a fairy tale, and he suddenly couldn't remember how to breathe. She was a vision. So beautiful and so dazzling that it almost hurt to look at her.

"Daphne." Jack clutched a hand to his chest. "You are…"

He shook his head. There were no words, really—no words to describe the need shooting through his veins. The need for more…

More of this crazy roller coaster ride they'd embarked on over a week ago. More *life*. More…love?

His jaw clenched. He shouldn't be having these thoughts about Daphne, of all people. They were cowriters, that was all. At best, friends.

"I think the word you're looking for is *overdressed*." She scrunched up her face, and he had a forbidden urge to kiss the glittery gloss right off of her mouth and tangle his hands in her updo until all the tiny crystals in her hair fell at their feet like starlight.

"Actually, the word I'm looking for is—" he winked at her, and a surge of adrenaline shot through him when color rose to her cheeks, pink like cherries "—perfect."

Her lovely mouth twisted into a bashful smile. Jack had never seen Daphne quite like this before—so vulnerable and open. Not even earlier today in his office when she'd told him about why she didn't like to date…why she had such a hard time trusting people. Men, in particular.

It almost felt like he was seeing her for the very first time.

"Thank you." Her gaze swept over him, and her eyes sparkled. "You clean up pretty good yourself, Captain. I like the tux."

He flicked the satin lapel of his jacket. "This old thing?"

She rolled her eyes at him. *Good,* Jack thought. *Back to the usual back and forth.* But the desire flickering to life inside of him was anything but ordinary.

Enjoying Your Book?

Start saving on new books like the one you're reading with the *Harlequin Reader Service!*

Get Free Books In Just 3 Easy Steps

Are you an avid reader searching for more books?
The **Harlequin Reader Service** might be for you! We'd love to send you up to **4 free books** just for trying it out. Just write **"YES"** on the **Free Books Voucher Card** and we'll send your free books and a gift, altogether worth over $20.

Step 1: Choose your Books

Try *Harlequin® Special Edition* and get 2 books featuring comfort and strength in the support of loved ones and enjoying the journey no matter what life throws your way.

Try *Harlequin® Heartwarming™ Larger-Print* and get 2 books featuring uplifting stories where the bonds of friendship, family and community unite.

Or *TRY BOTH!*

Step 2: Return your completed Free Books Voucher Card

Step 3: Receive your books and continue reading!

Your free books are **completely free**, even the shipping! If you continue with your subscription, you can look forward to curated monthly shipments of brand-new books from your selected series, always at a discount off the cover price! Plus you can cancel any time.

Don't miss out, reply today! Over $20 FREE value.

Free Books Voucher Card

YES! I love reading, please send me more books from the series I'd like to explore and a free gift from each series I select.

More books are just 3 steps away!

Just write in "**YES**" on the dotted line below then select your series and return this Books Voucher today and we'll send your free books & a gift asap!

≫ _YES_ ≪

Choose your books:

☐ **Harlequin® Special Edition**
235/335 CTI G297

☐ **Harlequin® Heartwarming™ Larger-Print**
161/361 CTI G297

☐ **BOTH**
235/335 & 161/361 CTI G29A

FIRST NAME	LAST NAME

ADDRESS

APT.#	CITY

STATE/PROV.	ZIP/POSTAL CODE

EMAIL ☐ Please check this box if you would like to receive newsletters and promotional emails from Harlequin Enterprises ULC and its affiliates. You can unsubscribe anytime.

"What are you doing here, though? I told you I'd meet you at the party." She glanced over his shoulder at the taxi, still idling by the curb.

"I know you did, but Nanny Marie was early, Olivia and Buttercup were snuggled together in their blanket fort and I figured that maybe we should ride together." He looked away lest she see right through the blatant lie.

Her expression softened in a way that made his chest fill with warmth. She knew exactly why he'd come back. If he thought he could hide anything from Daphne, he was fooling himself.

"Thank you," she said, resting a hand on his chest, palm nestled against his heartbeat.

"Anytime, Cinderella." He covered her hand with his and gave it a gentle squeeze.

They stood there for a moment as the sun dipped below the horizon, bathing the city streets in a rosy light. Just a few blocks away, the lush, verdant sprawl of Central Park was changing from bright, vivid green to fiery red. Autumn in New York was beautiful by any standard, but Jack had never fully realized how lovely the city could be when it let go…when it allowed itself, ever so gently, to fall.

He tipped his head toward the taxi. "Your chariot awaits."

Chapter Eleven

Daphne fixed her gaze out of the backseat window of the car and tried to focus on the blur of yellow as other taxis streaked past them and the dizzying lights of the city skyline. But no matter how hard she tried, she couldn't shake the fluttery sensation that had swept over her when she'd spotted Jack waiting for her outside the *Veil* building.

He'd come back for her.

It was such a silly thing, just a small gesture that to anyone else, wouldn't have been a big deal at all. But to Daphne, it meant a lot—the world, almost. Jack knew it would. He knew why too.

Daphne should've kept her mouth shut about Emerson Academy, her father, the whole lot of it. Her fake fiancé knew far too much about her now. That's the only reason he was getting under her skin so badly—the only reason why her knees had gone wobbly when she'd spied the look on his face as he'd seen her in the dress for the first time.

This was all the gown's fault. The gown, plus Daphne

spilling her guts to her work husband. That's what she wanted so desperately to believe, anyway.

She did her best to paste an impassive look on her face as she swiveled to face him, but the sight of him in that tuxedo made her mouth water. He may as well have been a cupcake. The suit had to be custom-made. After a decade in the bridal business, Daphne knew a bespoke tuxedo when she saw one.

"We're all set on the backstory we came up with, right?" she said.

Maybe if she reminded them both of the night's actual purpose, she'd be able to focus on what really mattered—her career, *Veil*, their undercover series of articles. Not the way her heart was beginning to feel like a bird trapped in a cage every time she looked at Jack.

He nodded. "You work as a personal shopper at Bloomingdale's, and we met when I came in to buy a suit."

Had they stolen that particular meet cute from an old episode of *Friends*? Yes. Yes, they had. But Jack assured her that his parents and their crowd weren't hanging around in their sweats at night binge watching old sitcoms. Their loss, as far as Daphne was concerned.

"It's been a whirlwind courtship," Daphne added. Hence the speedy engagement—so fast that he hadn't gotten around to telling his family about his new relationship status.

"Love at first sight." He brushed a strand of hair from her eyes, and his fingertips traced a shivering trail down the side of her face.

Daphne's breath bottled up in her throat. "It's amazing what silly things some people might let themselves believe, isn't it?"

"Ridiculous," he said. "Utterly laughable."

But neither of them seemed to be laughing.

Jack's forehead crinkled, as if he'd just remembered something important. Like the fact that this entire narrative was completely made up. He moved his hand away from her cheek and reached into his pocket.

"I almost forgot. I have something for you," he said.

And before Daphne could register what was happening, he was handing her a small velvet box. A *ring* box, much to her mortification.

She reached for it and then, when she realized what she was doing, she snatched her hand back as if she'd been accidentally grabbing hold of a live explosive.

"What is that?" she asked, heart pounding.

"It's nothing." He shrugged and nudged the box closer to her. "It's just a…um…engagement ring."

"But I've already got a ring." She held up her hand, where the faux diamond from the fashion closet glittered on her all-important finger.

"I see that." His brows lifted. "I'm also pretty certain that rock can be seen from space."

"Oh, I get it. Your family might recognize it as a fake," she said.

"They might, yes." He laughed under his breath. "This one is a bit more believable. But if you don't like it, you don't have to wear it."

Believable was good. That's what they were going for, so Daphne relented and took the little blue box from him.

She snapped the lid open and gasped when she spotted the emerald cut diamond solitaire nestled against the dark velvet cushion inside. It was a smaller, infinitely more regal version of the fake she'd been sporting for the past week and a half. Unlike the ring from the fashion closet, there was no questioning the jewel's authenticity.

It shimmered like mad—an entire kaleidoscope of light contained in a single, perfect stone.

"I…" She cleared her throat. "I, um, I do like it, actually."

Understatement of the century. The ring was stunning.

"I don't get it, though. You just happened to have an engagement ring from Tiffany's lying around?" Her gaze flicked toward his.

He hesitated for a beat, and then reality dawned. This must be the ring he'd originally given Ashley.

"Silly me, I almost forgot. You've been engaged before," Daphne said as she busied herself with removing the ring from the fashion closet from her finger. She didn't dare let him see even a hint of disappointment in her expression. What on earth did she have to feel let down about?

He took her hand and slid the new ring in place. It felt different the second it sat on her finger—heavy, almost. Weighed down by its preciousness and everything that a ring like that was supposed to symbolize.

With this ring…

Wedding vows rang in the back of Daphne's head. Clearly, she'd been working at *Veil* too long.

"Look, it's a perfect fit," she said, holding her hand out for inspection. "What are the odds?"

Jack offered her a quiet smile and echoed the sentiment. "What are the odds?"

Jack's parents lived in a sprawling penthouse that took up the entire top floor of their apartment building. A private elevator led from the lobby directly to their foyer. Just like that…no front door or anything. Their own elevator.

"Here we go," Jack said as the doors swished open.

He slid his hand onto the small of her back and bent to whisper in her ear. "Let's make this quick and easy. We'll stay and chat for a while and then make our escape."

Quick and easy. Jack made it sound so simple, like they were about to pick up a latte at the corner coffee shop.

Daphne took a deep breath. She could do this. After all, she'd gone through countless reward cards at the coffee truck that always parked around the corner from the *Veil* office.

Daphne nodded and stepped out onto the dazzling black-and-white marble floor just as an older woman in a floor-length burgundy sheath dress headed their way. With a champagne flute in each hand and the impeccable posture of a beauty pageant contestant, she in no way exuded coffee shop energy.

Jack's mom. Daphne swallowed. It had to be her.

"Well, hello, Jack dear. I was beginning to wonder if you were coming." The woman handed them both a glass of champagne and gave Jack's shoulder a tender squeeze as he bent to kiss her cheek.

"We're not that late, Mother. It's not even quarter past the hour," Jack said.

"But you're the guest of honor." The woman's gaze strayed toward Daphne, and she gave the blue gown an appreciative once-over. Thank goodness Addison and Everly had convinced her not to wear the knockoff suit. "And my, don't you look enchanting? Hello, dear. I'm Eleanor King, Jack's mother. I promise I'm not nearly as terrible as he's undoubtedly made me sound."

She extended a graceful hand, and Daphne shook it.

"He's said nothing but lovely things." What was a little white lie when she was already faking her entire identity? "I'm Daphne Grace. It's a pleasure to meet you."

"The pleasure's all mine," Eleanor said and then narrowed her eyes in Jack's direction. "Although Jack's told us next to nothing about you. I'm so pleased you're here. You must tell me everything."

Daphne sipped her champagne. "Everything" was an awfully tall order.

"We've only just got here, Mother. Perhaps we should at least let Daphne all the way inside before you start interrogating her." He pulled her closer, and she burrowed into him like it was the most natural thing in the world.

"Ah, Jack and Daphne are here." A man with the same square-cut jaw as Jack's and salt-and-pepper hair strode toward them from the living room, where massive floor-to-ceiling windows overlooked the park and the glittering skyline beyond.

His brows rose as he took in Daphne, and then he flashed a broad smile. "You must be our future daughter-in-law. I'm Gordon King, Jack's dad."

They exchanged more pleasantries, and Daphne tried to reconcile these polite, well-mannered people with the versions of them that she'd created in her head. They seemed nice enough—not like the villains that she'd imagined them to be. Then again, neither of them asked after Olivia right away, which seemed strange, considering they were the child's adoptive grandparents.

"Will your family be joining this evening?" Eleanor asked as their small group hovered on the edge of the crown in the living room. "We'd love to meet them before the wedding planning begins."

"I'm so sorry, but no." Daphne shook her head. Wedding planning? Surely, they could put that off until after Elegantly Engaged was over. Two weeks plus one day. That's all they had left, and then she and Jack could fake a breakup, just like they'd faked everything else. As much as Daphne loved sugar, the last thing she wanted to do was go on wedding cake tastings and the like with Jack's mother. "My mother passed away when I very young. It's just my dad and me. He lives in Houston and couldn't get away."

She didn't like lying about her father—especially not here. Of all the lies she'd told in recent days, this one was by far the worst. It felt like a betrayal.

It's not personal. It's work, she reminded herself.

"What does your father do, dear?" Eleanor asked.

And there it was—the question Daphne had been dreading. She couldn't...*wouldn't*...lie about this. She'd rather expose herself as a fraud.

"We're being rude to the other guests," Jack said, deftly intervening and saving her in the process. "Shall we mingle, sweetheart?"

The mingle game, just like Elegantly Engaged.

Daphne nodded. "Yes, let's."

The next half hour was a blur of introductions. Daphne must have met at least fifty people, one right after another. Jack never left her side, and together they repeated the made-up version of their backstory until it rolled off of her tongue as easily as her name. The mingle game had prepared them well.

"Your parents have a lot of friends," she said in a rare moment of privacy as they stood on the terrace.

The city lights twinkled all around, and Central Park looked like a plush, decadent carpet spread at their feet far below. Daphne had never seen Manhattan like this before. From this angle, it seemed untouchable, as if nothing bad could ever happen here. How desperately she wanted to believe in that glittering dream...

But Daphne knew better. She didn't even belong in this building, much less the penthouse terrace. The only thing that had gotten her here was a big fat lie.

"Them?" Jack's gaze slid toward the party guests and the tinkle of laughter and polite conversation back inside the apartment. "They're not friends. Not in any real sense of the word. If my family were to lose everything, Mom and Dad would probably never hear from most of them again."

"Do you really think so?" Daphne didn't want to believe it. That sort of conditional friendship seemed incredibly sad. Empty. Nothing at all like what she shared with her *Veil* girls.

"Maybe I'm being overly harsh, but I do. For the most part, anyway. I'll just say this—not a single one of these people who act as if they're so invested in my happiness bothered to reach out to me after Ashley and I ended our engagement. For a few months, my mom's social calendar suffered too."

Daphne's mouth dropped open. "Are you serious?"

"I sure am." Jack nodded.

"It must be confusing to grow up in a world like that," Daphne said.

Jack's expression went tender. "I know what you're thinking. Don't."

"How can you possibly know what I'm thinking?" She gave his chest a little poke.

He arched an eyebrow at her, ever the know-it-all fact-checker. "You're thinking of cutting the boys who treated you so poorly some slack. Like maybe their cruelty was a result of their upbringing in some way."

Okay, so maybe the thought had crossed her mind.

She planted a hand on her hip. "So now you think you can read me like a book—just like I knew what kind of dog you had, where you went to college and what signature drink you preferred?"

"One." He ticked off a finger. "You were wrong about

the college thing. *Harvard?*" He shot her an exaggerated look of mock disgust. "As if."

Laughter bubbled up Daphne's throat.

"And two..." There was that tender look in his eyes again, and it all but turned her insides to mush. "Yes, I think I do know you now. I *see* you, sweetheart. You want to believe the best in people—even people who don't necessarily deserve it."

"What makes you think so?" she asked with a lump in her throat and her heart on her sleeve.

"For starters? The way you reacted when you found out about Olivia. You understood why I hadn't said anything, even before I explained myself. And that was back in our Post-it era."

"Our Post-it era?" She couldn't help but laugh.

"We've moved on," he said, eyes dancing in the darkness. "We're in a different era now."

"Dare I ask what this era is called?" She gave him a shoulder bump, and the wispy, off-the-shoulder sleeve of her pretty blue gown dipped lower.

Jack moved it gently back in place, fingertips leaving a blaze of goose bumps in their wake. "The omelet era."

"You really think I'm going to eat spinach omelets every day now, don't you?"

"Please, I know better. But you know what they say— you can't make an omelet without breaking a few eggs. Isn't that what we're doing? Breaking eggs? Smashing our assumptions about each other, peeling away the outer shell that everyone else sees and getting a glimpse of the good part?" He lifted an eyebrow. "While simultaneously pulling the wool over everyone's eyes in the process, naturally."

A warm, fuzzy feeling came over Daphne.

"Again with the charm offensive. Be careful or I just

might think you're trying to sweep me off my feet," she said. She'd meant it as a joke, but the smile died on her lips before she could even get the words out.

She liked the way he saw her. She liked it a lot. She liked *him*.

"We wouldn't want that now, would we?" A grin tugged at his lips, but his eyes were dead serious.

Is that what she really and truly wanted—for Jack King to sweep her off her feet? For real this time?

"No." *Liar liar, pants on fire.* She'd told so many whoppers lately that she couldn't seem to keep track of them. "Obviously."

"Obviously," he echoed. And then, just like clockwork, the telltale muscle in Jack's jaw flexed.

Daphne blinked, convinced she was seeing things. She had to be. If not—if his jaw had indeed just ticked—that meant he hadn't liked her answer. It meant he *wanted* to sweep her off her feet.

No. Her gaze bore into his, searching. Searching for some sort of hint to what he might be thinking. *It can't be.*

"Jack? Daphne?" Eleanor stepped out onto the veranda, shoulders sagging in relief when she spotted them. "Here you are. I've been looking everywhere. It's time for the toast, darlings. The caterers have already poured the champagne and the servers are passing it around. Come, come."

She waved a hand, beckoning them back to the party.

Daphne's gaze slid toward Jack as they followed, but his attention was fixed firmly in front of him. The bubbly lightness from their earlier conversation had gone.

"Hear, hear, everyone." Jack's father raised a glass from the center of the room. "Time for a toast."

Melanie Miller would've been proud. According to

what they'd learned at Elegantly Engaged, this was text-
book toast behavior.

The next few minutes seemed to happen in slow motion, like a dream. Someone handed Daphne a glass of
sparkling liquid while Gordon King gave a little speech,
peppered with words like *marriage* and *family* and *soul
mate*—words that made Daphne's stomach squirm. Jack's
relationship with his parents might not be as close as hers
was with her father, but they were still his family. The
smile on Eleanor's face was so happy and bright. Would
she be ostracized from her social circle again once she
and Jack faked their breakup in a few weeks?

Then, just as Gordon began winding down his remarks, Daphne's attention snagged on a familiar face in
the crowd. Her stomach flipped. *Ashley.* Jack's ex was
here after all. Of course she was. Their parents were family friends. Daphne hadn't seen her earlier in the evening.
She and Wesley must've arrived while Daphne had been
outside on the terrace with Jack.

They were here now, though. Ashley was looking
straight at her, and a ball of anxiety settled in the pit of
Daphne's stomach. Ashley and Jack had a long, complicated history. If anyone could see through this charade,
it was her.

Then Ashley's gaze strayed to Daphne's ring finger,
laser focused on the emerald cut diamond Jack had slipped
onto her finger in the backseat of the taxi. Daphne braced
herself to be on the receiving end of a smirk or, at mini-
mum, a loaded glance. The ring was basically Ashley's
hand-me-down, after all.

But there wasn't even a hint of recognition in her expression as her eyes moved over the diamond. It was almost as if she'd never even seen it before.

Daphne barely had time to register her surprise, much

less make sense of it, before Jack's arm tightened around her waist.

"Are you okay with this?" he murmured, his breath warm against her neck.

Daphne blinked. "What?" She'd been so focused on Ashley that she'd missed the last few words of Gordon's speech.

"They want us to kiss," Jack said under his breath as he cupped her face, thumb caressing her cheek in what Daphne could only assume was a bid to stall for time.

"Oh." Daphne let out a little gasp. *Oh.*

She and Jack had gone over things in such detail. They'd walked into this party prepared for anything... Anything but this.

It had never crossed her mind that they might be expected to kiss—right here, in front of everyone. How could they have forgotten such an important detail? And wasn't Jack being chivalrous, asking her permission first, even as they were being put on the spot in front of his family and their high society friends?

They had to, right? They really didn't have a choice in the matter. At least that's what Daphne told herself as she grabbed hold of the satin lapels of his tuxedo jacket and hung on for dear life as she rose up on tiptoe and pressed her lips to his.

She felt him rear back a little in surprise at first, and then his hand splayed on the center of her back, pulling her flush against him. Fingertips dug into the delicate fabric of her dress, sending a wave of sensation skittering over her skin as if he too was trying to anchor them both to this moment...to make it as believable as possible. To make it real.

The kiss was tender at first. Gentle and reverent. Then

heat gathered deep in her belly as it moved into something different…something new.

This is just for show, she tried to remind herself through the fog of desire. *He's not mine. He's just something borrowed.*

But her body didn't seem to get the message. She felt herself opening for him, inviting him in, holding him so close that she could feel his heartbeat crashing against her rib cage. Wedding vows spun through her mind—words she'd heard so many times at work but that had never really made sense before.

To have and to hold. To love and to cherish. Until death do us part.

This feeling…this sense of sweet relief…this is what it meant to be cherished. Maybe even loved.

She heard a kittenish sound, a helpless little whimper, and was astonished to realize it had come from her. But she didn't dare pull away and end the kiss. Couldn't if she'd tried. So she surrendered to the moment…to the man who seemed to keep surprising her in the most wonderful ways as he kissed her like he meant it. Like it was the most honest and true thing in the world.

Like it was a vow.

Chapter Twelve

The following morning, Jack got up early to make Olivia pancakes before he left for work. As surprisingly enjoyable as last night had been, he'd left the party feeling like something was missing—and that something was the little girl who'd become such an important part of his life. The party had been the first family function that Jack had attended in quite some time, and his family included Olivia now.

He'd told himself he was being ridiculous. He wasn't actually engaged, and his earlier decision still stood. There was no reason to introduce Olivia to a woman whose presence in their lives would only be temporary.

Except Daphne no longer felt altogether temporary. She'd become important to him in ways that had little or nothing to do with their work assignment. Despite their vastly different upbringings, she seemed to understand him in a way that Ashley never had. He liked making her laugh, seeing her smile. In the magic moments they stole every so often in the midst of the subterfuge, he felt himself letting go. Inch by inch. Little by little. Maybe being surprised every so often wasn't such a bad thing.

"Like that kiss," he heard himself say as he flipped a pancake with his spatula.

Buttercup's big golden head cocked at the sound of Jack's voice. The dog was positioned immediately to Jack's left, her paws mere inches from his bare feet. Prime position for catching any dropped food.

"What did it mean, though?" Jack asked.

The kiss certainly hadn't felt temporary. It felt real in every sense of the word—dazzling, free and wildly passionate, just like Daphne. In its aftermath, Jack had come to the conclusion that control as a concept might just be a tad overrated.

The kiss didn't need to be that way. At a party like that, just a tender peck would've been completely acceptable. Daphne wasn't one for doing things halfway, though. Why have one cupcake when she could have two? Why settle for a glass of rosé when she could drink a wedding cake martini? Why wear a simple, modest gown when she could turn up dressed like a fairy tale and render him undone in the process?

Daphne ate life up with a spoon, and when she was finished, she licked the bowl. In most respects, anyway. And it was growing on Jack big-time. He no longer found it irritating. In fact, he was beginning to realize he'd envied it all along.

She still wasn't ready for a relationship, though. That much was obvious. Every time they danced around the topic, she withdrew. And maybe that was for the best.

That kiss had been real, though. There was no denying it. And now here Jack was, trying to talk through it with his dog.

Buttercup's ears pricked forward. The golden retriever was an excellent listener. Too bad she didn't have the same affinity for dispensing relationship advice.

"There *is* no relationship," he muttered as he slipped a bite of pancake to Buttercup. "And I'm talking to a dog."

"I talk to Buttercup too sometimes, Uncle Jack."

Jack's head swiveled toward Olivia, who was rubbing her eyes and carrying her teddy bear by a tattered arm as she tiptoed into the kitchen in her pajamas. Buttercup wasted no time abandoning Jack in favor of the little girl. She made a beeline for Olivia, tail wagging like a pendulum.

"You sure do, pumpkin. And something tells me Buttercup likes it," Jack said.

Buttercup licked the side of Olivia's face with a wet swipe of her tongue and the child let loose with a stream of giggles. Music to Jack's ears.

"How do pancakes sound this morning, kiddo?" He flipped a pancake up in the air and caught it with Olivia's favorite Angelina Ballerina plate.

"Pancakes are my favorite." She grinned, and dimples flashed in her chubby little cheeks. "Do it again, Uncle Jack!"

"Will do. In the meantime, why don't you get started on this one?" He slid the plate in front of Olivia's preferred chair at the table. He'd already set the table with silverware, napkins and three different flavors of syrup.

Olivia scrambled into her seat, and when Jack turned his attention back toward the stove, the bear's voice box recited its recorded message.

Mommy and Daddy love you, Vivi.

Jack's grip tightened around the handle of the spatula. No matter how many times he heard it, the sound of

Marianne's voice coming from that stuffed animal always felt like a punch in the gut.

"You okay this morning, pumpkin? You didn't miss me too much last night, did you?" Guilt tugged at his heartstrings. Was Olivia regressing? Were they going to go back to the tearful nights of playing that message on repeat?

"Nanny Marie let me watch princess movies on the big TV. I missed you just a regular amount," Olivia said.

A regular amount. Jack would take it. Regular was progress. Regular was good. Regular was freaking fantastic.

"Sometimes I just like to hear Mommy, though." She held on to the bear by its neck with one hand while she picked delicately at her pancake with the other.

"I know you do, pumpkin. And I'm glad you still can, even now that she's up in heaven," Jack said. His gratitude for that talking bear knew no bounds.

"Me too."

Jack waggled his eyebrows. "Watch this."

He flipped another pancake in the air, but this time it narrowly missed the plate in his hand. Buttercup dove toward it, paws scrambling for purchase on the kitchen floor. The dog crashed into Jack's legs but still managed to catch the pancake before it hit the ground.

There went Jack's breakfast.

Olivia squealed with delight, and because the morning hadn't gotten quite chaotic enough, Jack's phone rang from somewhere on the kitchen counter.

He pointed the spatula at the dog. "Try not to get in any more trouble while I answer that."

Buttercup licked her chops, trotted back toward Olivia and splayed herself out under her chair, ever hopeful for another pancake accident. Jack turned off the stove and managed to find his cell buried underneath a dish towel. His mother's contact information lit up the screen.

"Good morning, Mother."

"Good morning, son." She sounded cheery for a change. That was a relief. "How did you and Daphne enjoy the party last night?"

Strangely enough, they had enjoyed it a lot. The kiss didn't hurt, that was for sure. Afterward, they'd played the mingle game for a bit longer and then Jack had whisked Daphne away for midnight pizza. He'd told himself he simply wanted to make sure she'd eaten something. Making the rounds at the party had left little time to enjoy the canapés.

In truth, he'd simply wanted them to do something normal together. Something that had nothing whatsoever to do with *Veil* or their pretend engagement. He was certain that once they had a chance to be themselves around each other again, the attraction simmering between them would cool to their usual, thinly veiled loathing.

No such luck.

"We had a very nice evening," Jack said, smiling to himself at the memory of Daphne laughing as she ate a slice of pepperoni pizza, all dressed up like she was going to a ball. The truth was, last night had one hundred percent felt like a date—the best damn date of Jack's life.

He knew better than to tell Daphne that, though.

"I'm glad. Your father and I enjoyed meeting Daphne, although I have to say, she wasn't at all what I expected," Eleanor said.

Careful there, Mother.

"Is that what you called to tell me? Or is this about the *Times* announcement? Because I told you we're not ready for that yet." The last time Jack had been engaged, his mom had wasted no time whatsoever making sure it was featured in a splashy announcement in *The New York Times*.

That couldn't happen again, for obvious reasons, so Jack had bought them some time by insisting that Daphne wanted to wait and have their engagement portrait taken at the Plaza in a few months when it was all decked out for the holidays. His mother had bought it, hook, line and sinker. Either that, or she wanted to make sure his surprise fiancée had been thoroughly vetted and deemed acceptable before the entire city read about the engagement in the newspaper.

Jack was betting on the latter.

"I know. I know. You've made that very clear, and I fully agree," his mother said.

So the latter, most definitely.

"Actually, I was calling to get Daphne's phone number. I didn't get a chance to collect her contact information last night."

Jack froze, and his gaze flitted to Olivia. He'd already been doing his best to speak in code, giving away little to no information. Little girls had big ears, and he didn't want the child to think there was really a new lady in his life—not when things finally seemed like they were settling down. Olivia hadn't had a nightmare in weeks. Jack almost felt like he could breathe again.

"I'm not sure that information is readily available," he said, then popped a slice of bacon in his mouth.

"Jack, honestly. You're going to marry the girl and you refuse to give me her phone number?" His mother let out a huff. "I suppose I'll have to drop by Bloomingdale's and get the number for myself."

Jack took a sharp inhale and the bacon lodged in the back of his throat. A coughing fit commenced.

"Uncle Jack, are you okay?" Olivia's eyes went as wide as saucers. She squeezed her teddy bear's hand.

Mommy and Daddy love you, Vivi.

Even Buttercup seemed alarmed. She leaped to her feet, bounded toward him and rose up to plant her paws on his shoulders in what Jack could only guess was a misguided attempt at a doggy Heimlich maneuver.

"Jack? What's going on over there?" his mother asked, clearly annoyed. "Jack? Answer me. *Jack?*"

"I'm here," he wheezed. "I'll text you Daphne's contact info when we hang up. Breakfast just went down the wrong pipe. Don't worry—everything is completely under control."

Completely under control...

Another lie, and this one just might be a whopper.

"Wait a minute." Addison held up a finger, eyes narrowing at Daphne. "That does *not* sound like a fake kiss."

Daphne squirmed on the tufted ottoman in the fashion closet. Addison and Everly had insisted on meeting before work to hear all about the engagement party, and of course Daphne had agreed. But now that the Monique Lhuillier gown was once again hanging on its designated rack and last night's proverbial glass coach had turned back into a pumpkin, Daphne wasn't entirely sure what to say about the night before. Or feel about it, for that matter.

"Well, it was." Daphne fanned her face. Why did it feel so hot in here, and why were her friends smirking at her like that? "There was a toast, people expected us to kiss and so we did. End of story."

Was it, though?

Try as she might, Daphne couldn't recall the prince taking Cinderella out for pizza after the clock struck midnight. In fact, she was certain that had never happened.

Which meant that at some point last night, she and Jack had gone off script. They'd waltzed straight off the pages of their fake fairy tale and into the land of reality.

Or maybe Daphne was simply making too much out of an innocent pizza date.

It wasn't a date, her subconscious screamed. It was just two people eating pizza after dark. In formal wear. At a time when they had no professional obligation to be together.

Oh, no. It had been a date.

"Describe the kiss again." Everly's eyes danced. Holly Golightly sat perched beside her, ears pricked forward with jaunty curiosity. "I'm just trying to wrap my head around this, because I never would've have imagined that straitlaced Jack King would be the world's best kisser."

Daphne's face went impossibly hot. "I never said he was the world's best."

Had she?

No, certainly not. She might've thought it—correction: she'd *definitely* thought it—but surely, she hadn't said it out loud.

"Besides, it was the other way around. *I* kissed *him*." At least that's the way Daphne remembered it. She could still feel the smooth satin lapels of his tuxedo jacket beneath her fingertips…the shock of pleasure that had sizzled through her as Jack's hand splayed low on her back.

Addison and Everly's brows rose in unison. Even Holly's eyes widened.

"It wasn't like that," Daphne said, but she couldn't maintain a straight face. It had totally been like that.

"But he kissed you back," Addison said.

Boy, had he.

A knock sounded on the door to the closet, saving Daphne from having to elaborate further. All three women frowned in its direction. Holly let out a high-pitched yip.

"Please don't let that be Colette's assistant looking for me again," Daphne whispered. Her life really couldn't take any more upheaval, professionally speaking or otherwise.

"Are you kidding? She never knocks." Everly nibbled on her bottom lip. "Come to think of it, no one does."

"Come in," Addison said warily.

The door opened and Jack walked in, looking as stiff and uncomfortable as Daphne had ever seen him. A thrill coursed through her all the same.

"Pardon the interruption," he said.

Holly—clearly more adept at hiding her excitement than Daphne was—scurried toward him. When she collided with his polished loafers, she rolled onto her back and gazed up at him, waiting for a belly rub. Jack crouched down to acquiesce.

Everly glanced at Daphne with a look that said, *World's best kisser* and *sweet to dogs. What more could you possibly want?*

Daphne fought back an eye roll.

"Hi there, Jack. I suppose you're here looking for Daphne?" Addison adjusted her black velvet headband. Shockingly unruffled, as if a man's presence in the fashion closet was an ordinary occurrence.

It wasn't. In fact, Daphne couldn't remember it happening before. Ever.

"Um, yes?" Jack's gaze flitted to Daphne.

"It's okay, they know," she said. There was no sense making him sweat and letting him think he might accidentally be revealing their identities as the authors behind the undercover articles.

"What was I thinking?" He aimed a charming smile

in Everly and Addison's direction. "Of course you do. There are no secrets among you ladies."

"Zero," Everly said, biting back a smile.

Daphne wanted to plunge headfirst in the nearby rack of wedding gowns and disappear.

Instead, she stood up, hoping her friends would take the hint, do the same and then slink straight out of the closet so she could figure out what Jack wanted. She crossed her arms.

"Come on, Everly. Let's go. There's a staff meeting in the conference room in less than half an hour," Addison said.

"It might take me that long to walk down there," Everly said, tidying the neat grosgrain bow at the empire waist of her black-and-white polka-dot dress. Even at nearly eight months pregnant—with *twins*—she still managed to give off strong Audrey Hepburn vibes.

Holly pranced after her as she and Addison slipped out of the closet, clicking the door shut behind them.

Alone, at last.

Daphne hummed with nervous energy. *It's just Jack, you goofball.* Her hands balled into fists, itching for the feel of satin tuxedo lapels again. His hand on her back. Her lips on his.

"How did you know where to find me?" she asked in a wobbly voice.

"Seriously?" The corners of his mouth quirked upward. "Everyone in the office knows you guys hang out here."

So much for secrecy. "They do?"

"Yes, you three are legendary around here—*Veil*'s very own glitterati. You know everyone thinks that you, Addison and Everly are going to take over this place someday."

"That was before the Peloton," Daphne said.

Confusion crossed Jack's face. "I don't know what that means."

"Never mind. It's not important." She screwed up her face. "Although why does it feel like the tables have turned and instead of me instinctually knowing everything about you, you seem to know everything about me?"

"I suppose that's a mystery." Jack tucked his hands in his trouser pockets and came to stand closer—further into the inner sanctum. "Let me know when you figure it out."

They were talking in circles, and she still had no idea why he'd come looking for her.

"Did you want to see me about the class tonight?" she asked.

Their second Elegantly Engaged session was this evening. Daphne prayed this week's topic would be wedding cake—choosing it, slicing it, smashing it into each other's faces at the reception. A girl could dream.

"No, actually." His expression turned serious as he removed a hand from his pocket and scrubbed the back of his neck. "I—"

The ringtone on Daphne's cell phone cut him off.

"Weird. Who on earth could be calling me at this hour?" Daphne fished around in the pocket of her voluminous skirt—hot pink taffeta. Her power skirt.

"Before you answer that—" just as Daphne's grip tightened around her phone, Jack reached to rest a hand on her forearm "—it's my mother."

"What? *No.*" Daphne somehow stopped herself from tossing the phone at him, like they were playing a game of hot potato. Impossible, though. Why would Jack even think that? "It can't be. She doesn't even have my number."

"She does now and trust me. It's her. That's what I came to tell you. She cornered me this morning, and I had no choice. She mentioned stopping by Bloomingdale's."

"She can't do that." Panic swirled in Daphne's belly. She felt sick. "I don't really work there."

Jack nodded. "Exactly."

"This is *craziness*."

Daphne's cell continued to ring. She'd better answer it before Eleanor King turned up at Bloomingdale's in search of her son's lying fiancée.

"Hello?" she said as chirpily as she could manage while Jack looked on, straining to hear. "Hello there, Eleanor. It's so wonderful to hear from you. Such a lovely surprise."

Jack's lips twitched, like he was trying his best not to laugh.

Stop it, Daphne mouthed. They weren't supposed to be having fun. This was serious. This was work.

Still, she had to look away and fix her gaze on a shelf of satin bridal pumps so she wouldn't crack up if he lost his composure.

"Mmm-hmm." She tried her best to concentrate on what Eleanor was saying instead of her son. So near. So handsome. So newly irresistible. "That sounds perfect. See you then."

Jack narrowed his gaze at her as she ended the call. "What was that all about? When, exactly, will you see her?"

"In about six hours." Daphne sighed. She didn't need a fact-checker to tell her that her life had gotten completely ridiculous. "I'm having afternoon tea at the Plaza with your mother."

Chapter Thirteen

Daphne slid a cucumber sandwich from the bottom layer of the three-tiered stand that the waiter had placed between her and Eleanor. Their small table practically groaned beneath the weight of all the china and cutlery, and Daphne didn't know what to do with half of it. She wished she'd written more articles on etiquette before she'd been nicely slotted into the beauty department at *Veil*. Her encyclopedic knowledge of lipstick wasn't the least bit helpful at the moment.

Eleanor dabbed the corners of her mouth with her napkin and then reached for the tiered stand. This time, she chose a scone from the middle layer. Daphne finished her finger sandwich and did the same.

So far, she'd simply done her best to emulate Eleanor, who wore an enormous Hermès scarf like a shawl around her shoulders and somehow managed to stir her tea without making a single *clink* sound. When Daphne tried that move, she'd sloshed tea onto the crisp white tablecloth.

She'd slid her plate on top of the stain lest anyone notice, especially Jack's mother.

"Thank you for inviting me today," Daphne said between nibbles of scone.

Afternoon tea at the Plaza was served in the Palm Court, the very same room where Elegantly Engaged took place on Friday evenings. It looked so different, all decked out in pristine white linen and fine china emblazoned with the hotel's famous gold crest. Daphne wondered how long it would take the staff to transform the space into the configuration she was more familiar with. Then she reminded herself that if she was the type of woman who would really be engaged to Jack King, she probably wouldn't be worried about the housekeeping staff's problems.

"I'm so pleased that you could join me. You should've heard Jack on the phone this morning. Getting him to share your contact information was like pulling teeth." Eleanor reached for her teacup and took a dainty sip.

"I'm sure he didn't mean any harm. He's just a little… protective," Daphne said, and as she did so, she realized it was true.

He'd gone out of his way to make sure she felt comfortable the first night of Elegantly Engaged, and that had been before he knew anything about her past or her father. Once he did, he'd been adamant about making her dad feel comfortable at the engagement party. He'd never once pressured her to bring him, though. And he'd turned up with a cab instead of letting her meet him at his parents' penthouse last night. Daphne had appreciated that kind gesture most of all.

"He's *overly* protective." Eleanor leaned forward and lowered her voice. "That poor little girl of his has been through so much, but he babies her. I'm sure you've noticed."

Uh-oh.

Daphne was in no way equipped to discuss Olivia. Even if she had been, she wouldn't have felt right doing so behind Jack's back.

"I think Jack is just doing his best," Daphne said. The tea party food she'd ingested was beginning to feel like a lead weight in the pit of her stomach. "He has a very strong work ethic."

Eleanor regarded her through narrowed eyes. "I'm not sure what his work ethic has to do with this particular situation."

"Maybe I should have said his sense of duty? Honor? He wants to make sure Olivia feels as happy and secure as possible, given the situation. I think that's admirable," Daphne said.

Eleanor tilted her head. "You really are quite smitten with my son, aren't you?"

"What? No," Daphne blurted, as if on some sort of autopilot leftover from the Post-it era. Then Eleanor's gaze went steely, and Daphne snapped back to the present. "I mean, of course I am. I'm marrying him."

"It appears so, yes." Eleanor's gaze flitted to the diamond on Daphne's ring finger. "The ring is stunning, by the way. I didn't get a chance to tell you so last night."

Daphne swallowed. Was this a test? Why was Jack's mother pretending she'd never seen the ring before?

"Thank you. It was a real surprise." Daphne smiled. Best to keep things as truthful as possible. The ring *had* been a surprise, and she had no desire to get into a discussion about Ashley.

She was having enough trouble trying not to think about how many times Jack's ex might have sat in this very room, sipping tea with his mother. Not that it mattered. Daphne had no reason whatsoever to be jealous of the woman.

Then why are you?

Eleanor's gaze bore into Daphne's, as if she were trying to read her mind. Thank goodness she couldn't. Daphne's thoughts were all over the place lately, even more so than her feelings. This entire charade was getting confusing. She'd be grateful when it was over.

No more pretending to be someone she wasn't. No more tiptoeing around the truth. No more awkward teas with Eleanor.

No more Jack.

"He's a caring and compassionate man." Daphne heard herself say. Her throat went so thick that the thought of taking another bite was inconceivable. "I care about him very much."

Eleanor's expression softened. "Of course you do, dear."

"I know the situation with Olivia is relatively new, but I think it would really mean a lot to Jack if you and Gordon tried to spend some more time with her. Get to know her a little bit better?" *Kind of like what we're doing right now.*

Daphne couldn't help but wonder if Eleanor had ever invited the little girl to tea at the Plaza. If not, it seemed like a huge missed opportunity. Daphne had never met the child, but what little girl growing up in Manhattan didn't want to be Eloise from the children's books?

Eleanor frowned into her tea. Great. Daphne had shoved her stiletto-clad foot entirely into her mouth.

She waved a hand. "Never mind. I'm sure you've already done that. Don't listen to me. I'm…new on the scene…so I'm sure I don't know what I'm talking about."

"Actually, you might." Jack's mother set her teacup down on its saucer with a whisper.

Daphne bit her lip.

"Gordon and I have always wanted the best for Jack—the best schools, the best social circle, the best career..." Eleanor's gaze swept over Daphne.

The best fiancée.

She didn't need to say it. They were both already thinking it.

"And over the past few years, Jack has made it clear that his idea of what's best doesn't always align with ours. It started when he took the job at *Sports World* instead of joining his father's investment firm. I really should've realized back then that he and Ashley might not be the best fit." She shot Daphne a questioning glance. "He did tell you that he'd been engaged before, yes?"

Daphne nodded.

"That fell to pieces when Olivia came along. Then he got the dog and switched jobs and somewhere along the way, we just started drifting further and further apart." Eleanor's shoulders sagged, as if her Hermès scarf was suddenly bogged down with the weight of the world. "And then I found out he was engaged through the grapevine."

"That couldn't have been easy. I'm really sorry." Daphne's chest tightened with guilt. "I promise that had nothing to do with how Jack feels about you and Gordon. You have my word on that. Jack loves you both very much."

A glimmer of affection shone in Eleanor's gaze. She had the same gray eyes as Jack, and it made Daphne think that perhaps she and her son weren't so different after all. It had taken some relentless prodding and a fake engagement to get to know the real man behind the red editorial scribbles that regularly made her work product look like a crime scene. Beneath the cool, society matron exterior, Eleanor was a mom—a parent. Just like Daphne's dad. Just like Jack.

"Just because Jack doesn't want to work at the family business and he's doing things differently as a parent doesn't mean he's turning his back on you and Gordon. Maybe the fact that he chose journalism as a profession just means that he wants to make his own way in the world." Daphne tried to imagine Jack sitting behind a desk on Wall Street. She just couldn't fathom it. He was a talented writer. She hoped he'd get the opportunity to keep working as a reporter after their anonymous series was over. "That's a pretty admirable quality, don't you think?"

Eleanor gave a reluctant nod. "I suppose so."

"Or maybe he just really, really likes sports," Daphne said in an effort to lighten the mood. "And correcting other people's grammar."

The older woman laughed—and not just a polite little titter. "I'm beginning to think you understand my son really well, Daphne."

The compliment pleased Daphne more than it should have. Happiness bloomed inside of her.

She wasn't supposed to be enjoying this time with Jack's mother. They definitely weren't supposed to be bonding. She didn't belong here at all.

But she couldn't help saying one last thing, even though none of this was any of her business whatsoever.

"As far as Olivia is concerned, maybe try thinking of it this way…she's Jack's family now. Family is clearly important to him, and in all likelihood, that's something he learned from his parents." She smiled at Eleanor because she really meant it.

No one was perfect. And whether a person came from money or had to work overtime just to put food on the

table, most moms and dads just wanted the same thing—
for their children to feel loved. To feel like they belonged.
To be happy.

Was Jack happy? A month ago, Daphne would've said
no. Emphatically. But he'd certainly seemed happy last
night, eating pizza off a paper plate with his bow tie loosened and a grin on his face. He seemed happy when he
talked about Olivia and his whole face lit up. He'd even
seemed happy in the fashion closet this morning, trying not to laugh while Daphne spoke to his mother on
the phone.

Daphne's heart twisted thinking about all those moments. She wasn't sure why she felt so misty-eyed all of
the sudden.

"Do you really think so?" Eleanor pressed a hand to
her chest, and the expression on her face was so hopeful that Daphne's vision grew blurry with unshed tears.

"I do," she said.

I do.

Wedding words.

Look who was beginning to sound like a real bride
after all.

"Gee, why do I feel like I was just here two hours ago?"
Daphne said later that evening as she and Jack made their
way through the glittering lobby of the Plaza. "Oh, right,
because I *was*."

Jack took in the sight of his fake bride and couldn't
help but smile. "I don't think anyone has ever so thoroughly charmed my mother as you did at tea today."

Daphne glanced at him. A hint of a smile danced on
her lips and then she looked away. "That can't possibly
be true."

"Oh, trust me." Jack straightened his tie. He needed

something to do with his hands. He kept wanting to weave his fingers through Daphne's, as if it was natural or appropriate to do so when no one was looking.

This urge was becoming a problem, in much the same way as his unrelenting desire to kiss her again—just for them this time, not for a crowd. This morning in the fashion closet, it had taken every shred of Jack's willpower not to press her against the soft, billowy fabric of all those wedding gowns and claim her mouth with his.

He wondered what HR would have had to say about that. At least he and Daphne weren't at each other's throats anymore. The entire office should've been breathing a collective sigh of relief.

"It's true. She called me straight afterward, gushing about you." Jack shot her an exaggerated look of irritation. "It was quite annoying, actually."

"It was not, you big faker." She dug her elbow into his side, and even that brief contact was enough to send heat coursing through his veins. "You should be thrilled that your mother loves me. You should love it."

He knew she was only teasing him. What difference did it make how Eleanor felt about Daphne? Her opinion was certain to change once they faked a breakup less than a month after their splashy engagement party.

He couldn't help feeling a sense of relief, though. It had been a long time since he and his mom had a meaningful conversation like the one they'd shared after Eleanor and Daphne's tea. She'd told him he'd found a special girl in Daphne, but the part that had really blown him away was when she'd said she wanted to start having a regular weekly tea date with Olivia. Just the two of them—grandmother and granddaughter.

It didn't take a genius to figure out where that idea had come from.

"Honestly?" Jack paused near the entrance to the Palm Court.

He needed Daphne to understand he was being serious now. No more pretending. No more make-believe.

"I do love it. More than I can properly express. I don't know what you said or did to get through to her, but I feel like my mother has a much clearer understanding of things now. Instead of seeing everything I do as an act of defiance against my upbringing, she seems to want to be more involved. I couldn't be more surprised. So..." He pressed a hand to his heart. "Thank you."

Jack blew out a breath. He wasn't accustomed to spilling his guts like that, but it had to be said. He wouldn't have been able to keep it in while they played the mingle game or whatever was in store for them tonight.

A few other couples slid past them as they hovered near the entrance to the class. Daphne's entire face lit up...

And then she seemed to catch herself. She tried—and failed—to tamp down her beaming smile. "Well. You really owe me now. Having to suffer through finger sandwiches, tea and clotted cream was much harder than it sounds. The yummy *petit fours* at the end weren't half bad, though."

The sweet tooth strikes again.

Jack shook his head and laughed under his breath.

"Even if they could've used more frosting," Daphne added.

"Duly noted, Cinderella." And then he went ahead and gave into temptation—he reached for her hand and squeezed it tight.

Their eyes met, and for a loaded second, the air between them swirled with all the things they couldn't... *wouldn't*...say. Neither of them let go. Daphne's eyes grew shiny, and Jack pretended not to notice that Melanie Miller had already started her welcoming remarks near the bar.

Class was starting. They needed to get to work.

"If I buy you a can of store-bought frosting the next time I'm at the market, will that suffice?" He ran the pad of his thumb over the back of her hand in tender circles. "I wouldn't want you walking around deprived of your daily dose of cake icing."

"It's a start," she said, and Jack couldn't be sure, but he thought he heard a hitch in her voice—a telltale break in her resistance.

"Consider it done." Jack tipped his head toward the cluster of Elegantly Engaged students. A few people were glancing at them with open curiosity. Weren't they still supposed to be flying under the radar? "Shall we?"

Daphne nodded. "Let's do this."

The topic of the evening was wedding reception dining. As topics went, it was far more tedious than champagne etiquette. Between samples of hors d'oeuvres and instructions as to which appetizers required cutlery and which could be served as finger foods, participants learned about various reception seating arrangements. At one point, Melanie Miller put Daphne and Jack on the spot when she asked them if they were planning to serve a full meal at their wedding reception, a buffet or canapés.

"Full meal. The whole nine yards," Daphne said.

While Jack simultaneously said, "Light hors d'oeuvres with a heavy emphasis on cake."

Their classmates eyed them dubiously. A titter of nervous laughter made its way through the group.

"Well then." Melanie tutted. "It appears that the two of you aren't exactly on the same page."

"She has no idea," Daphne murmured just as Jack popped a square of mini avocado toast into his mouth.

"You might want to take a moment to discuss your individual expectations after class this evening," their instructor said.

Once she'd turned her attention to a different couple, Jack pressed a kiss to Daphne's hair and whispered as quietly as he possibly could, "We'll get right on that, won't we? Right after we cowrite another article about this thing that breaks the internet."

He'd expected a laugh. A conspiratorial grin. Something…

But Daphne's forehead crinkled, and she didn't seem to have heard him.

"What's wrong?" he asked under his breath.

Daphne's gaze slid toward his. She shook her head, as if to brush off his concern, but she still appeared preoccupied. "I'm sure it's nothing, but my phone keeps vibrating in my handbag. It just went off for the fourth time since class started. I never get this many calls in such a short time period."

"Go ahead and take a look at your notifications," Jack said. He would've done the same if his phone was blowing up, despite Melanie Miller's frequent reminders that phones were to be kept out sight during class.

Supposedly, etiquette was the reason behind this rule. But Jack suspected it had more to do with the air of secrecy that drove the months-long waiting list for Elegantly Engaged. So long as phones were tucked away in handbags and pockets, no one could film the lesson and post it on YouTube or TikTok or whatever social media site everyone was flocking to nowadays. Now that someone was spilling all of Melanie Miller's secrets, she was sure to be extra vigilant about keeping the Palm Court cell phone free.

Daphne shot a cautious glance in the instructor's direction. Luckily, their teacher was busy waxing poetic about prosciutto-wrapped goat cheese and beluga caviar. "Just a quick peek. It's probably only the *Veil* girls."

She clicked open her purse—an ivory, heart-shaped bag encrusted with approximately fifteen pounds of pearls, rhinestones and glitter—and slid her phone into her palm. Just as she bowed her head to scan through her many notifications, Jack caught a glimpse of a string of words that made his heart stop.

New York-Presbyterian Hospital, Queens.

"Jack." Daphne blinked up at him, and her aquamarine eyes were huge in her face—the frightened eyes of a lost little girl. "It's my dad."

Chapter Fourteen

Jack wrapped an arm around Daphne in the hospital hallway as a doctor explained what had happened.

He hadn't set foot inside a hospital since the night of Brian and Marianne's accident, and the sickeningly familiar antiseptic smell made his stomach churn. He tried to breathe through his mouth, but the scent still managed to permeate his senses, clogging his throat and making his eyes water.

"Your dad, Mr. Ballantyne, was brought in earlier after suffering a fall at his workplace." The ER physician—a tall, reed-thin man with a head of shaggy blond hair and the name Oliver Carson, M.D. stitched near the lapel of his crisp white coat—consulted the clipboard in his hand. "According to the EMS report, he fell from a six-foot ladder while changing a light bulb and subsequently hit his head on a metal school locker."

Daphne's dad rested quietly in a room a few feet away. A thin cotton blanket covered his still form, but even from this distance, Jack could see the steady rise and fall of his breathing. This wasn't like the accident. He was going to be okay. *Everything* was going to be okay.

"But he's out of danger now?" Daphne pressed her fingertips to her lips. She still had the lost, haunted expression that had come over her when she'd first read the string of texts and voice mail notifications from the hospital.

It was an expression Jack knew all too well. He'd seen it on Olivia's sweet round face that fateful night back in March. Even six months later, on particularly bad days, he still saw it.

"He's going to be fine. He's got a mild concussion. We're going to discharge him here in the next hour or so and he'll need to rest this weekend, but I don't foresee any complications." The doctor gave Daphne a reassuring smile. "He's actually lucky he hit the lockers on his way down. They broke his fall, to a certain extent. Your dad is a lucky man. This could've been a lot worse."

Daphne shook her head. "I can't even think about that. It's terrifying."

"Not to worry. He's fine. It's just a bump on the head." Dr. Carson shook each of their hands. "It's nice to meet you both. Have a nice evening and try not to worry."

He tucked the clipboard under his arm and headed toward the nurse's station, and Daphne blew out a long, trembling breath.

"I can't believe this."

Jack pulled her toward him, and she dropped her head onto his chest. "Hey, sweetheart. I'm so sorry. I know how scary this is, but try and concentrate on what the doctor said. Your dad is okay."

She lifted worried eyes to Jack. "He is, isn't he?"

"He sure is. He's strong." Jack brushed a strand of hair from her eyes. "Just like his daughter."

Daphne gave a half shrug. "I'm feeling anything but strong at the moment."

"No problem. I'll be strong for all of us," Jack said.

Too much? Maybe. He wouldn't even be here if Daphne hadn't gotten the call while they'd been at Elegantly Engaged.

But Jack wouldn't have had it any other way.

Daphne took him in, and some of the tension in her body loosened. The worry lines on her forehead smoothed away. "Thank you for coming with me. You really didn't have to…"

Jack's jaw clenched. Had she honestly expected him to put her in a cab by herself and send her off to the hospital alone after everything they'd been through together the past ten days?

"Please don't thank me, Daph," he said in a voice that sounded raw and rusty, even to his own ears.

He tried his best not to feel disappointed, to take her lack of faith in him personally. In so many ways, she was still the same heartbroken teenage girl she'd been on prom night. Afraid to trust, afraid to lean on anyone but herself, afraid to believe that anyone—least of all a man who came from the same world as the boy who'd hurt her—could really and truly care.

He cupped her face in his hands, tilted her chin upward to force her to look him in the eyes. *It's me, Cinderella. I'm here, and I'm not going anywhere.*

But he didn't want to spook her, didn't want to give her even the slightest reason to push him away. So he kept things light, like they always did. That's what people who were only pretending to care about each other did.

He pressed a kiss to her forehead—tender, chaste, innocent. "I owe you one, remember?"

"That's right. You do, don't you?" She smiled, but it wobbled off of her face almost before Jack could take a single, relieved exhale.

"We're even now." He gave her a lopsided grin. "You can forget the can of frosting."

She laughed under her breath and shook her head. "It feels good to smile again. But Jack, what are we going to do? I've got to get my dad home, and I'll probably stay with him here in Queens this weekend. How are we going to get our article written? It's due Sunday."

"The article is the last thing you should be thinking about right now. We'll get it done in the same way we did the last time…" Jack lifted a brow. "Together."

They would make it happen, just like they had last week. Texts, video chats, collaborative word documents. It had all worked before. They'd make it work again.

Daphne fixed her gaze with his and nodded. "We've got this."

"Indeed we do."

She wrinkled her nose, and her expression turned uncharacteristically shy. At last, another glimpse of the real Daphne Ballantyne. Guard down, heart open wide. "In the meantime, would you like to meet my dad?"

An unexpected release of tension flooded Jack's body. He could breathe again—even here, amid the sterile fragility of a hospital hallway. "I'd love to."

Daphne took him by the hand and led him into her father's room. Side by side, they peered over the bed rails. The patient slept peacefully, face slack, to the rhythmic lullaby of the nearby blood pressure monitor.

"Dad?" Daphne gave his shoulder a gentle shake. "Hey, Dad. I'm here."

The older man's eyes fluttered open and his gaze passed briefly over Jack before landing on Daphne. He gave her a shaky smile. "Daphne? What on earth are you doing here?"

"Seriously, Dad? The hospital called me when you were admitted to the ER. I'm your emergency contact, remember?"

Her father waved a hand and then let it drop back down onto the bedsheets. "No need. It was just a little spill. I'm fine."

"Dad, stop. You fell off a ladder and hit your head. You *passed out*. You have a concussion." Daphne's bottom lip started to tremble, and she bit down on it until she regained her composure. "You were very lucky. The doctor says it could've been a lot worse."

"It's a tiny bump on the head." Her father gingerly touched his salt-and-pepper hair. "See? No bandage. It didn't even break the skin. And I didn't pass out—I'm just a little drowsy from the painkillers. Your dear old dad is as good as new."

"Well, you scared me to death." She took a ragged inhale. "And from now on, we have a new family rule— anything requiring a doctor's visit, and you call me right away. Understand?"

Daphne leaned over the bed rails and pressed a kiss to her father's cheek. Then she took his hand in both of hers and held on to him so tightly that her knuckles turned white.

She'd said she wanted them to meet, but Jack wondered if he should slip out of the room and give them some privacy. This was an intimate moment, and he wasn't family. Jack wasn't sure what he was to Daphne. He couldn't have put an accurate label on their relationship if his life depended on it.

But then her dad shifted his gaze toward Jack, and his face split into a grin. "Sweetheart, I think you've forgotten to introduce me to your friend."

Jack held up a hand. "Hello, sir. I'm Jack King."

"Abe Ballantyne. It's a pleasure to meet you."

A flush rose to Daphne's porcelain cheeks. "Sorry, I'm such a mess right now. Dad, this is Jack. He's—"

Her words came to an abrupt halt, and she frowned. She searched Jack's face, as if the answer she was looking for was written right there in bold, black Magic Marker. But nothing about their relationship was black and white. They'd moved so far into the murky gray shadows that Jack couldn't see how they'd ever find their way back again.

"He's my...um..."

Jack arched an eyebrow.

Work husband. Mortal enemy. Fake fiancé.

They all applied, but Daphne couldn't seem to force any of the litany of descriptors out of her mouth.

"Go ahead, my darling girl. You can say it. I might have a concussion, but the old ticker is just fine. I can take it," Abe said.

Jack and Daphne exchanged a glance. At first, Jack assumed her dad was confused. He had, after all, suffered a recent blow to the head. But then Abe's eyes shifted downward, toward Daphne's hands, still clutching his. All at once, Jack understood.

The ring.

Daphne was still wearing the emerald cut diamond on the ring finger of her left hand, and its all too meaningful presence hadn't escaped her father's notice.

Abe smiled down at it, awestruck, until at last Daphne followed his gaze.

"Oh." Her eyes widened in alarm. "Um."

She stared at the ring, as if trying to make sense of how it had ended up on her finger. Then she swiveled her attention toward Jack like maybe he had the answer she was searching for.

Maybe he did. Maybe he *was* the answer.

Daphne swallowed, then she turned bright eyes on her father and repeated the lie that somehow, despite their best efforts, kept inching closer and closer to the truth.

"Jack and I are engaged."

The following Thursday, Daphne gathered with the *Veil* crew at Bloom for their weekly Martini Night. At their usual high-top table, once she'd finally gotten a much-needed wedding cake martini under her belt—an Hermés knockoff, complete with a flashy *H* buckle that Eleanor King probably would've instantly identified as a fake—Daphne confessed her latest nonsensical sin in the continuing saga of her make-believe courtship with Jack.

"Wait just a minute. I can't believe what I'm hearing right now." Addison held up a hand, fingers splayed in the universal gesture for *stop*.

Daphne wished she could stop. But it was too late for that now. The engagement train had already left the station, and there was no getting it back. It kept chugging along, making random stops along the way to…where exactly? The actual altar?

"Oh, my gosh." She dropped her head in her hands. "What have I done?"

"From what you just said, it sounds like you lied to your dad and told him you and Jack are engaged." Everly snickered.

Daphne picked her head back up so she could glare at her. "Pardon me if I fail to see the humor in this situation."

"Oh, it's humorous," Addison said with a snort. "It's freaking hilarious. Just a few weeks ago, you wanted him to 'choke on a pad of Post-it notes,' and now you're introducing him to your family as your fiancé."

Daphne gave her drink an overly aggressive stir with a swizzle stick. "First of all, those annoying air quotes aren't necessary. I remember what I said. And second, it didn't exactly come out of the blue. We've been pretend engaged for several weeks now. Things have somehow just snowballed a little."

Addison cast her a sideways glance. "Honey, this is bigger than a snowball."

"It's more like an avalanche," Everly said, and the two of them clinked their martini glasses.

"So happy to see that you two are getting such a kick out of this. Meanwhile my dad thinks I'm marrying an Emerson alumnus. I've never seen him so excited. I stayed with him in Queens over the weekend to make sure he got some rest after being discharged from the hospital, and Jack was all he wanted to talk about." Daphne gnawed on her bottom lip. How had she let this charade get so outrageously out of hand? She and Jack were simply supposed to attend a few etiquette classes and write about them. Now she was having tea with his mother at the Plaza and her dad was waxing poetic about Jack like he was the son he'd never had. "Did I tell you Jack got Knicks tickets for Dad for next week? Courtside. Right down on the floor."

Joy welled up in Daphne's heart every time she thought about it. It was the sweetest thing anyone had ever done for her dad, and the minute Jack sent them over on Saturday afternoon, she'd promptly forgotten all about the promise she'd made to herself to sit her father down and tell him the truth.

How could she?

"Courtside Knicks tickets? Wow." Everly blinked. "Your dad must be in hog heaven. He adores the Knicks."

"Yep, and now I've got to somehow figure out how to tell him the truth." Daphne squirmed on her bar stool. "It's going to crush him."

Addison shrugged. "Not necessarily."

"Oh, it will. Trust me on this." Daphne couldn't bring herself to even think about what her dad might say when she told him the truth, the whole truth and nothing but the truth. She hadn't dreaded a conversation with her father this much since the time she'd gotten caught letting a classmate cheat off her paper on a spelling test in third grade.

This was so much worse than that, though.

"That's not what I meant. Think about it—do you really need to tell him the truth?" Addison sipped from her martini glass with all the nonchalance of someone who hadn't just suggested that Daphne marry Jack for the sole purpose of avoiding an uncomfortable confrontation with her dad.

Daphne's mind reeled. "I'm sure Jack would love that idea. *Surprise! We're really getting married after all.*"

Addison's eyes narrowed. "That's not what I was suggesting at all. I just meant that you could go with the same breakup plan that you're planning on using with Jack's family."

"Oh." Daphne reached for her martini, face flaming.

"But it's super interesting that your mind jumped straight to the wedding chapel," Addison said.

"Occupational hazard." Daphne squared her shoulders. "Don't read into it."

There was no stopping Everly, still aglow with newlywed bliss from her marriage to Henry, from reading into things, though. She was practically giddy as she swirled her mocktail. "You know, Jack might not be as opposed to the wedding chapel plan as you think."

Daphne cast a pointed glance at Everly's martini glass. "Are you sure there's no alcohol in that thing? Because you sound beyond crazypants right now."

Everly held up her hands. "I call it as I see it. I can't even remember the last time you two argued anymore."

"That's because we have a cease-fire for the duration of the undercover assignment. He made me promise. I had to, or else he wasn't going to do it," Daphne said. It felt like a century had passed since they'd struck that deal. "Once this is all over, the gloves are off again."

She wasn't sure she wanted to argue with Jack anymore, though. Now that she knew him, it didn't seem all that fun anymore. The man had a lot on his plate. He should be able to keep his stapler in perfect alignment with his desk blotter if that's what helped him get through the day.

Oh, no. I have it bad, don't I? She was actually beginning to think Jack's annoying quirks were cute. This couldn't be good.

Everly eyed her up and down like she was mentally planning their rehearsal dinner. Maybe it was time for Daphne to get some new friends who had nothing whatsoever to do with the bridal industry. "From where I'm sitting, Jack looks like he's over your office war. In fact, I think he's smitten."

"With me?" Daphne laughed. Or at least she tried to, but now that Everly had uttered the impossible out loud, it no longer seemed like a laughing matter.

Everly and Addison exchanged a glance.

"No." Daphne shook her head. She needed to nip this conversational detour right in the bud. "That's absurd.

He's not. We're coworkers who have excellent chemistry *on the page*. That's all."

"I'll say. The second article in your series is still the top ranked piece on the *Veil* digital site, and it's been up for four days already. Your first article is still sitting at number two. Nothing anyone else writes can compete." Addison gave a little half shrug. "Face it—you and Jack are a power couple."

Daphne cut her a look. Power couple? She and Jack weren't even a *couple*—powerful or otherwise.

When they worked together, though, they were pure magic. There was no denying it. Before the second article went live, Daphne had wondered if their initial success had only been a fluke. She and Jack had cobbled the second piece together much like they had the first. She'd fired off paragraphs while her dad napped, and once he'd woken up and she spent hours playing board games with him or watching movies, Jack had taken over. He filled in the gaps, moved things around and sent everything back to her for another pass. It was crazy how they could stitch it all together in pieces and end up with something that far exceeded the sum of its parts, like a patchwork heirloom quilt.

"I mean 'power couple' in the professional sense, of course." Addison wrapped a dark curl around her finger.

That's not all she'd meant, but Daphne wasn't going there. Not now.

Everly splayed her hands on the table. "You still haven't told us why you lied to your dad. I think your reasoning is key to understanding what's really going on between you and Jack."

"Excellent point." Addison held her glass aloft. "Explain yourself, Daphne, and we'll gladly psychoanalyze everything you say."

Which is exactly what Daphne was afraid of. "Gee, thanks."

Everly gave her hand a tender squeeze. "Come on, Daph. We're your best friends. No judgment."

"The truth is…" Daphne sighed. "I don't have an explanation. I'm not sure what happened. Dad saw the ring on my finger, he jumped to conclusions and, in my head, I knew that I needed to pump the breaks and tell him what was going on. But then I looked at Jack, and I just couldn't say it. I think for a minute there, my heart wanted to believe the lie so badly that the words just wouldn't come."

And there it was—the God's honest truth.

Daphne groaned. "How pathetic is that?"

"Hon, it's not pathetic at all. It's a bit telling, though, don't you think?" Everly said.

Desperate for a different opinion, Daphne swiveled her gaze toward Addison, girl boss extraordinaire. For as long as Daphne had known her, Addison hadn't had the time nor the inclination for romance. At. All.

Addison scrunched her face. "Sorry, but I actually agree with my little sis on this one."

"I can't have feelings for Jack King." Daphne shook her head, as if she could rattle the very idea right out of her thoughts. "I just can't. That could ruin everything. We've worked so hard on the Elegantly Engaged articles, and we still have two left to write. All of this fairy tale stuff—the etiquette classes, the engagement party, the Cinderella dress…"

The kiss!

"It's just getting confusing, that's all." And more than a little bit overwhelming. They only had two classes left, though. Class three was scheduled to take place tomorrow night and then the last one next week. She just needed to hang on for eight more days.

And then what?

Then she could write her own ticket at *Veil*. After the numbers the undercover series had pulled in, Colette would probably let her do whatever she wanted. Daphne might even be able to convince her to take a look at the new secret project she'd been working on in what little free time she'd had in recent weeks. Right now it was just pages full of handwritten scribbles in a spiral-bound notebook, but it had the potential to be something special. Something different… Something she never would've let herself try, if not for Jack.

How had he gone from being the bane of her existence to…whatever he'd become in just a matter of weeks? Not only did it defy logic, but it went against everything Daphne believed about dating, relationships and people like Jack. Once upon a time, she thought that growing up in a fancy penthouse on Central Park South meant that life was easy. Charmed. But sadness, loneliness, feeling misunderstood—those things had a way of finding everyone, it seemed.

Only eight more days…

She twisted the engagement ring on her finger. "Once this undercover business is over, everything will go back to normal."

But tears stung the backs of Daphne's eyes as she forced herself to stop toying with the ring and reach for her frothy wedding cake martini, because she'd left out one crucial detail—normal suddenly seemed far less appealing than it used to.

Chapter Fifteen

Jack struck a red line through the opening sentence of Daphne's latest article for *Veil*'s beauty vertical. Then another…and another. It was a shame, really. The piece was a listicle about the best beauty masks for brides and bridesmaids for the night before their big day, and Daphne's prose was snappy and fun. He was probably sitting at his desk with a goofy smile on his face, even as he marked up her copy.

But had she really expected him to approve her claims that such and such mask would "literally make a bride look like J.Lo's hotter twin sister" on her wedding day? Or that the main ingredients of a particular high-end mask from Sephora were "unicorn horns and fairy dust"?

Yeah, no.

"Is that my mask story?"

Jack gave a start. He'd been so wrapped up in his work that he hadn't realized Daphne had just swept into his office in a cloud of sparkle and sweet-smelling perfume.

His gaze shifted to her feet and snagged on her shoes. He squinted at the round acrylic heels of her glittery footwear. It looked she was walking around on a pair of snow globes. And was that a *wedding cake* he spied inside each sparkly globe?

It was. A delicate, three-tiered mini cake piled high with ceramic icing, right there inside the heel of each shoe.

Only Daphne, he thought. Unless this was a *Veil* crew thing and Addison and Everly each had a matching pair. Jack wouldn't have been surprised.

"Nice shoes," he said, mouth curving into a bemused smile.

"Thank you." She crossed her arms, gaze homing in on the red-slashed pages on his desk. Her pillowy lips flattened into a straight line. "So, that *is* my beauty mask article, isn't it?"

Jack nodded. "I'm almost finished with it. I'll have it back to you in plenty of time to get it revised before we have to leave for class."

Tonight was the third Elegantly Engaged session. Jack had made arrangements to get off early so he could go home, eat dinner and get Olivia settled for the evening before heading to the Plaza. Daphne had already told him she planned on working straight through and meeting him at the hotel. He'd seen her writing furiously in a spiral bound notebook a few times in the break room at lunch, and early this morning, she'd exited the fashion closet with the same notebook tucked under her slender arm.

Stalker, much?

Oh, how the tables had turned since he'd caught Daphne lying in wait for him at the dog park. Jack wasn't really stalking her, though. He was simply observant. The fact that most of his observations these days centered around Daphne Ballantyne was purely coincidental.

Or, more likely, his keen sense of observation where Daphne was concerned had more to do with the fact that he wanted her. He wanted her so much it hurt.

"How very optimistic of you to think I can revise that by the end of the day," Daphne said, glaring down at the red ink covering her pages. "Given that it looks like I'm going to have to rewrite the entire thing."

"Not the entire thing," he corrected. "Just the references to mythical creatures and magic wands...of which there are more than half a dozen."

Her gaze flitted to his stapler, and Jack could see the wheels turning in that beautiful head of hers.

He pointed at her with his red pen. "Don't."

"Don't what?" she asked, resting the tip of her pointer finger on the end of the stapler. Her fingernails were covered with enough glitter to choke an elephant. Or, ironically, a unicorn.

Jack's annoyance flared. What was she doing? This was a flagrant violation of the terms of their truce, and she knew it.

"Daphne." He said her name like it was a warning.

She cocked her hip. "Jack."

And then she did it. She nudged the stapler out of place—just an inch or two askew from proper alignment with his other office supplies, but more than enough to get under Jack's skin.

He stood, planted his hands on his desk and leaned over the pages of Daphne's article, still bleeding all over his desk blotter. Their faces were suddenly so close that he could see the way her eyes went dark as her pupils dilated, hear her sudden intake of breath while her lips parted...ever...so...slightly...

Heat flushed through Jack's body. The back of his neck tensed, and his heart began to pound hard in his chest. If Jack hadn't known better, he would've thought he was aroused instead of royally ticked off.

Maybe he did know better.

Maybe he was both.

"I know what you're doing, Daphne," he said as his gaze drifted slowly, achingly, to her mouth. The scent of crushed strawberries and longing wrapped its way around him, tightening around his chest like a band.

He took a tense inhale.

I want her so much it hurts...

But the pain was so delicious, so exquisite, that sometimes he never wanted it to end.

"Just what is it that you think I'm doing, exactly?" she asked, voice breathy and furious all at once. "Other than messing up your desk."

She knocked over a silver cup on his desk, sending paper clips scattering all over the place.

Jack didn't even flinch. "You're purposely trying to pick a fight with me."

"Why would I do that?" Daphne's gaze flicked toward his letter opener. What was she planning on doing with that? Stabbing him with it?

Jack wrapped his hands around her wrists like bracelets, anchoring her in place and thus preventing her from making a bigger mess or inflicting bodily harm.

Why would she want to pick a fight?

Because in a week, everything they'd built together would come to an end. The charade would be over. She'd go back to her life, and he'd go back to his. They wouldn't have any reason to text each other on the weekends or talk on the phone. He wouldn't know what was going on with her dad or her personal life, and Daphne would no longer go to tea with his mother or ask after Olivia. The next time she got an emergency text, he wouldn't be standing by her side. Life would be a lot less chaotic. A lot more peaceful.

And lot more lonely.

Jack understood perfectly, because he felt the same way. He wasn't sure when exactly it had happened—probably sometime around the night of the engagement party or the moment when he'd slipped the very real diamond onto his fake fiancée's finger—but the looming deadline of the last Elegantly Engaged class had begun to feel like a great big clock—tick-tick-ticking its way to midnight, Cinderella-style.

Jack fully expected to end up all alone on the crimson carpeted steps of the Plaza with nothing but an empty shoe in his hand.

"Because you're afraid," he said, voice losing its edge. An anguished tenderness took its place. "You're afraid of what's going to come after. Most of all, you're afraid that if we're no longer at each other's throats, we're eventually going to do this."

He leaned closer...and closer...until their mouths were just a whisper apart. Her lips were right there for the taking, perfectly inviting. Perfectly kissable.

But they were in the office, and as much as Jack wanted to prove his point, he'd meant it when he told Daphne that he'd never force her to do anything she didn't want to do. So in the sliver of a moment before their lips met, he paused and looked her straight in the eyes. Everyone said the eyes were the windows to a person's soul, and in that tortured moment, Jack believed it. He could see everything right then and there—all Daphne's hopes and fears, all the love she held deep inside, all the ways she wanted him.

Just as fiercely as he wanted her.

Jack's body went as hard as granite.

"Yes?" he whispered.

"Yes," Daphne murmured. A plea. A prayer. "*Please.*"

That was all it took. In one swift motion, Jack released his hold on her wrists, cradled her head in his hands and crushed his mouth to hers. Her lips were sweet, hot and every bit as wanting as he knew they would be. And even though he knew he hadn't been imagining the sparks that always seemed to fly between them, the evidence of her desire was intoxicating.

A shudder of pleasure coursed through him, and he let out a low moan. Daphne responded in turn by grabbing on to his shoulders and somehow climbing on top of his desk so she was kneeling on its surface. Paper clips skidded over the dark wood and flew to the floor. Jack had no idea what happened to the stapler. It could've leaped straight out the window for all he cared.

"Wow," Daphne murmured against his lips.

Yeah...wow.

Never in his life had Jack experienced such a flood of sensation—passion, abandon and sweet relief, all rolled into one. And simmering beneath the hot, molten surface was a feeling that Jack wasn't sure he'd ever felt before. A feeling that felt an awful lot like...

Love?

"Jack? Are you in there, man?" Three sharp knocks sounded on his door.

And as quickly as the kiss had accelerated, it came to a sudden, screeching halt. They pulled away and looked at each other for a beat, frozen in panic. What were they *doing*? They were at work, and as far as the majority of their coworkers knew, they were supposed to hate each other.

"Oh, my gosh. We're both insane. This can't be happening." Daphne scrambled off of his desk, red-faced.

"Is everything okay in here?" The door swung open, and Henry Aston, the magazine's recently appointed travel editor, strode into Jack's office.

Henry was also Daphne's good friend Everly's husband, so Jack had a feeling that this little episode would be the talk of the fashion closet come morning.

"Oh, hey, Daphne. Fancy seeing you here." Henry took in Daphne's flushed features, the mess on Jack's desk and the various office supplies littering the floor. He blew out a breath. "Okay then. You guys are fighting…again."

"That's *exactly* what we're doing," Daphne blurted before shooting Jack a ridiculously over-the-top dirty look.

"Sorry to interrupt. It's nothing important or even work related for that matter. It's about Knicks tickets…" Henry's brow furrowed, and he pointed at something in Jack's hand. "Is that a shoe?"

Jack looked down, and sure enough, one of Daphne's wedding cake snow globe shoes rested in his palm. Of course. He'd known he was going to end up with an empty shoe in his hand. He just hadn't realized it would happen so soon.

"Did you *throw a shoe at him*, Daph?" Henry gaped at Daphne.

"I sure did." She marched toward Jack and plucked the shoe in question out of his hand. "And I'll be taking it back now, thank you very much."

Then she stormed out of Jack's office without bothering to put the shoe back on her foot. She just limped out of sight with a puzzled Henry watching her retreat.

He turned his gaze slowly back toward Jack, and Jack braced himself for questions. His office looked like a bomb had just gone off. He couldn't take a step without the crunch of a paper clip underfoot. The red-lined pages of Daphne's beauty mask article were fanned all over floor, out of order. He *really* needed to locate the stapler.

But when Henry finally spoke, he didn't mention the mess at all. He just shrugged and hitched a thumb over his shoulder in the direction where Daphne had just disappeared. "You know what? I'm pretty sure Everly has that same pair of shoes."

Jack could only shake his head and laugh under his breath, despite the catastrophic state of his surroundings. *Sounds about right.*

Daphne didn't dare show her face for the remainder of the day. She didn't want to see anyone—not her *Veil* crew, not Henry, not Colette and not Jack.

Especially not Jack.

She was a total mess. One look at her and anyone would know she'd just had a make out session with the magazine's fact-checker. Her messy bun was no longer artfully tousled, but messy in a bad way. Her winged eyeliner was smudged. *Note to self: never recommend this brand to readers again.* And her lipstick was flat-out nonexistent.

What had *happened* back there in his office? Her hands wouldn't stop shaking during the entire limp of shame to the fashion closet. She knew she had to look ridiculous, clutching her shoe to her heart, but she didn't want to stop walking long enough to put it on. All she wanted was to disappear among all the soft tulle and wispy organza fabrics for a little while and try to get her bearings.

Jack had seen right through her, just as she'd always suspected he could. He'd known what she was up to even before she did.

Daphne hadn't initially gone to his office with the

intention of violating their cease-fire—at least not con-
sciously. She'd wanted to ask him how Olivia's first afternoon tea with Eleanor had gone. Today was the first
of their weekly tea dates at the Plaza, and if Daphne
knew Jack, he'd rung Eleanor the second she'd dropped
the child off with the nanny at his apartment afterward.
Daphne couldn't wait to hear the report.

But she'd been feeling unsettled since Martini Night at
Bloom last night. The thought of what life would be like
after their cowriting arrangement was over had taken root
somewhere deep inside of her, and she couldn't shake the
sadness that came over her every time she allowed herself
to think about it. So she didn't. She tried to pack it away
in a neat little box, just like prom night at Emerson. Just
like she did anytime she worried about something happening to her father. Better to concentrate on the here and
now—on things that she could control, things that she
was good at, like her career. Hadn't she already proved
to herself that she didn't need a relationship to be happy?

But when she'd walked into Jack's office, he'd been
striking through a line in her beauty mask article with
one of his beloved red pens. Truthfully, Daphne didn't
care much about that article. Any writer on the staff
could've thrown it together. It was a silly little listicle,
and she had new goals here at *Veil* that she was more
emotionally invested in.

But before she knew it, she was provoking Jack over
all the red ink and toying with his stapler. When the muscle in his jaw ticked in response, the feeling of satisfac-
tion that washed over her had been like a balm. Sweet
relief. Then she completely lost her head and knocked
over the silver cup—engraved with Jack's initials, no
less—that held his paper clips. She couldn't have said
what made her do it.

But Jack knew.

You're purposely trying to pick a fight with me...
You're afraid of what's going to come after.

Bingo! What better way to ease her anxiety than force an ending now, so she wouldn't have to dread the inevitable moment when they went back to being each other's archenemies?

That had certainly backfired.

Daphne collapsed onto the ottoman and pressed a hand to her chest. Her heart was still galloping wildly out of control. Now she knew what it was like to kiss Jack for real, and she wasn't sure she'd ever recover. If she'd been scared of the ending before, now she was flat-out terrified.

Minutes passed, then hours. She fixed her makeup with samples from *Veil* advertisers that she found in the drawer beneath the light-up makeup mirror that was part of the closet's custom shelving unit. There was even a mini fridge stocked with fizzy water and tiny bottles of Prosecco. She could live in here the rest of her life if she had to and never face Jack King again.

But of course she wouldn't. They had their Elegantly Engaged class tonight, and there wasn't a thing in the world that could make her miss it. She was a professional. She'd show up and pretend to be Jack's fiancée, just like she'd been doing the past couple of weeks. If she lost a little piece of her heart in the process, so be it. That's what ice cream was for.

Then, just as she was about to emerge from her brief hibernation, her cell phone chimed with an incoming text message. The lavender baby doll dress she'd worn today had a tulle overlay dotted with multicolored glitter, so it took some maneuvering to get the device out of her pocket. When at last she read the message, she couldn't believe her eyes.

I'm so sorry, Daphne. I can't make it tonight.

Jack was bailing on their work assignment. She didn't know whether to feel devastated or furious. She aimed for the latter and failed. She just couldn't believe it.

Yes, Daphne had broken her promise to never rearrange his desk again, and she'd broken that promise in an absurdly spectacular way. But never in a million years did she think Jack would ever let her down like this. It wasn't like him.

She'd ruined everything, hadn't she?

Then her phone pinged with another text, and this time, she didn't have to read through the lines. Everything was suddenly crystal clear.

Something's happened and I can't leave Olivia.

Chapter Sixteen

It was the talking bear that did him in. On a day that had started out with so much promise, the toy that had been a savior to both Jack and Olivia these past six months swiftly and suddenly lost its voice.

Little Olivia had come home from afternoon tea with her grandmother, grinning from ear to ear. She'd been a chatterbox, describing the yummy tea cakes in so much detail that Jack had wondered if he might have a future Daphne-level cake enthusiast on his hands.

That wouldn't be so bad, would it? he'd thought. He couldn't think of a better role model than Daphne for a young girl like Olivia. If they'd ever met, he would've had a bona fide case of hero worship on his hands. But they hadn't, which was for the best. Jack knew this with absolute clarity. He was just having trouble remembering the reasoning behind that prudent decision.

"Uncle Jack, help!" There was silence for a beat, and then a soul-deep cry that Jack had never heard from Olivia before—not even on the night at the hospital when he'd been the one to break the news that her mommy and daddy hadn't made it. "Nooooooooooo!"

He'd been in the kitchen with his sleeves rolled up, preparing dinner for them to eat together before Nanny Marie returned so he could meet Daphne at the Plaza for their Elegantly Engaged class. Buttercup had been sitting right at his feet, sniffing the air—par for the course whenever food was involved. The second Olivia's mournful wail pierced the air, the dog had taken off like a shot. Jack was only a heartbeat behind. A sickening dread had mired down his steps, making him feel like he was moving through murky brown water.

When he reached Olivia's room, he'd found her clinging to the dog's thick neck, sobbing into her fur. The child's fist was wrapped around the talking bear's paw, squeezing again and again, until her tiny knuckles went white. But her mother's voice was gone, leaving nothing but silence in its place—and an emptiness so dark and thick that it was like Olivia's parents had died all over again.

"I can't leave her," Jack whispered into the phone when Daphne called to check on them after he'd sent her the cryptic text. "The bear is broken. Or the voice recording is worn out. I'm not sure which, but Olivia is inconsolable."

Back pressed to the wall in the hallway just outside Olivia's room, Jack slid to a crouching position and dropped his forehead to his knees. Daphne said all the right things—she was sorry, she understood, she didn't want him to worry a bit about missing the class. She'd write the article on her own. But nothing she said registered, because Jack could still hear Olivia crying softly in her room. If he listened closely enough, he could also

hear the repetitive click of the bear's voice box and then…
nothing. He wasn't sure which was more heartbreak-
ing—Olivia's tears or the absence of the sound coming
from the bear's paw.

Mommy and Daddy love you, Vivi.

He could hear those words so clearly in his mind—
every subtle inflection of Marianne's voice as familiar to
him as breathing. What good did memory do him now,
though? Why hadn't he thought to record the message on
his phone in case something like this happened? A good
father—a *real* father—would have known to do that before it was too late.

This was all Jack's fault. He'd gotten complacent. He'd
actually allowed himself to believe that Olivia was okay
and that their little makeshift family was going to work—
that they were going to be all right. He'd even convinced
himself that he was doing a better job at parenting than
his mom and dad had done when he'd been a boy.

Now he knew better. Jack had taken his eye off the
ball. He'd let himself get so caught up in his fake courtship with Daphne that he'd let his guard down. He knew
he should've said no when Colette first asked him to go
undercover.

"I messed up," he whispered into the phone. "I messed
up and there's no way to fix it."

But again, he was too late. He and Daphne had already ended the call. Jack could barely remember doing
so, could barely remember Daphne's strained good-bye.
There was no one on the other end to hear his tortured
confession—no one to tell him everything was going to
be okay.

Was it wrong that the one person Jack wished was
there to reassure him was Daphne? He didn't know any-

more. All he knew was that he'd never felt so alone in his life. He needed someone. He needed *her*.

He dragged himself off the floor, raked a hand through his hair and went back to Olivia's room. She cried until she made herself sick, and Jack never left her side. He pressed a cool, damp cloth to her head while she retched, and Buttercup sprawled her long, furry body across the entrance to the bathroom like a sentry.

When, at last, Olivia wore herself out, Jack cradled her in his arms until her dainty chest began to rise and fall in a deep, deep sleep. Spent, at last.

He carried her to the living room and placed her gently on the sofa amid the remnants of her blanket fort. Buttercup leaped onto the cushion beside her to rest her big head on Olivia's lap, and then the dog let out the saddest whine that Jack had ever heard. It barely sounded canine.

"Good dog." Jack scratched the golden retriever behind the ears. "You watch over our girl, okay?"

Buttercup swiveled her soft brown eyes toward Jack and released a bone-weary sigh. Jack had never related to a dog so much in his life.

What am I going to do?

He could try to get the voice box repaired. A quick Google search on his phone told him the problem likely wasn't fixable, but he had to try. Beyond that, he was at a loss.

Jack slumped onto the sofa, closed his eyes and leaned his head back against the cushions. He'd thought he'd had everything figured out. Somewhere deep down, he'd even thought that maybe, just maybe, he and Daphne might have a shot at making things real. That's what the kiss in his office this afternoon had been about. When Daphne had tried to provoke him into one of their old squabbles, Jack knew there were only two ways forward. Either he could respond in turn and they'd fall straight back into their old pattern of barely tolerating one another, or he could force her to face facts.

He cared about her. A lot. He knew she had feelings for him too, whether or not she was ready to admit it. And for one bright, shining moment, he'd thought they might have a future together.

Now everything was such a mess that he didn't know what to think. Come morning, when Colette found out he'd been a no-show at the Elegantly Engaged class, he might not even have a job at *Veil* anymore. It was possible he might never see Daphne again.

The thought settled in the pit of his stomach like a stone, weighed down by a heaping dose of guilt. He shouldn't be thinking like this. He shouldn't care about anything but Olivia right now.

Jack's chest went tight. It hurt to breathe. It hurt to think…to feel. His jaw ached from clenching his teeth, and he had a splitting headache. He pressed the heels of his hands against his eye sockets, desperate for relief.

And then he heard it—a gentle knock on the front door to his apartment.

It was so quiet that, at first, Jack thought he was hearing things. He'd simply mistaken the beat of Buttercup's tail against the soft leather sectional for a knock at the door. Then it happened again. A little bit louder this time. A little bit more insistent.

Buttercup hadn't budged an inch. The dog's paws twitched, as if she were chasing rabbits in her dreams. Jack hadn't imagined the knock, after all.

He rose to his feet and checked to make sure Olivia was still asleep before padding to the front door in his sock feet. He was still dressed in the clothes he'd worn to work—tie loosened, and oxford shirt wrinkled beyond all recognition. There was no telling what had happened to his cuff links. A glance at the clock on the mantel told him it was only half past seven, even though it felt like midnight. The dinner he'd been in the middle of making two hours ago sat in a state of disarray on the kitchen counter, untouched.

"Yes?" Jack bowed his head, speaking softly into the crack between the door and the frame so as not to wake Olivia.

The building had a doorman. Jack couldn't remember the last time he'd had an unexpected knock at the door. It shouldn't be happening, especially tonight of all nights.

"Are you home, Jack? It's me," a voice said from the other side. "Daphne."

Daphne could barely breathe as she waited for Jack to open the door.

Would he open the door? She had no business being here. He'd told her in no uncertain terms that he didn't want to involve Olivia in their ruse, and Daphne had assured him that she understood.

He'd sounded so bereft on the phone, though. Utterly and completely heartbroken. Daphne couldn't take the thought of Jack dealing with a situation like this all on his own. Every time she pictured Olivia squeezing her teddy bear's hand to no avail, she felt like she might be sick.

And so, when the time had come to leave the *Veil* offices and head to the Elegantly Engaged class, she couldn't do it. It had just seemed too silly and unimportant—*all* of it. Pretending to be engaged, playing the mingle game, worrying about things like how many hits the articles got and if she might end up with a promotion once the charade was over…did any of it really matter?

No.

A child was hurting, and so was Jack. Daphne couldn't pretend otherwise and run off to the Plaza to drink champagne and eat wedding cake. Maybe she was overstepping. Maybe she'd let herself get too attached.

Or maybe she'd had enough pretending. She didn't think she could do it for one more minute.

The door swung open, and there he was, looking every bit as tortured as he'd sounded on the phone.

"Oh, Jack. I'm so sorry." Her breath hitched. *Get it out. Just tell him why you're here so he can either tell you to go away or let you in.*

"What are you doing here, Daphne?" he asked, but there wasn't even a hint of anger in his tone. He sounded awestruck almost, like her presence might be the answer to a prayer he hadn't dared utter out loud. "*How* are you here? The doorman didn't ring to ask if he should send you up. Or if he did, I missed his call."

Right. That.

"It's actually kind of a funny story." She swallowed hard. "Your doorman sort of thinks we're engaged now."

"Of course he does." Jack shook his head. Was that a laugh she heard out of him?

She held up her hand and wiggled her fingers. The diamond engagement ring sparkled like crazy. "This rock does some pretty heavy lifting. It's probably a good thing you held on to it after Ashley gave it back to you."

Jack's gaze bore into hers. His eyes went serious, and Daphne wished she hadn't mentioned his ex.

"That ring was never Ashley's," he said, as if that made any sense whatsoever.

"I don't understand."

He blew out a breath. "Never mind. We can talk about that later."

Of course, because she still hadn't explained why she'd turned up on his doorstep out of the blue.

"I'm supposed to be at class. I know," she said.

He nodded. Neither of them needed to elaborate. They both knew what missing Elegantly Engaged would mean. Daphne had just shot both of their futures at *Veil* right in the foot.

"I wanted to help, so I gathered up some things from work that I thought Olivia might like." Daphne swallowed hard. It seemed like a presumptuous move, given the fact that she'd never met the child. But Jack had told her more than once that he thought Olivia would adore her.

I'm fairly certain she'd think you're Cinderella.

He'd said those exact words, and if playing at being Cinderella might help Olivia feel better, then Daphne knew just how to deliver.

Jack nodded at the overflowing tote bags she'd slung over each arm. "It looks like you have the entire contents of your desk in there."

"I do." Bubble baths, lipsticks…the bedazzler she used on her hair. Daphne had brought it all. "I've also got flower girl dresses from the closet in case Olivia wants to play dress-up. I might have also snagged a tiara or three."

"Of course." The corner of Jack's mouth quirked into a grin, and Daphne's heart soared. "Why steal one tiara when you can steal three?"

"One for Olivia, one for me and one for Buttercup." Daphne winked. "Honestly, it's like you've never had a girls' night before."

He held up a hand. "Guilty as charged."

Daphne shifted from one foot to the other. The fact that she was still standing in the hallway wasn't lost on her. "Truly, though, Jack. It's okay if you don't want me here. I can just leave this stuff and go."

"Believe me, sweetheart. I want you here." Jack's gaze went tender, and all of Daphne's breath bottled up tight in her lungs. Why did she get the feeling that this was the most genuine moment they'd ever shared? "And not just for Olivia."

Then he took a backward step and held the door open wide.

Chapter Seventeen

"Look at me, Uncle Jack!" Olivia twirled, and the frothy dress she'd slipped on over her pajamas swished around her legs.

Jack's chest hitched. Over the course of the past hour, as Daphne bedazzled Olivia's hair and helped her try one dress after another, his living room had become almost unrecognizable. Sheer pastel fabrics littered every surface. Wedding veils hung from the light fixture. Shoes in various sizes and heel heights lay scattered all over the floor. If Jack hadn't known better, he might've thought he was looking at some sort of bridal-themed obstacle course.

Even Buttercup had gotten in on the action. After Daphne had used her bedazzling tool to apply a generous amount of sparkles to Olivia's hair, Olivia "felt sorry" for the dog because her fur looked plain. Jack had patiently explained that dogs and tiny rhinestones that could be easily mistaken for food didn't exactly mix, so

Olivia had settled on a thick padded headband instead. It currently sat atop Buttercup's head with a little net veil pulled down over the golden retriever's eyes.

None of that bothered Jack, though. Once Daphne had swept into his home toting all manner of princess paraphernalia, it was like Olivia had come back to life.

The change hadn't been instant. At first, the child had been bashful around Daphne. Jack had wanted her to sleep as long as possible, but she'd stirred awake within minutes of Daphne's arrival. Olivia had simply stared at Daphne for several long minutes until the lure of Daphne's sparkly hair and big eyelashes were too powerful to resist.

"You look beautiful, kiddo," Jack said, taking Olivia's dainty hand in his and spinning her around. His gaze fixed on Daphne's over the top of Olivia's head. "And so do you."

He winked.

Daphne blew him a smacking kiss. She'd let Olivia apply her lip gloss and it had strayed significantly out of the lines, but to Jack, Daphne had never looked more lovely.

Life could be like this, couldn't it? Real, *everyday life*.

Hours ago, Olivia had been inconsolable. All it took was an open door—an open heart—and everything had changed.

"Why don't you try this one on, Vivi?" Daphne held up a white tulle dress with straps made from interlocking silk daisies.

Olivia's eyes lit up. Daisies had always been her favorite flowers.

"Did you bring the entire contents of the *Veil* fashion closet with you?" Jack asked Daphne as Olivia scrambled out of one dress and let Daphne pull another one on over her pj's. "There can't be much left back at the office."

"Oh, you'd be surprised. I doubt anyone will be able to tell I borrowed a few things. That closet is the fashion equivalent of a clown car." Daphne fluffed the fabric around Olivia's slender legs.

And so it went until Olivia could no longer keep her eyes open. She asked Daphne to read her a bedtime story, and the sight of his little girl lying with her head on Daphne's shoulder and a smile on her face as she drifted off to sleep seemed like nothing short of a miracle to Jack.

"Are you glad you opened the door for me?" Daphne asked in a hushed voice when it was just the two of them in the darkened living room.

"It was never a question," Jack whispered, moving to cradle her face in his hands so he could slide his thumb along her bottom lip and brush away the smudged lip gloss. "I couldn't have turned you away if I'd tried. Haven't you figured it out yet?"

"'Figured it out.'" Daphne searched his gaze. "That's the exact phrase you used the other day when I asked how the tables had turned and you seemed to suddenly know everything about me instead of the other way around. You told me to let you know when I figured it out."

"And have you?" Jack tucked a strand of hair behind her ear. He couldn't seem to stop touching her.

Maybe he needed to convince himself that she was really here—that tonight hadn't just been a dream or wishful thinking on his part. Or maybe when he'd swung that door open earlier, it hadn't just been the door to his home. He'd opened his heart to Daphne too.

"I'm not sure." She peered up at him through the thick fringe of her eyelashes. "You might need to give me a hint."

Desire radiated between them. Not urgent, like before in his office. This time it was tender. Sweet. Like waking up slowly—achingly—to discover everything you'd ever wanted was just an arm's length away.

Jack took a deep breath, savoring the way she looked at him now. Had she always watched him like that—with her lips slightly parted and eyes dark with yearning?

"I'm crazy about you. How's that for a hint?" he said.

There was a beat of stillness, and all of Jack's senses went on high alert. He was hyperaware of the sound of his own heartbeat and a catch in Daphne's breath. Then her lips curved into a smile as she wrapped her arms around his neck and kissed him slowly and thoroughly.

Like he was the man she wanted to marry.

"Daphne." He groaned into her mouth, and then it was she who led them to the bedroom, where they made love as if their fake engagement had simply been some strange form of courtship and the real fun was only just beginning.

She whispered his name in the wee hours of the morning, and Jack woke to find her looking at her engagement ring as a shaft of moonlight cast a rainbow of colors from the diamond onto his bedroom walls.

"Yes, sweetheart?" He pushed her hair from her eyes and kissed the little pucker in her forehead that told him her wheels were spinning.

"What did you mean last night when you said this ring had never belonged to Ashley?"

"I meant it's yours. I bought it for you." Jack's mouth went dry, and he wasn't even sure why. He'd done a nice thing. Why would that be a problem?

"You did *what*?" Daphne shook her head. "I don't understand."

"I saw how much you loved wearing the ring from the fashion closet, and then you told me about Emerson, and…"

"And you felt sorry for me?" She shifted in the bed so she was sitting up against the pillow ever so slightly out of Jack's reach.

"No. I mean, a little, I suppose. I wanted to do something for you—something to show you how special you are. You deserve to be happy, Daphne," Jack said.

"Then why didn't you tell me that instead of spending a fortune on a diamond ring?" She slid the ring off and set it on the nightstand.

A spike of panic hit Jack right around the region of his heart. What was happening? They'd had a breakthrough tonight. They'd just made love…

And now Daphne was running scared again.

"Because I wanted to show you," he said, stopping short of admitting the whole truth.

He hadn't just wanted to show her that she was special. He'd wanted to show her that he had feelings for her and buying her the ring was the only way he knew how—especially when he knew she wasn't ready to hear the truth.

She *still* wasn't ready, apparently.

"Jack, what are we doing?" she whispered. The fear in her eyes was palpable.

And just like that, Jack understood. The ring was a lavish gesture. To her, it represented the fact that he came from a world where she'd never belonged. A world that had gone out of its way to make her feel less than.

"We're making things real," he said. Couldn't she see that? "You and me. I'm in love with you, Daphne. That's what last night was all about."

Wasn't it? It sure as hell had been for him.

Her eyes were suddenly huge in her heart-shaped face. "Jack, I—"

A shrill ringtone pierced the air, jarring them further into the light of day.

"That's my phone." Daphne wrapped a sheet around herself as she scrambled out of bed and searched for her cell amid the glittery pile of her discarded clothing. "I don't know who could be calling this early. I need to check in case it's my dad."

Jack climbed out of bed to find her a robe from his closet, and when he came back, she was nodding as she spoke to whoever was on the other end of the call.

"I'll get to the hospital as fast as I can." Daphne fixed her gaze with Jack's. Something was definitely wrong. "See you soon. If I can catch a taxi, I'll be there in less than half an hour."

She hung up the phone, and Jack sprang into action.

"I'll call the doorman and have him get you a car. He'll have a cab waiting for you by the time you get downstairs," he said, and Daphne blew out a relieved breath. It felt good to fix that one small problem, even when everything else seemed to be spinning out of control. "Is it your dad? I can't leave Olivia right now, but I'll see if I can get the nanny to come and I'll meet you there."

"It's okay, Jack. It's not Dad." Daphne smiled, and it broke Jack's heart a little that he hadn't been able to put a smile like that on her face moments ago when he'd told her he loved her. "Everly is in labor. The twins are coming!"

"What is this? It tastes vile." Daphne frowned into the paper cup of brown liquid that Addison had just handed her in the waiting room of Everly's birthing suite at the hospital.

Over three hours had passed since Daphne swept into the maternity ward, wearing the same lavender tulle dress she'd worn to work the day before. With Everly still in the early stages of her labor, the *Veil* girls had been able to spend time at her bedside. Daphne had painted Everly's toenails—Tiffany blue, of course—while they'd watched *Friends* reruns that Henry had downloaded on his tablet especially for the occasion. He'd chosen all of Everly's favorite episodes, starting with the one where Monica, Rachel and Phoebe hang out in wedding gowns all night, eating popcorn and watching television. The "*Veil* Girls Episode," as Henry called it. The atmosphere had felt almost like a slumber party until the time between Everly's contractions grew shorter and the pain intensified.

Things felt more real now. More serious. Daphne knew Henry was taking good care of Everly back in the delivery suite, but now that she and Addison had moved into the waiting room, worry had begun to set in. Having twins was serious business. There were all sorts of things that could go wrong. Daphne wouldn't feel better until all of this was over and she got to see Everly holding two healthy babies in her arms.

"Did you just ask me what's in your coffee cup? Because news flash—it's coffee." Addison sat down in the chair beside Daphne and crossed her denim-clad legs.

Addison had paired jeans with quilted Chanel ballet flats and a plain white T-shirt. She looked fresh as a daisy, like a style blogger who was ready to ride around Paris on a bicycle with a baguette in a wicker basket between the handlebars—as opposed to Daphne's crumpled morning-after look, which—thus far—everyone had graciously pretended not to notice.

Daphne had a feeling that was about to change.

"This is coffee?" She pulled a face.

Addison smirked. "Yes, hon. This is what coffee tastes

like when you don't add equal parts cookies-and-cream flavored creamer to it."

"Then you know what?" Daphne choked down another sip. "I might not actually like coffee."

"Next time one of us has a baby, I'll be sure to pack a cooler with the essentials—flavored coffee creamer and wedding cake samples," Addison said.

Daphne nodded. A slice of wedding cake would hit the spot right about now. "Sounds perfect. Although, do we really think there's going to be a next time anytime soon? Everly and Henry are about to have their hands full."

"Who says I was talking about Everly and Henry?" Addison cast a sidelong glance at Daphne's attire. "Because you obviously didn't go home last night after Elegantly Engaged. It seems like this fake engagement of yours is getting more and more real every day."

Where to start? So much had happened since Daphne had last chatted with Addison at the office yesterday that she didn't know where to begin.

She took a deep breath. "I didn't go to the Elegantly Engaged class last night. Neither of us did."

Addison's perfectly groomed eyebrows drew together. "I don't understand."

That makes two of us.

Daphne still couldn't make sense of her decision to go straight from work to Jack's apartment. In doing so, she'd probably thrown both of their careers straight under the bus.

Colette was going to lose her mind when she found out they had nothing to write about this week. Good-bye, feature article splashed across the *Veil* home page. Good-bye, viral success. Good-bye, promotion.

Good-bye, paycheck.

"Jack had a family emergency, and instead of going

alone like I was supposed to, I went to see if I could help him and Olivia." A lump lodged in Daphne's throat. She tried to swallow it down but couldn't.

Then, for the first time since she'd seen poor little Olivia's red-rimmed eyes and swollen face, Daphne let her own tears fall. Between sniffs and dabbing her eyes with the scratchy napkin that had come with her coffee from the hospital café, she told Addison the entire story—all the way from the crazy kiss in Jack's office yesterday to earlier this morning when he'd told her he wanted to keep what they had…to make it real.

She talked and talked, until Addison finally had all the facts. The entire picture. Daphne had to give credit where credit was due—as much as she and Everly teased Addison about being a mini Colette, she didn't fixate at all on the fact that Daphne had blown up all the hard work she and Jack had done on the *Veil* undercover series.

She just had one question. "Do you love him, Daph?"

Daphne bit her lip. *I think I might.* She hadn't asked to fall in love with Jack. It was the very opposite of what she wanted, and now she didn't know what to do with herself. "I can't answer that. It's more complicated than a simple yes or no."

Addison shook her head. "It doesn't have to be."

"But it is. Everything is a mess. I don't know what I'm going to do about the article. Colette is probably going to fire us both. And for what? Jack and I can't be together for real. We're too different." Had it just slipped Addison's mind that until Colette forced them into a writing partnership, they could barely stand the sight of each other?

"For two people who have nothing in common, you and Jack sure work well together. What you've created these past few weeks is special. That's why the response has been so overwhelming—not because you've spilled any secrets about the Elegantly Engaged class. Frankly, it doesn't sound all that riveting. But the way you and Jack write about it… I don't know. It's just…"

Magic, Daphne thought, and when Addison met her gaze, she knew her friend was thinking the same thing.

"Being different isn't such a bad thing, you know. You and Jack complement one another perfectly," Addison said.

"In the land of make-believe, maybe." Daphne wrapped her arms around herself. It was getting harder and harder to hold herself together when everything had fallen so spectacularly apart. "Reality is a different story."

Addison's gaze narrowed. "What are you even talking about?"

"Me and Jack. There *is* no us. It's been fake all along." How was she still having to explain this?

"It might have started out that way, but you're fooling yourself if you think things haven't changed. The ring, the engagement party, midnight pizza, tea with Eleanor at the Plaza, Jack going with you to the hospital when your dad got hurt, everything that happened last night at Jack's apartment… Do you know what all those things have in common?" Addison looked at Daphne long and hard. "Not one of them had anything to do with your writing assignment."

"But—" Daphne started to object, and then let her voice drift off when she realized Addison was right.

"You say that you and Jack come from different worlds, but you've already started blending your families. You're becoming a part of his world, and he's becoming a part of yours. If it can work now, when you're not even really trying, imagine how good it could be if you commit to a real life together." Addison took both of Daphne's hands in hers and squeezed them tight, as if doing so could impress what she was saying straight onto Daphne's heart. "Can't you see that you've already decided? When you turned up at his apartment last night instead of going to Elegantly Engaged, you chose Jack and Olivia over *Veil*. That right there tells me all I need to know. You love him, hon. You and Jack are the real deal, whether you realize it or not."

Daphne went as still as stone.

Was that true? It certainly made sense. Day by day, their very real lives had gotten more and more intertwined. And every time it happened—every time Jack had been there for her when he really didn't have to and vice versa—Daphne had fallen just a little bit more. And now here she was, hopelessly in love with Jack King.

But when Jack told her he loved her, she hadn't been able to say it back. She'd been all too happy when the call came about Everly going into labor so she could escape and try to talk herself out of what she was feeling. She'd even left her ring behind.

"Addison? Daphne?"

Daphne blinked, startled back to the present by the sound of Henry rushing into the waiting room and saying their names.

Addison flew to her feet. "Is everything okay?"

"Everything is perfect. The babies are here." Henry beamed. "Everly sent me to come get you. Are you two ready to meet the newest members of the *Veil* crew?"

They were, of course. And when Daphne walked back into Everly's hospital room, all it took was one look at her friend, surrounded by so much love—her newborn daughters, her husband Henry, and the framed photo of her precious dog Holly Golightly on her bedside table— for Daphne's head to catch up with her heart.

It hit her in a rush of emotion so powerful that her knees buckled.

This. Her eyes filled with tears, making the heart-warming scene before her look like a watercolor painting—too soft and too dreamy to be real. But it was. What could be more real than true love? *This is what I want with Jack. This is real life, and it's better than a make-believe happy ending. Better than a fairy tale.*

But how could she tell him, after the way they'd left things?

And what on earth was she going to do about *Veil*?

Chapter Eighteen

My office. 30 minutes.

Daphne dragged her eyes open and scanned the text bubble lighting up her phone screen. After getting home from the hospital right around midnight the night before, she'd subsequently stayed up until dawn writing her article for *Veil*. She hadn't wanted to lose the spark of inspiration that had struck her while rocking one of the twins to sleep in the gliding rocker in Everly's maternity suite. Plus, she knew what she wanted to write was a departure from the actual assignment. A big one. Better to get it finished and off to Colette with plenty of time for changes in case the editor in chief wasn't on board.

When Daphne had finally nodded off, she'd done so with fresh hope in her heart. The article was different than what Colette originally wanted, but it was better. It was *real*. Daphne had included her byline at the top instead of hiding behind *Anonymous*, and she had a feeling the piece would resonate with readers even more than the first two articles in the series had.

She hoped so, anyway.

That hope took a serious hit as she read the text. It was from Colette—*Colette*, who'd never, ever messaged Daphne's personal number before—and it was time-stamped less than two hours after Daphne had pressed send on her article.

Panic fluttered in Daphne's chest. She hadn't even been aware that her boss knew her contact information. Ordinarily, Colette preferred to communicate via e-mail or through her assistant. Daphne would've been less surprised to find herself on the receiving end of an engraved invitation on gilded parchment than she was to see a text that read as if she'd been summoned to the fashion closet by one of her best friends. And on a Sunday morning, no less.

This couldn't be good.

She gnawed on her bottom lip as she glanced at the clock on her nightstand and did the math. Thirty minutes? That barely left time for Daphne to wash her face and shower before heading to the office. She wouldn't even have the bandwidth to try out the "Bridal-luncheon Ready in Under Ten Minutes" makeup application she'd written about recently for the magazine.

It was just as well. The very thought of Colette firing off this text message within minutes of reading the article was enough to leave Daphne shaking in her stilettos. There was no way she'd be capable of executing winged eyeliner in this state. Even a simple swipe of lipstick seemed like a pipe dream.

She jumped in the shower, scrubbed her face and smoothed her wet hair into a low twist at her nape. Taking a page out of Addison's minimalist book, she grabbed

a pair of skinny jeans, a plain white tee and a pair of ballerina flats—encrusted with silver glitter and definitely
not Chanel, because she was still Daphne Ballantyne,
after all—and headed to the office.

The building was eerily quiet. She could have heard
a pin drop as she made her way up the elevator, past the
vacant receptionist desk and through the empty cubicle
area. Daphne's desk was almost unrecognizable without
its usual clutter of beauty products. When she'd packed
everything up in hopes of cheering Olivia up, she'd really done a clean sweep. The pristine workspace looked
as if whoever occupied it had been roundly dismissed,
along with all their office supplies.

Daphne's stomach tumbled at the thought.

Whatever happens is for the best, she told herself. For
the first time in her career, she'd written with total abandon. Every word of that article had come straight from
her heart. She'd been more vulnerable on the page than
she'd ever allowed herself to be in person—not with Jack,
not with her dad, not even with the *Veil* girls. She'd taken
a chance, and it was either going to pay off big-time or
she was about to lose everything she'd worked so hard
for since she'd first breezed through the hallowed halls
of the *Veil* offices.

Besides, she hadn't really written the piece for the
magazine. She'd written it for Jack. The fact that it might
run beneath the masthead just meant there was a chance
he'd actually read it instead of writing her off completely
after she'd walked out of his apartment and left her engagement ring behind.

"In here, Daphne." Colette beckoned from her office,
as if Daphne was purposefully dragging her feet, afraid
to enter.

She totally was, but that was beside the point.

"Hi, Colette." Daphne hitched her Kate Spade tote higher up on her shoulder as she took in the sight of her boss and tried her best not to let her shock register on her face.

Colette was dressed in *athleisure wear*—specifically, black leggings, a stretchy black tank top and white sneakers dotted with tiny white pearls. As athletic shoes went, they were definitely fashionable, but still. Daphne had never seen Colette in anything but lady-boss clothes that bordered on haute couture. Her wardrobe probably *was* bespoke, come to think of it. As editor in chief of *Veil*, Colette was one of the most powerful women in the fashion industry.

And here she was, wearing spandex. This day was getting more bizarre by the second.

"Please, have a seat." Colette flicked a hand toward the white faux fur guest chairs situated opposite her desk, the same ones where Daphne and Jack had sat side by side when Colette first suggested they work together.

Suggested as in *ordered*, basically. But who cared about something as trivial as details at a time like this?

A sharp pang of longing coursed through Daphne as she lowered herself into one of the chairs. She wished Jack was there, sitting beside her again.

"Thank you for coming in. I thought we needed to have a chat about your article in person and given the timing for publication, it couldn't really wait until Monday. You understand, yes?" Colette folded her hands on top of a stack of typewritten pages that Daphne instantly recognized as her article. The title was centered right there at the top of the first page in all caps, text-speak for yelling. Which seemed appropriate, given the context.

ELEGANTLY IN LOVE: HOW I FELL FOR MY FAKE FIANCÉ

Daphne was outing herself as half of the undercover team behind the Elegantly Engaged exposé and proclaiming her love for Jack in one fell swoop, for all the world to see.

"I understand." Daphne nodded, and then she turned Colette's words over in her head. "Wait, I'm not sure I do. You just mentioned the timing for publication. Does that mean you're going to run it?"

She'd hoped, but she hadn't quite allowed herself to fully believe. If Colette was prepared to run the story, that meant Daphne wasn't fired. She might still be in trouble for messing up the remainder of the series, but surely Colette wouldn't publish the article if she was planning on letting her go.

"Yes, Daphne. I'd love to run it. I'd be crazy not to. This is the best work you've ever done. You should be extremely proud of this story." Colette tucked a wayward strand of her signature bob behind her ear. Again, strange. Daphne had never seen Colette with a hair out of place.

"But I went rogue. I didn't even go to class last night," Daphne said.

Colette arched an eyebrow. "Are you trying to talk me out of accepting this article in lieu of what we'd initially agreed on?"

Daphne gulped. "No, not at all. I—"

Colette held up a hand, effectively cutting her off. "You don't need to explain. The quality of this story far exceeds the excellent work you've already done on this series, so I'm willing to overlook the fact that you and Jack strayed from the original assignment. This time and this time only. Understood?"

Daphne heaved a sigh of relief. "Absolutely."

"But Daphne, I want to make sure you've given this some serious thought. This is a highly personal story, and the second it gets published, it's going to blow up. I expect it to get double the hits the other articles in your series have gotten." Colette tapped her polished nails on the shiny surface of her white lacquer desk. "So I'm going to ask you one last time, face-to-face—are you ready for this to go live tonight? There's still time to pull it and write something else if you're not sure."

Colette had a point. Once the story was out, there would be no turning back. Everyone with a Wi-Fi connection would know how hard and fast she'd fallen for Jack King, and she still didn't know for certain that they had a future together. What if this entire thing blew up in her face?

What if it doesn't?

Love—*real* love—required vulnerability. Daphne had been guarding her heart for far too long. It was time to let someone in, and that someone was Jack.

"I'm sure." Daphne nodded toward the massive computer monitor sitting on the credenza behind Colette's desk. "In fact, you can upload it right now if you want to."

Colette's brows rose. "Okay then. It's already typeset and ready to go. I just have to click publish."

She swiveled in her chair, and with a few taps on her keyboard, it was done.

Daphne took a deep breath and braced herself for a feeling of elation to wash over her or, at the very least, relief. But in that moment, all she felt was a bone-deep exhaustion. She was tired...so very tired, like she'd been running and running for a very long time and had finally allowed herself to stop and take a breath.

"Before you go, I'd like to talk to you for a moment about your future here at *Veil*." Colette leaned back in her chair, and a smile tipped her lips. "I understand that Everly gave birth to her twins yesterday. I wondered if you might be interested in taking over as the interim features editor while she's out on parental leave. When she returns to work, we can revisit things and find you another suitable role…if you're interested, that is."

Daphne took a beat before she answered. A few weeks ago, she would've jumped at this chance without giving it a second thought. Even now, she was tempted.

But for weeks, she'd been unable to shake something Jack said to her that night at Bloom. He'd called her wildly creative and talented, and he'd hinted that she might be a good fiction writer. The more Daphne thought about the idea, the more she liked it. She liked it so much that she'd taken pen to paper and started writing something new, something unlike anything she'd ever written before.

This is your chance. You might never get the opportunity to write your own ticket at Veil ever again.

"Actually, I had something different in mind. I've been working on a serialized fiction column, and I was hoping you might take a look at it." Daphne pulled her spiral notebook from her leather tote and slid it across the desk toward Colette. "It's about three best friends who work at a bridal magazine. I think it might be great as an ongoing series. If not for the print edition, maybe for the *Veil* digital site?"

There, she'd said it. She'd put herself out there. Again.

"A continuing fiction series? It's an interesting concept. Unexpected…but intriguing." Colette flipped open the notebook and scanned the first page. Then the second. When she got to the third and laughed at something halfway down the page, she gently closed the notebook. "I'll read the rest of this by Monday morning. It's rough, but it's good, Daphne. It's really good. I'm sure we can figure something out. You've earned this chance, and what you have here is a completely fresh concept."

Was this really happening? When Daphne walked into the building, she'd wondered if it might be the last time she'd ever set foot in the *Veil* office, and now she was getting promoted to a role she'd created herself.

It never would've happened without Jack. She couldn't wait to tell him.

"Colette, can I make one last suggestion?" Daphne swallowed. She knew she was pushing her luck. Colette wasn't exactly known for her patience and if the athleisure wear was any indication, she hadn't planned on sitting at her desk all day on a Sunday.

"What is it, Daphne?"

"Jack would make an excellent interim features editor," Daphne said. "In fact, I think he'd be better at the job than I would."

"I agree. But when he was here earlier, he asked to be moved to a features writer position." Colette shrugged. "He wants to write. He says working with you on this four-part series reminded him how much he loves it. He's not interested in editorial."

Wait.

What?

Daphne's stomach fluttered. Colette wasn't making sense. Jack had been there in the *Veil* office...*today*?

"Three-part series," Daphne corrected, although why she'd homed in on that insignificant detail was a mystery she couldn't begin to fathom.

Colette frowned. "Pardon?"

"You said 'four-part series.' That was the original plan, but now that we've published my article, I can't go back to Elegantly Engaged. So the series will end with only three installments." Daphne shrugged.

Colette's look of confusion was slowly replaced with a knowing smile. "He didn't show you, did he?"

A shiver ran up and down Daphne's spine. Colette had to be talking about Jack. He'd been here earlier. He'd been here, and Daphne had missed it. "Show me what?"

"Jack wrote his own article for your series. He outed himself, just like you did. He sent me the pages this morning, and the story is going to run tomorrow as the final installment. The grand finale." Colette's gaze flitted to her computer monitor. "Would you like me to pull it up and show you the title?"

Daphne started nodding before Colette could get the full question out. She didn't trust herself to speak without crying. Tears were already gathering behind her eyes, and she didn't even know what Jack had written about their time together.

She hoped, though… Oh, how she hoped.

Colette clicked a few keys on her keyboard and then turned the monitor so Daphne could get a full, unobstructed look at the screen.

FAKING A FAIRY TALE BUT HOPING FOR A REAL HAPPY-EVER-AFTER

Daphne choked on a sob as her gaze darted from one paragraph to the next. Words like *love, future* and *real* jumped out at her. Words that featured heavily in the article that had just gone live—the one that *she'd* written about *him*.

"This is really something. Your stories are practically mirror images of one another." Colette shook her head. "When Jack's article hit my inbox right after yours did, I assumed you two had come up with this plan together. Are you telling me that's not what happened?"

Daphne shook her head. "No, it's not. We just…"

We just belong together.

Colette's smile turned tender around the edges. "Say no more. I understand."

"You said Jack was here at the office earlier?" Daphne brushed a tear from her cheek. She couldn't believe they'd narrowly missed seeing each other.

"Yes, he was here with his little girl and his big rambunctious dog. I'm surprised you didn't run into him. I told him you were on your way." Colette tipped her head in the direction of Jack's office. "You might check his workstation."

"I'll do that right now," Daphne said, but she'd passed Jack's office on the way to Colette's. The light had been turned off, and his desk, as usual, was neat as a pin.

Daphne stood. She *had* to find him. How far could he and Olivia have gotten? But once she was on her feet, she paused as her gaze landed on Colette's Peloton. Daphne had been so consumed with saving her job, she hadn't even noticed it sitting there like a giant, mechanical thorn in Addison's side. Now the athleisure wear made a bit more sense.

"Thank you so much for everything, Colette." Daphne tipped her head toward the exercise bike. "Nice Peloton, by the way. I'm curious what made you decide to get one. Is there some kind of fitness contest going on between you and the editor in chief at *Cosmo*? We've all heard about her treadmill."

Daphne couldn't believe she'd just gone there. Colette didn't engage in office chitchat—certainly not about her personal life.

But was the exercise bike really a personal matter, given that she'd plunked it down right here in her office? Also, its presence was making Addison crazy. Daphne owed it to her friend to find out what she could if she had even the teeniest tiniest opening. The spandex qualified.

"There's no fitness contest," Colette said. "Although if there were, I would obviously win."

"Obviously," Daphne echoed.

"The bike is here because I've signed on for a six-month bicycle tour through Europe, starting in January. As I'm sure you're aware, I don't believe in doing things halfway. It's always best to be prepared." Colette tilted her head, and her glossy bob skimmed her jawline, razor-sharp. "Is that all Daphne, or are there more burning questions you'd like to ask me?"

So, so many.

But now wasn't the time. As much as Daphne loved *Veil*, she didn't belong here in Colette's office on a Sunday morning. As Addison said, Daphne made her choice the moment she'd picked Jack and Olivia over the magazine. This time was precious, and it belonged to them...

If only she knew where he'd gone.

Jack wasn't in his office. He wasn't in the break room. He wasn't waiting for Daphne in the fashion closet.

He wasn't *anywhere*.

Daphne's spirit, already in tatters after all the breathtaking highs and lows she'd experienced over the past few days, couldn't take it. Even the wonderful fantasyland of the fashion closet failed to cheer her up. Without Jack, the room that had once felt so comforting and so much like home just seemed...empty. Much like Daphne's heart.

She tried calling Jack's cell, but the calls kept rolling to voice mail. If Colette hadn't shown her Jack's article, Daphne might have been tempted to think he was ghosting her. But that couldn't be true. It just couldn't...

On the sidewalk in front of the *Veil* building, Daphne took a deep inhale of crisp, fall air. Leaves swirled in the air, and it almost seemed like if she just closed her eyes and spread her arms open wide, the autumn wind would carry her straight to him, charmed by the same magic that had inspired their writing. Those articles meant something. Daphne knew it with her whole heart.

She had no choice but to go back to Jack's apartment building, charm the doorman and talk her way up to Jack's floor again—a feat that would likely be far more challenging without the engagement ring on her finger. The thought of it was exhausting. Daphne couldn't remember the last time she'd eaten anything. She'd hardly slept a wink in the past forty-eight hours, and the last caffeine she'd consumed had been the tragic cup of coffee from the hospital café.

Her situation was dire—dire enough that the only thing that could possibly help was a cupcake.

Magnolia Bakery was only a block away. She'd pop in to grab a coffee and sustenance to tide her over while she walked to Jack's building. Maybe she'd even get a whole box of cupcakes to take with her. Today called for a celebration, and what kind of celebration would it be without cake?

A tiny part of her wondered if she was dragging her feet. After all, if Jack truly loved her and wanted to build a real life together, why had he left the office before she got there? Colette said he knew she was on her way. Why hadn't he waited?

Don't go there. It was all going to work out, just like a fairy tale. Just like Cinderella.

The memory of Jack's voice rang in the back of her mind, squeezing her heart with a fresh ache. She loved it when he'd called her that. It had never failed to send a shiver coursing through her.

"Going somewhere, Cinderella?"

Daphne's steps slowed. She felt herself frown. That

had almost sounded real…not just a figment of her imagination or a treasured memory.

No, it couldn't be. It wasn't…was it?

She looked up and there he was. Jack. Walking straight toward her with a smile on his face and a small, white paper bag in his hand. Buttercup trotted alongside him, tongue lolling out of the side of her mouth. Olivia was there too, clutching what looked like a brand-new teddy bear in her arms. When the little girl spotted Daphne, she broke away from Jack and skipped toward her. The tiny rhinestones in her hair glittered like diamonds in the soft morning sunshine.

"I was trying to find you, actually," Daphne said, gaze fixed on Jack's as Olivia hugged her knees and the dog pranced in happy circles around them.

The corner of Jack's mouth twitched into a half grin. Daphne had never been so glad to see that smirk in her entire life. "The fact-checker in me wants to ask why you're headed in the opposite direction of my apartment if that's really where you were going."

"Well." She scrunched her face. "I might've been making a tiny stop on the way."

"Let me guess." Jack held up the paper bag. It was printed with Magnolia Bakery's familiar logo.

Joy blossomed within Daphne, as the last vestiges of her anxiety melted away. If there was a spinach omelet in that bag, she was going to hide every single office supply the man owned. "Is that for me?"

"We wanted to surprise you. Colette told me you were coming into the office, and it seemed like a good idea." Jack's expression softened, and the tenderness in his eyes made her want to cry again. "But our trip to the bakery took longer than expected. I got sidetracked by an alert on my phone letting me know a new article had been up-loaded to *Veil*'s home page."

He'd read it.

Daphne couldn't have felt more exposed if she'd been standing naked in the middle of Times Square. But right here—without her armor, face bare and heart open wide, was the only place she wanted to be. Today, tomorrow, forever...

"Daphne, look. Uncle Jack got me a new bear," Olivia said, finally releasing her hold on Daphne's legs.

"You did?"

Olivia nodded and thrust the stuffed animal at Daphne for inspection.

Daphne bent down so she was eye to eye with the little girl. It was good to see her smile. Daphne knew Olivia's struggles weren't over. Healing was like that...it didn't happen all at once or even in a straight line. There were good days and there were bad ones, and gradually, the former outweighed the latter.

Today was a good day, though. A very, very good day.

"He talks, like my old bear does." Olivia pointed at the bear's paw. "Squeeze him right there."

Daphne wasn't sure what to expect. Jack had mentioned trying to get the voice box from the other bear fixed, but she doubted that would've been possible in such a short time. Given that this bear looked brand-spanking-new, she had a feeling Jack and Olivia had made a trip to the toy store on their way to *Veil* this morning.

She gave the bear's paw a gentle squeeze. A clicking noise sounded, followed by the soft static of a recorded message.

Uncle Jack loves you, Vivi. Jack's voice—strong, comforting, unmistakable—followed immediately by little Olivia's. *Vivi loves you too, Uncle Jack.*

"I know it can't replace the original one, but it's something," Jack said quietly.

Olivia tugged the bear from Daphne's hand and held it to her heart. She squeezed the paw again, and Buttercup's head cocked at the sound of the voice message.

"It's not just something," Daphne whispered. "It's everything."

He was finding his way as a parent, and it was beautiful to see. Olivia was going to be okay. They all were.

"Go ahead and tear into this. I know you want to." Jack handed her the bag and winked.

In all honesty, she'd forgotten about the cupcake. There were far more important things to say and do, but once she caught a whiff of buttercream coming from the bakery bag, Daphne couldn't resist. Plus Jack seemed awfully eager for her to dig in. Too eager.

Daphne couldn't say why, exactly, but her heart started to race as she opened the bag. She spied a hint of pink icing. Jack had obviously noticed that vanilla cupcakes were her favorite. She reached inside to pull it out, and then gasped at what she saw.

There, nestled right on top of the little cake, was her engagement ring—propped in the center of a swirl of pink frosting, glittering like mad in the sunlight. She broke into a wide smile, but when she glanced back up to meet Jack's gaze, he was no longer standing right in front of her.

He'd dropped down on one knee, hand to heart.

"Jack?" Daphne nearly dropped the cupcake. It wobbled in her grasp, but she caught it just in time.

"Oopsie," Olivia said.

Oopsie was right. They'd made so many mistakes along the way but, in the end, none of that mattered. Everything they'd done over the past few weeks—every lie they'd told, every scattered paper clip, every feeling they'd tried their best to deny—had led them here….to this moment. And Daphne wouldn't trade any of it for the world.

Buttercup licked the side of Jack's face and nudged him in the side with her big muzzle, like she was trying to figure out what he was doing on the ground like that.

But Daphne knew. This was how good fairy tales ended, even the real kind.

"I'm sorry I didn't think to ask you this way before. You deserve a proper proposal. I know it's soon, but I love you and I can't imagine my life—" Jack paused to smile at Olivia "—*our* lives, without you. This ring belongs to you, and if you'll let me, I want to slide it back onto your finger for good. Let's make this real, Daphne. Will you marry me?"

Daphne nodded, not quite trusting herself to speak. Passersby had begun to gather around, and a collective *aw* went up from the crowd. *Let them look*, Daphne thought. *Let them all look, but this moment isn't for them. It's for us.*

Daphne Ballantyne and Jack King were finished putting on a show.

"What do you think about this?" Daphne winked at Olivia.

The little girl gave her a shy smile. "I think yes."

"I think yes too." Daphne said, and when Jack rose to his feet to slide the ring onto her finger, the air seemed as sweet as candy.

She cupped Jack's face as he lowered his head to kiss her, and in the moment just before their lips met, she whispered against his warm mouth. "We don't need to make it real, my love. It's been real all along."

Epilogue

Veil Magazine, November Issue

Wedding Report

Veil's own Daphne Ballantyne and Jack King tied the knot this month in a private ceremony for family and friends at the Plaza Hotel. The bride and groom, known best for their viral series of articles about the Elegantly Engaged etiquette class, fell in love while posing as an engaged couple for this very magazine. Their true identities were revealed just three months ago.

The couple exchanged vows in the hotel's Palm Court, where the class that brought them together took place last autumn. The ceremony was a family affair, with the bride escorted down the aisle by her father, Abe Ballantyne. Jack's adopted daughter,

Olivia, served as flower girl, accompanied by the family dog, Buttercup, who wore a collar of fresh pink peonies and white roses. The bride's veil was a King family heirloom, passed down from generation to generation of King brides since World War II. A delicate confection of blush-colored organza, it was worn most recently by the groom's mother, Eleanor King.

Courtiers at Monique Lhuillier designed the bride's bespoke gown in shades of pastel pink, lemon yellow and powder blue. In a heartwarming twist, the flower girl's dress matched—down to the very last, sparkly detail.

Daphne Ballantyne is the author of Veil's new ongoing fiction column "Love Unveiled." Jack King was recently promoted to senior features writer and continues to explore wedding-related stories from a fresh perspective. The couple has been nominated for a Fashion Media Award for their coverage of Elegantly Engaged.

Everyone here at Veil wishes them a very real, very joyful happy-ever-after.

* * * * *

For more stories of antagonism turning to love,
try these other great romances:

Heir in a Year
By Elizabeth Bevarly

The Business Between Them
By Mona Shroff

The Soldier's Refuge
By Sabrina York

Available now from Harlequin Special Edition!

SPECIAL EXCERPT FROM

The baby was only the first surprise...

*Retired rodeo cowboy Dean Hunter has escaped to
Charming, Texas, for some solitude, some surf and a
new start. But his plans are interrupted by his
stunning—and sparring—neighbor next door...and the
baby he discovers on Maribel's doorstep!*

Read on for a sneak preview of

A Charming Doorstep Baby
by Heatherly Bell.

Chapter One

"Another drink for Maribel."

Maribel Del Toro held up her palm. "No, *thanks*. I might not be driving, but I have to worry about walking while under the influence."

For an establishment that was a historical landmark, the Salty Dog Bar & Grill had mastered the art of a modern twist. The ambience fell somewhere between contemporary and classic, with a long bar of gleaming dark wood, one redbrick wall and exposed ceiling beams. Separate and on the opposite side of the bar the restaurant section was filled with booths. To top it all off, a quaint sense of small coastal town community infused the bar. Maribel loved it here.

Her brother, Max, was the occasional bartender and full-time owner. Situated on the boardwalk in the quiet town of Charming, Texas, it was the kind of place where everybody knew your name.

Especially if you were the younger sister of one of the

three former Navy SEALs who owned and operated the establishment.

"You had one beer. Even I think you're skilled enough to make it to the cottages without falling." Max grinned and wiped the bar.

"Ha ha. My brother, the comedian. I'll have a soda, please and thank you."

Afterward, she'd take a leisurely walk down to her beach rental a short mile from the boardwalk. Lately, she'd been digging her toes in the sand and simply staring off into the large gulf. Her father had once said if she ever got too big for her britches, she should consider the vastness of the ocean. She often had from her childhood home in Watsonville, California. The Pacific Ocean was an entirely different feel from the Gulf Coast, but both reminded her of how small her own problems were in comparison.

The doors to the restaurant swung open and some of the customers called out.

"Val! Hey, girl."

"When are you gettin' yourself back to work?"

"Soon as my husband lets me! Believe me, I miss y'all, especially your tips." Valerie Kinsella stopped to chat with customers and let a few of them check out the bundle in her front-loaded baby carrier.

She sidled up to the bar, her hand protectively cradled on her son's head of espresso brown curls that matched his mother's. "Hey, y'all. How's it goin'?"

"Hey there." Max hooked his thumb in the direction of the back office. "If you want Cole, he's in the back checking the books. We want to give the staff a nice bonus around the holidays."

"Well, dang it, I'm going to miss out on that, too. But I didn't just come by to see Cole. I sleep next to him every night." Valerie elbowed Maribel. "How are you enjoying your vacation?"

"Loving it. The beach rental unit is just perfect."

"And even if it is hurricane season, the weather seems to be cooperating."

Oh yeah. By the way, somebody should have told Maribel. When she'd eagerly booked this vacation for November, everyone forgot to mention the tail end of hurricane season. But this part of the Gulf Coast hadn't been hit in many years, so it was considered safe. Or as safe as Mother Nature could be. In any case, the lovely row of cottages near the beach were being sold to an investor, according to her sister-in-law, Ava, and this might be Maribel's last chance to stay there.

She nodded to Valerie's baby. "What a cutie. Congratulations again."

"Wade is such a sweet baby. We're lucky." Valerie kissed the top of his head.

He was a healthy-looking kid, too, with bright blue curious eyes the same intense shade as his father's. Maribel didn't have any children of her own, but she had plenty of experience. Loads. More than she'd ever wanted, thank you. In a way, that was why she was here in Charming, taking a sabbatical from all the suffering and gnashing of teeth. It went along with her profession like the ocean to the grains of sand.

"When do you go back to teaching?" Maribel gently touched Wade's little pert nose.

"Not until after the holidays. I've had a nice maternity leave, but it's time to get back to my other kids. The students claim to miss me. I have enough cards and drawings to make me almost believe it."

Maribel spent a few more minutes being treated to Valerie's "warrior story," i.e., her labor and delivery. She was a champ, according to Cole. Valerie claimed not to remember much, which to Maribel sounded like a blessing in disguise. Mucus plug. Episiotomy. Yikes. Maribel had reached her TMI limit when Cole, the former SEAL turned golden surfer boy, came blustering out of the back office looking every bit the harried father of one.

"Hey, baby." He slid his arm around Valerie, circling it around mother and child.

Maribel had known Cole for years since he'd been a part of the brotherhood who for so long had ruled Max's life. She imagined Max and his wife would be headed to Baby Town soon, as well. And though it was information still being held private, Jordan and Rafe were newly pregnant. Maribel had been given the news by a thrilled Jordan just last week.

Maribel slid off the stool. "Well, folks, I'm going to head on back to my little beach shack now."

Shack wasn't quite the right word. She'd been pleasantly surprised to find a suite similar to resort hotel villas. It contained a separate seating area and flat-screen, attached kitchenette and separate bedroom with a second flat-screen and a king-size bed. The bedroom had sliders opening up to a small patio that led to the private beach.

"Need a ride?" Cole asked.

"Nah. Part of the ambience of Charming can only be enjoyed by strolling."

Max gave a quick wave. "Don't forget, Ava wants you over for dinner soon."

"I'm here two weeks. Plenty of time." She slid a pleading look Valerie's way. "I'm hopeful for another invite to the lighthouse, too."

"Anytime!" Cole and Valerie both said at once, making everyone laugh.

Max rolled his eyes, but he should talk. He and Ava often finished each other's sentences.

Outside, the early November evening greeted her with a mild and light wind. Summers in the gulf had resembled a sauna in every way, but autumn had so far turned out to be picture perfect. Except for the whole hurricane season thing. Still, it was warm enough during the day for trips to the beach. When she dipped her toes in, the gulf waters were less like a hot tub and more like a warm bath. Maribel ambled along the seawall, away from the boardwalk side filled with carnival-style rides for children. The succulent scent of freshly popped kettle corn and waffle cones hung thickly in the air. She passed by shops, both the Lazy Mazy kettle corn and the saltwater taffy store. The wheels of an old-fashioned machine in front of the shop's window rolled and pulled the taffy and entertained passersby. In the distance, Maribel spotted a group of surfers.

The views were everything one would expect from a bucolic beach town with a converted lighthouse, piers, docks and sea jetties. The first time she'd been here was for Max and Ava's wedding six months ago, and she'd fallen in love with the area. It was the only place she'd considered escaping when she'd decided to resign from her position as a social worker. The offer from a multi-author doctor corporation was one she'd consider while here. They wanted a psychologist on board to assist with their heavy caseload, and that meant Maribel would put her hard-earned PhD to use. Although she wasn't excited by the prospect. Maybe after this vacation, she'd be able to clear the decks and finally make a firm decision. The offer was attractive, but it would be a huge change for her. She wasn't sure she'd be able to do much good and felt at a crossroads in her life. And this was the perfect location to decide what she'd do for the rest of her professional life.

The small row of beachfront cottages were rented year-round by both residents and tourists. Maribel had lucked into a rental during the off-season, meaning she had the peace and quiet she craved. As far as she could tell so far, she had only one neighbor, immediately next door. He was the most irritating male she'd ever had the misfortune of meeting. Sort of. There was, in fact, quite a list. He was, at the moment, in the top five.

On the day she'd arrived, she'd been to the store to stock up on groceries for all the cooking she'd planned to do. Hauling no less than four paper bags inside, she'd set one down just outside the heavy front door, propping it open.

When she'd returned for it, a huge cowboy stood outside her door holding it.

"Forgot something." He'd brushed by her, striding inside like he owned the place.

"Hey," she muttered, following him.

The man spoke in a thick Texan drawl, and he hadn't said the words in a helpful way. More like an accusatory tone, as in "You dingbat, here's your bag. If you need any other help getting through life, let me know."

She'd caught him looking around the inside of her rental as if apprising its contents. But he didn't *look* like a burglar.

"I didn't forget." Maribel snatched the shopping bag from him, deciding in that moment he'd made it to the top five. Of all the nerve. She hadn't been gone a full minute.

"You might not want to just leave anything out here unattended. Unless you want someone to steal it."

Steal? Here in the small town of Charming, Texas?

She flushed at the remark. "I don't think anyone is going to steal my box of cereal or fresh fruit."

"Regardless, you should care for your property. Don't invite trouble."

Okay, so he'd figured out she was a single woman and wanted to look out for her.

"Great. If you're done with your mansplaining, I'm going to cook dinner."

"Are you liking this unit well enough? Everything in working condition?"

Now, he sounded like the landlord. *Good grief.* Top three most irritating men, easily.

"Yes, thank you, I have located everything I need." She rolled her eyes.

"I'm next door if you need anything else."

"I won't."

He'd tipped his hat, but she'd shut the door on him before he could say another word.

Since that day, she saw little of him, and that was fine with her.

Twenty minutes of an invigorating walk later, she arrived at her cottage. There was her neighbor again, the surly surfing cowboy, coming up from their lane to the beach carrying a surfboard under his arm. He might be irritating as hell, but he looked like he'd emerged from the sea shirtless, ready to sell viewers the latest popular male cologne.

She wondered whether he was attempting to cover two hero stereotypes at once. He wore a straw cowboy hat, and though this was Texas, after all, the hat didn't *quite* match with the bare chest and wet board shorts he wore low on his hips. A towel slung around his neck completed the outfit of the salty guy who once more simply nodded in her direction. Before she could say, "Howdy, neighbor," he stared straight ahead like she no longer existed.

No worries. She hadn't come here to make friends. Even if he resembled a Greek god. Thor, to be more specific—who wasn't actually from Greek mythology. This demigod had taut golden skin, a square jaw and a sensual mouth. His abs, legs and arms were chiseled to near perfection. But she was going to ignore all this because it didn't fit into her plans.

Focus. Men were not part of the plan. Even sexy irritating males, her weakness. She was here to unplug and had turned off her cell, giving her family the landline for emergencies. In her plan for mindfulness and peace, she was practicing yoga every morning before sunrise. And reading. Not from her e-reader but actual print she had to hold in her hands.

Rather than dwelling on her problems, Maribel would set them aside for now. Since months of dwelling on her problems hadn't given any answers, she was trying this new approach.

Once she'd spent enough time away from her situation, her mind would produce fresh results and ideas.

Because she had to decide soon how she would spend the rest of her life.

Dean Hunter hopped out of the shower and wrapped a towel around himself. Another day completed in his attempts to hit the waves and master the fine art of surfing. All he had to show for it? Two more fresh cuts, five new bruises and a sore knee. He had to face facts: he was a disaster on the water, having spent most of his life on a working cattle ranch. He'd been bucked off many a horse, and how interesting to find it wasn't any less pleasant to slam into the water than the ground. Seemed like water should give a little, and of course it did, more than the ground ever would. Still hurt, though, equal to the velocity with which a person slammed into a wave.

Why am I here?

A question he asked himself twice a day.

He should have simply backed out of this vacation and lost his deposit. This time was to have been a getaway with Amanda, where he'd get down on bended knee and pop the question. The cottages were going to be a surprise wedding gift to her. A way to show her all he'd accomplished. They'd have a vacation home every summer, a whole row of them. He was a damn idiot thinking that maybe he'd finally found the right woman. He and Amanda were both part of the circuit and had been for years. They had a great deal in common, and eventually they'd decided moving out of the friend zone made sense.

Then, six months ago, he'd walked in on Amanda showing Anton "The Kid" Robbins the ropes. And by "the ropes," he meant he'd walked in on her and the twenty-six-year-old, Amanda straddling him like a bucking horse. No way a man could ever unsee that. He'd walked out of his own house and moved into a hotel room. One more race to win, he'd told himself, and maybe then he'd go out on top. But that hadn't happened.

To think that Anton had been his protégé. Dean hadn't been ready to retire, but he saw the sense in training the new kids, giving them a hand up. Someone had done this for him, and he would return the favor. He couldn't ride forever, but he'd thought he would have had a little more time. Now Dean was the old guard and Anton the new. He didn't have as many injuries (yet) as Dean and was also ten years younger.

Dean still had no idea how he'd gotten it all so wrong. He hadn't been able to clearly see what had been in front of him all along. His manager had warned him about Amanda, who was beautiful but calculating. Dean had wanted to believe he'd finally found someone who would stick by him when he quit the rodeo. He'd had about six months with her, during which time she convinced him he'd found the right woman. *Yeah, not so much.*

Their breakup happened right before his last ride. He'd already been reeling when he'd taken the last blow, this one to his career. In some ways, he was still trying to get up from the last kick to his ego. At thirty-six, battered and bruised, he'd been turned in for a newer model. Anton still had plenty of mileage left on him, time to make his millions before a body part gave out on him.

So Dean should have let the opportunity to buy this investment property go. There were ten cottages, and in anticipation of his stay here to check them out thoroughly, they'd kept them vacant for him. All except Cute Stuck-up Girl next door. The moment he'd noticed he wasn't here alone as expected, he'd phoned the real estate agent.

"Thought I was going to be here by myself."

"You were, but Maribel Del Toro apparently has some influential friends in this town, friends who know the current owner and have some pull. We thought it best not to reschedule her reservation like we did the others."

"How am I supposed to inspect her unit?"

He'd already found an excuse by hurrying to help bring in a grocery bag in before she had a chance to say anything. You would have thought he'd wrecked the place instead of tried to help. He'd obviously insulted her in the process, but how else was he supposed to check inside? He never bought a dang thing before he inspected every nook and cranny, and that included a horse.

"We will give you a clause to back out if something is wrong in that unit. These deals fall apart all the time."

"And why is she right *next* to my unit?"

The real estate agent sighed. "Remember, you asked for new storm windows if you were even to consider buying. Progress on the others was not complete, and hers was the only unit available when she arrived."

By nature, Dean was a suspicious sort, and he couldn't help but wonder why these units were going far too cheaply for ocean-front property. But as a kid who'd grown up in Corpus Christi to a single mother who never had much, it would be a nice "full circle" gesture to buy this. And after years of punishing his body and garnering one buckle after another, he was a wealthy man. Still, he didn't like anyone to know it, least of all women. So he dressed like a cowboy even if he was technically a multimillionaire. At his core, he was a cowboy and always would be.

While the injury was said to be career ending, he could have gone through rehab and come back stronger than ever. Having come from nothing, he'd been wise about his investments, and while others enjoyed buckle bunnies, gambling and drinking, Dean had socked away every nickel. He had investments all over Texas, including his ranch in Hill Country.

In the end, he'd forced himself to walk away from the rodeo before he didn't have a body left to enjoy the other pleasantries in life. Oh yeah. That was why he was here in Charming trying his hand at surfing in the Gulf of Mexico during hurricane season. It was just the shot of adrenaline a junkie like him needed.

He would find his footing in his new world with zero illusions he'd find a second career as a competitive surfer. Instead, it was time for the second part of his life to begin, the part that was supposed to matter.

Life *after* the rodeo. Life after poverty.

He'd already been coming here for a short time every summer just to remember his roots. He'd drive from Corpus Christi to Charming, counting his blessings. Enjoying the coastal weather.

Remembering his mother.

Once, he could recall having ambitions that went beyond the rodeo. An idea and a plan to fix for others what had been broken in his own life. Somewhere along the line, he'd forgotten every last one of those dreams. He was here to hopefully remember some of them in the peace and quiet of this small town. Here, no one would disturb him. No one except his feisty neighbor, that is, who behaved as if he'd deeply insulted her by carrying in her groceries. She'd immediately put him on the defensive, seeing as it had merely been an excuse to get inside her unit. It was as if she could read his mind. He didn't like it.

He often watched Cute Stuck-up Girl from a distance as she sank her feet in the sand and read a book. Two days ago, he'd seen her fighting the beach umbrella she'd been setting up for shade. It was almost bigger than her, which was part of the problem. She'd cursed and carried on until Dean was two seconds away from offering his help. He'd walk over there and issue instructions on how to put the umbrella up until she got all red in the face again with outrage. The thought made him chuckle. He'd put the umbrella up *for* her if she'd let him. Not likely.

Finally, she got it to stay up and did a little victory dance when she must have assumed no one was watching.

And he'd found a laugh for the first time in months.

After changing clothes and towel-drying his hair, Dean plopped on his favorite black Stetson and headed to the local watering hole. A little place along the boardwalk that he'd discovered a few years ago sandwiched between other storefronts and gift shops. At the Salty Dog Bar & Grill, the occasional bartender and owner there was a surfer who'd given Dean plenty of tips. Cole Kinsella had even offered Dean one of his older boards, since as a new father, he wasn't taking to the water as often.

Safe to say, Dean liked the bar and the people in it from the moment he'd strode inside and momentarily indulged in one of his favorite fantasies: buying a sports bar. It was one of the few investments he didn't have because he'd been talked out of it too many times to count. This place resembled a sports bar, but was more of a family place that also happened to have a bar. The restaurant section sat next to the bar separated only by the booths. Instead of huge flat-screens on every spare amount of space, there were chalkboards with the specials written out in fancy white cursive.

Everyone was friendly and welcoming. The first night Dean had come in, he'd met a group of senior citizens who were having some kind of a poetry meeting.

The only gentleman in the group, Roy Finch, had offered to buy Dean a beer.

"Don't mind if I do." Dean nodded. "Thank you, sir."

"You're a cowboy?"

"Yes, sir. Born and bred." Dean tipped his hat.

"Don't usually see that many of you here on the gulf."

"Our profession usually keeps us far from the coast."

"What you doin' in these parts?"

"Good question." Dean took a pull of the beer the bartender had set in front of him. "I guess I'm lookin' for another profession."

"All washed out?"

"That obvious?" Dean snorted. "I was part of the rodeo circuit longer than I care to say."

"Thought I recognized you. Tough life."

They'd discussed the rodeo and the current front runners, which unfortunately included Anton. The man thought he was God's gift to women, overindulging in buckle bunnies and earning himself quite a reputation both on and off the circuit.

Dean had gone over a few of his injuries with Roy, but held back on the worst ones. Mr. Finch had introduced him to his fiancée, Lois, and some other women who were with him and were all part of a group calling themselves the Almost Dead Poets Society. Every night since then, Dean met someone new.

Now, he sidled up to the bar, but the surfer dude wasn't behind it. A dark-haired guy named Max, going by what everyone called him, was taking orders.

"What can I get you?" he asked Dean in an almost-menacing tone.

"Cold beer."

"We have several IPAs, domestic and imported." He rattled off names, sounding more like a sommelier than a bartender.

"Domestic, thanks."

"Here you go," he said a moment later, uncapping a bottle and taking Dean's cash.

This guy wasn't quite as chatty and friendly as Cole had been. He was also busy as the night wore on and, after a while, got grumpy.

"Max," someone called out. "C'mon! I ordered a mojito about an *hour* ago."

This was a great exaggeration, as Dean had listened to the man order it no more than fifteen minutes ago.

"And if you ask me again, you're not getting it *tonight*."

Dean would go out on a limb and guess this man was one of the owners of the bar. Cole had explained they were three former Navy SEALs who had retired and saved the floundering bar from foreclosure.

Turning his back to the bar, Dean spread his arms out and took in the sights. A busy place, the waitresses in the adjacent dining area flitted from one table to the next. He saw couples, families and a group of younger women taking up an entire table.

"Hey there, cowboy," a soft sweet voice to his right said. "I'm Twyla."

Dean immediately zeroed in on the source, a beautiful brunette who looked to be quite a bit younger than him. He shouldn't let that bother him, but for reasons he didn't understand, only younger women hit on him. He guessed it to be the fascination with the cowboy archetype, which usually happened when traveling in urban cities or coastal areas. He happened to know men who'd had nothing to do with ranches or rodeos who wore Western boots, a straw hat and ambled into a bar. They never left alone.

But a beautiful woman would only take time and attention away from Dean's surfing. Besides, were he to take up with any woman, it would be with the girl next door. Literally. She was as gorgeous a woman as he'd ever laid eyes on. Dark hair that fell in waves around her shoulders, chocolate brown eyes that made a man feel…seen.

"Dean. It's a pleasure." He nodded, failing to give her a last name. She didn't seem like the type to follow the rodeo, but one never knew.

He intended to remain anonymous while in Charming, though a few had already recognized him. The night before, he'd given out his autograph and taken a few photos with a family visiting from Hill Country. He ought to ditch the hat and shoot for a little less obvious.

"You're on vacation?" Twyla asked.

"How did you guess?"

"Not many cowboy types around here."

"Actually, I'm a surfer."

Speaking of exaggerations...

"You're kidding. Well, you're in the right place. Pretty soon the waves are going to kick up, depending on whether a system hits us. But don't worry, we haven't had a direct hit in decades." She offered her hand. "I own the bookstore in town, Once Upon a Book."

Her hand was soft and sweet, making Dean recall just how long it had been since he'd been with a woman. *Too* long. And even though it seemed like bookstores had become as out-of-date and useless as broken-down cowboys like him, he didn't feel a need to connect with this woman.

She had a look about her he recognized too well: she had a *thing* about cowboys. He wasn't interested in indulging in those fantasies. Been there, done that, bought the saddle. He was done with women who were interested in the part of him he was leaving behind. Rodeo had been fun, his entire life for two decades.

And now it was over.

They chatted a few more minutes about nothing in particular, and then Dean set his bottle down on the bar, deciding to call it an early night.

"Nice meeting ya."

"I'll see you around?" she asked.

"You will." He waved and strode outside.

The sun was nearing the end of its slow slide down the horizon, sinking into the sea, assuring him the sky would be dark by the time he drove to his rental. He looked forward to another night of peace and quiet, retiring to bed alone and hogging the damn covers. There were good parts of being alone, few that they were, and he needed to remember them lest he be tempted to remedy the situation.

He arrived to find a basket in front of Cute Stuck-up Girl's house she'd obviously forgotten to bring inside, again, and Dean figured he'd knock on the door and finally introduce himself. This time, he wouldn't be as irritated and try on a smile or two. Maybe even apologize for their rough beginning.

Just a quick hello, and he'd be home lickety-split. He stepped over the crushed shell walkway between them, heading toward the front door.

Then the basket made a tiny mewing sound.

What the hell?

Dean approached and bent low to view, with utter horror, that his neighbor had left her baby on the doorstep.

Chapter Two

Maribel was in the middle of chopping onions for her mother's arroz con pollo recipe when she heard a loud pounding on the front door. This was odd, because everyone she knew in Charming would call or text first. But she'd told Ava to drop by anytime. Maribel dried her hands on a dish towel, then walked toward the door. The pounding had become so fierce it could not possibly be her sweet sister-in-law. This was more like a man's fist. Or a hammer.

There was urgency in the knocking. She could feel it, like a pounding deep in her gut. With an all too familiar deep sense of flight-or-fight syndrome coursing through her, she swung the door open.

There stood her neighbor, holding a large basket.

His expression was positively murderous. "Forget something?"

Wondering why he was still so concerned about her

forgetting stuff and ready to tell him off, she peered inside the basket. "Oh, you have a baby."

"Your baby." He snarled, then pushed his way inside, setting the basket down.

"*Excuse* me?"

"It was right on your doorstep. This is dangerous. How absent-minded are you, exactly? Are you going to tell me you didn't even realize?"

Her hackles went up immediately at even the suggestion that she, of all people, would forget a *baby*. He didn't know her or her history. He quickly went from top five to number one most irritating male she'd ever met.

"Number one!" she shouted.

"*Excuse* me?"

"I don't have a baby, *sir*!"

"Well, it's not *my* baby!"

They stared daggers at each other for several long beats. His eyes were an interesting shade of amber, and at the moment, they were dark with hostility. Aimed at her, of all people. Because he didn't know her and that she'd sooner be roasted over hot coals than put a child at risk.

Her mind raced. In the past few days, she'd never seen him with a baby. No sign of a woman or child next door, so her instinct was to believe him. It probably wasn't his baby. And either he was certifiably insane, or he really was indignant that she would have forgotten her baby.

Which meant… Realization dawned on Maribel and appeared to simultaneously hit him.

They both rushed out the front door, him slightly ahead of her. Maribel ran to the edge of the short path in one direction, and Cowboy went in the other.

"Hey!" he shouted after whoever would have done this terrible thing. "Hey! Get back here!"

"Do you see anyone?"

"You go back inside with the baby. I'll go see if I can find any sign of who did this." He took off at a run, jogging down the lane leading to the beach.

Her breaths were coming sharp and ragged. Maybe this was a joke. Yes, a big practical joke on Maribel Del Toro, the burned-out former social worker. But she didn't know of anyone who'd leave a baby unattended outside as a joke. It wasn't funny. Who would be this stupid and careless?

Inside, the baby lay quietly in the basket, kicking at the blanket, completely unaware of the trauma he or she had caused. Why *Maribel's* door? And who was this desperate? Almost every fire department in the country had a safe haven for dropping a baby off, no questions asked. Of course, Charming *was* small enough to only have a volunteer fire department, and she wasn't sure they even had a station in town. But Houston was only thirty minutes away and had a large hospital and fire department.

Dressed in pink and surrounded by pink and white blankets, a small stack of diapers was shoved to one side of the basket. The baby looked to be well cared for. Two cans of formula and a bottle were on the other side. Obviously, a very deliberate, premeditated attempt to get rid of a baby. Maribel unwrapped the child from the soft blanket and unbuttoned the sleeper. As she'd suspected, due to the baby's size, she found no signs of a healing umbilical cord. Not a newborn. The belly button had completely healed. Maribel's educated guess would make the infant around two to three months old.

Someone had lovingly cared for this baby for months and then given up. Why?

The question should be: Why this time?

Drugs? Alcohol? Homelessness? An abusive home? For years, Maribel had witnessed situations in which both children and infants had to be removed from a home. Usually, the need became apparent at first sight. Garbage inside the home, including drug paraphernalia. Empty alcohol bottles. Both kids and babies in dirty clothes and overflowing diapers. No proper bed for the child or food.

But she'd never seen a baby this well cared for left behind.

"Where's your mommy?" Maribel mused as she checked the baby out from head to toe.

A few minutes later, Cowboy came bursting through Maribel's front door slightly out of breath.

"I couldn't find anyone."

"I don't understand this. Why leave the baby at *my* front door?" Then a thought occurred out of the blue, and she pointed to him. "Hang on. What if they meant to leave the baby at *your* front door but got the wrong house?"

"Mine?" He tapped his chest. "Why *my* house?"

"Let's see. What are the odds somewhere along the line you impregnated a woman? Maybe she's tired and wants *you* to take a turn with your child."

Even as she said the words, Maribel recognized the unfairness behind them. She'd made a rash conclusion someone this attractive had to be a player with a ton of women in his past. And also, apparently, someone who didn't practice safe sex.

And from the narrowed eyes and tight jawline, he'd taken this as a dig.

"That's insulting. I don't have any children. If I had a baby, believe me, I'd *know* about it."

"It doesn't always work that way, Cowboy." She picked up the baby and held her close, rubbing her back in slow and even strokes.

"My name's *Dean*, not Cowboy." He pointed to the diapers. "What's that?"

"Diapers," Maribel deadpanned. "Are you not acquainted with them?"

"This." He bent low and, from between the diapers, picked out a sheet of paper.

"What is it?" Maribel said.

Dean unfolded and read. As he did, his face seemed to change colors. He went from golden boy to gray boy.

He lowered the note, then handed it to Maribel. "It's not signed."

Maribel set the baby in the basket, then read:

Her name is Brianna, and she's a really good baby. Sometimes she even sleeps through the night. The past three months have been hard, but I want to keep my baby. I just need a couple of weeks to figure some things out. Please take care of her until I come back. Tell her mommy will miss her, but I promise I'm coming back. I left some formula and diapers, and I promise to pay you back for any more you have to buy. She likes it when I sing to her.

"Figure a few things out" could mean anything from drug addiction to a runaway teen.

And this troubled girl had left the baby...with Maribel.

"I swear, I... I don't know who would have done this. I don't even live in Charming. I'm here on vacation."

"She must know you somehow. More importantly, she trusts you with her baby."

"She's trusted the wrong person if she thinks I'm going to allow this to happen."

He narrowed his eyes. "What does that mean?"

"We have to call the police."

"No. We *don't.*"

"Just one week ago, I was an employed social worker with the state of California. I know about these things."

"Sounds like you're no longer employed, and we're in the state of Texas, last I checked."

"That doesn't change facts. This is child abandonment, pure and simple."

"Except it's *not*." He snapped the letter out of Maribel's hands and tapped on the writing. "It's clearly written here that she'll be back. She's asked you to babysit. That's *all*."

"Are you kidding me? She left the baby on my *doorstep*. Babysitting usually involves *asking* someone first. An exchange of information. Anything could have happened to her baby. You were upset when I left a bag of *groceries* on the doorstep."

"Is it possible she rang the doorbell, and you didn't hear? You took your sweet time coming to the door for me, and I was about to knock it down."

"It's…possible." She shook her head. "I don't know. We should call the cops. At the very least, get her checked out at the hospital and make sure she's okay."

"No. If we take her to a hospital, too many questions will be asked."

"Those questions *need* to be asked! We don't know what we're dealing with here."

"We know *exactly* what we're dealing with here, thanks to the note. A probably young and overwhelmed single mom is asking you to babysit. You're the one person who could stand between her ability to ever see her baby again."

You're the one person who could stand between her ability to ever see her baby again.

His words hit her with sharp slings and a force he

might have not intended. They felt personal, slamming into her, slicing her in two.

"Nice try. But I refuse to be guilt-tripped into abandoning my principles."

He snorted. "Principles. That's funny."

"What's funny about principles? Don't you have them?"

"Principles won't work if there's no real intent behind them. Or is family reunification a myth?"

She crossed her arms. Interesting. Her analytical brain took this tip and filed it away for future use. The man seemed to know a few things about the system.

"Of course it's not a myth. It's the goal, but too many times, the parents are unable to meet their part of the deal. The children come first. Always."

"And the children want to be with their parents. It's the number one truth universally acknowledged. If you call law enforcement, that's going to complicate everything."

"That will simply start the clock ticking, and she'll have forty-eight hours to return."

"I can't let you do that. This mother clearly wants her baby back."

Everything inside Maribel tensed when this total stranger told her what she could and couldn't do. He didn't know how many times she'd had faith in a parent, worked for their reunification, only to be burned time and again. The last time had nearly ruined her. She was done rescuing people.

"I can't… I can't take her."

"You're choosing not to. Do me a favor? Stay out of this. I'll take the baby."

"*You* will. You?"

For reasons she didn't quite understand, the surfing cowboy had strong feelings about this. And she got it. A baby in need brought out universal emotions. She wanted to help, but the right thing to do was to call the authorities. Eventually, if the mother *proved* herself to be worthy, she'd get her baby back through the proper channels. Parents should prove they were capable of caring for their children. That way, all could be reassured this wasn't simply a temporary lapse in the girl's judgment. Everyone could be certain the baby was returned to a safe environment.

Dean took the baby from Maribel, then bent to pick up the baby's basket. He moved toward the front door. "Don't let us bother you."

"Wait a second here. What do *you* know about babies? Have you ever had children?"

"No, but I know enough. The rest I'll learn online."

"Online? So, you're going to *google* it?"

"Listen, there are YouTube videos on everything. I guarantee you I can figure this out. You don't need a PhD to change a diaper."

Her neck jerked back. It was unnerving the way he seemed to read her, to know her, before she'd told him a thing. No, you didn't need a *PhD* to change a diaper, but to understand why people reacted in the ways they did. To meet them in their dysfunction and try to help. The problem was all bets were off when addiction was part of the picture. Then parents didn't behave logically. They made decisions not even in their *own* best interest, let alone a child's. And Maribel didn't know whether this mother was an addict who could no longer care for her child. She didn't know anything at all about this mother, and the thought filled her with anxiety.

She cocked her head and went for logic. "This is going to interfere with your precious surfing time, you know."

She'd noticed him on the beach with his board every day, like it was his religion.

"Not a problem." He turned to her as though giving her one more chance to reconsider. "But if that's an offer to babysit a time or two, I'd take you up on it."

"Babysit? For all practical purposes, that's *my baby* you're holding. She left her for me to take care of."

"And you've said you can't violate your principles, so…"

"I also don't know whether I can trust you to watch YouTube videos and figure out how to take care of a baby."

"Well, damn. Looks like your principles are in conflict with one another."

Really? Tell me about it!

Not long ago, this had been her life. A desire to help but forced to follow rules set in place with the best of intentions. Foster care was never the horrible place pop culture and the news media led people to believe. It was only meant to be a temporary and safe home. Too many negative stories made the press, and did not acknowledge those angelic foster parents who cared for children with what amounted to a pittance of a salary.

"While you cuddle up with your principles tonight, I'll be next door with Brianna." Then he left with the baby.

"Number one!" she shouted behind him, but either he hadn't heard or decided not to acknowledge it.

She wasn't cuddling up to her principles, she was *living* with them. Doing the right thing. And yet…procedure would involve alerting the police. The problem was she seemed to be in a gray area, but ethics were always important, regardless of whether legalities were involved.

You're here to unplug. Mindfulness is the key. You're going to teach yourself to cook. Read feel-good fiction.

Stay off your cell, all social media and recharge. You have a major decision to make.

Last month, an old headhunter friend had approached and offered Maribel a position with a six-figure salary. She'd be taking over the caseload of a therapist who had counseled the children of the Silicon Valley elite. Anxiety, depression and ADHD were core issues. Maribel had a knee-jerk reaction to the proposition: no. But maybe she could do some good there. It would be something so different from what she'd been doing for years. A chance to use her education and experience in a different way.

She only had a few more weeks to decide before they looked for someone else.

Maribel went back to her dinner of arroz con pollo, so rudely interrupted by both her neighbor and a baby. As she opened cans of tomato sauce and stirred them into the rice, she relaxed and unwound. Her breathing returned to normal, and her shoulders unkinked. Routines were good to employ in the aftermath of shock. They soothed. They reminded a person life would go on.

On the day Maribel discovered the toddler she'd helped reunite with his mother had been rushed to the hospital with dehydration, she'd brushed her teeth in the middle of the day. Later, she would come to doubt every decision she'd ever made, including the one to become a social worker.

Despite the fact Dean had let Maribel off the hook, she couldn't ignore the mother's request. The baby was her responsibility, and she never shirked her duties. Not from the time she was working with her parents in the strawberry fields of Watsonville to the moment of her PhD dissertation. She, Maribel Del Toro, was no quitter.

She didn't want a surfing cowboy dude who had to google *diapering* to take care of the baby. And even if

Maribel had a good sense of people, she didn't know this man. She'd let him take a baby next door, where he might hopelessly bungle it all. In all good conscience, she couldn't just stand by.

Ten minutes later, she turned off the stove and banged on the door to *his* cottage.

He opened the door, almost as if he'd expected her. But then he walked toward the connected bedroom with barely a glance, simply leaving it for her to choose to walk inside or not.

"I can't walk away from her. It's my responsibility," she said.

Since he didn't say a word, she closed the front door and followed him past the sitting room area, the kitchenette and into the bedroom. He'd emptied a dresser drawer and placed Brianna in it, surrounded by her blankets.

"This is a temporary bed for her." He ran a hand through his hair, looking more than a little out of sorts. "Maybe I should buy a crib."

He'd removed the hat, and she wasn't surprised to find golden locks of hair had been under it, curling at his neck and almost long enough to be put in a short ponytail.

Hands in the pockets of his jeans, he lowered his head to study the baby as if mulling over a complicated algebra word problem.

Brianna cooed and gave him a drooly smile. Aw, she was such a cute baby. Beautiful dark eyes and curls of black hair. Her beautiful skin was a light brown. She could be African American, Latina or multiracial.

"As you said, babysitting her is temporary. You don't need to invest in a crib. Maybe this, um, drawer will do for now."

"You *approve*?"

The corner of his lip curled up in a half smile, and

something went tight in Maribel's belly. The cowboy's eyes were an interesting shade some would call hazel, others might simply call amber. But they were no longer hot with anger.

She tilted her chin and met his eyes. "Let's just say I'm in new territory here, but so far, so good."

"You're going to help me?"

"It would be irresponsible of me to let you do this on your own."

He shook his head. "Those principles in conflict again. Pesky little things."

"Don't make fun of me. This is serious."

"Yeah, it is. A baby needs you. I know what I'm going to do. What about you?"

She still didn't know, but maybe she didn't *have* to make an immediate decision. It was entirely possible the mother would be back by tomorrow at the latest, regretting what she'd done and missing her baby. Unfortunately, Maribel was too jaded to believe this a real possibility.

But she wanted to.

"We don't even know if she'll be gone the full two weeks. She could come back sooner."

"Exactly." Dean picked up a diaper. "The way I look at this, Brianna is going to need more diapers. I already went through two of them."

"*Two?* You've been in here for fifteen minutes."

He scowled and scratched his chin. "She wet while I was changing her. Is that…normal?"

Oh boy. This guy really didn't know a thing. Then again, how often did men babysit siblings, nieces or nephews even if they had them? Not often, at least not in her family.

Dean had already explained he had no children of his own. *That he knew of.*

"It's normal. You're lucky Brianna isn't a boy. Sometimes the stream goes long and wide."

"Okay." Dean crossed his arms and gazed at her from under hooded lids. "Thanks for the four-one-one."

"Um, you're welcome." Self-consciously, Maribel pulled on the sleeve of her sundress and chewed on her lower lip.

She didn't usually wear dresses, and that might be the reason she was so ill at ease here with him. Usually she wore pantsuits, her hair up in a bun. Men were still occasionally strange creatures to her, who had ideas she didn't quite grasp.

Watching this particular man from a safe distance had been comfortable. Easy. She could ogle him all she wanted from the privacy of her own cottage and realize nothing would come of it. Now, standing next to him, there was a charge between them. He'd really *noticed* her. She suddenly felt a little...naked. And a lot...awkward.

"You mind watching her while I go buy some diapers and formula?" he said.

"Go ahead."

A perfect opportunity. While here alone, Maribel planned on surreptitiously checking out Dean's unit. It wasn't that she had trust issues, no sir, but if he was going to watch the baby *she'd* been entrusted with, she should make sure he could be relied on with any child. She wouldn't call it snooping, exactly. More like a light criminal background check.

"Be right back." He grabbed his keys.

"And don't forget baby wipes."

"Okay. Wipes."

She pointed. "*Baby* wipes. Don't get the Lysol ones."

"Speaking of mansplaining." He quirked a brow and gave her the side-eye before he walked out the door.

Snooping commenced immediately. First, she checked on Brianna, who, with a clean diaper, had gone back to snoozing. Admittedly the drawer was an ingenious and scrappy idea from a man who'd probably had to figure things out in the wilderness when all he had for supper was a stick and a rabbit.

Okay, Maribel, he's a cowboy, not Paul Bunyon.

She knew little of life on the range, where she assumed he lived. Checking through his luggage, she found plenty of shirts and jeans. Interesting. He wore dark boxer briefs. Not even white socks but dark ones. Wasn't that against cowboy regulations?

Put the underwear down and back away, Maribel.

His underwear and clothes told her nothing about the man. Importantly, she hadn't found a gun or a buck knife. She rifled through drawers in each room, finding real estate flyers and Ava's "Welcome to Charming" Chamber of Commerce handout. But nothing embarrassing, dangerous or disgusting. She checked the medicine cabinet and under the mattress for those pesky recreational drugs. On her principles, she'd whisk this baby away in a New York minute even if she found the (ahem) legal stuff. Nothing. So far, he checked out.

Then she found a pack of condoms in his nightstand drawer, and it snapped her back to reality.

What am I doing?

She sat on the bed and stared at the wall, covering her face. If only her colleagues could see her now. They'd no longer have any doubts that she'd done the right thing by resigning from the California Department of Social Services.

They'd no longer have any doubt that she'd lost all faith in humanity. She no longer believed in people. She no longer believed in second chances.

This poor man was trying to do a good thing here, and she'd found his condoms, violating his privacy in every way. None of her business. Hey, at least he was prepared. She could find nothing wrong with the man who'd offered to care for the baby, so she didn't have an excuse to call the authorities. He was right to hope. Maybe. There was a memory nagging at the edge of Maribel's mind, but she couldn't pin it down. Last week, when she'd been to the Once Upon a Book store with Stacy Cruz, Maribel might have mentioned her former career in social services. There had been a teenage girl there looking through the mystery section.

She could give this mother at least twenty-four hours.

One day to regret her decision and come running back for her baby.

The mother would be back, and if she didn't return, *then* Maribel would call the police.

Chapter Three

Dean stood in the middle of aisle fourteen, feeling like a giant idiot. He'd asked for wipes and the clerk sent him straight here, but this wasn't right. These were the Lysol cleaning wipes Maribel had warned him about, as if he didn't know any better. The clerk had simply assumed *he* didn't have a baby, but obviously must have a bathroom or a kitchen to clean. And he hadn't been specific enough. *Baby* wipes.

Maybe babysitting Brianna wasn't such a great idea. If only his pretty neighbor would have agreed to watch the baby and let him off the hook. What was wrong with her, anyway? He expected most women would want to babysit a cute baby, but then again, he'd wager she wasn't most women. It turned out she was a social worker with an inherent bias against mothers who made mistakes.

People like Maribel had changed the trajectory of Dean's life.

He wandered down the aisles and finally found the

baby stuff. There were packages of diapers in all manner of sizes. Newborn, the smallest, and then differing numbered sizes by weight. He had no idea how much the baby weighed. In two seconds, he was overwhelmed. He didn't even know how old this baby was and hadn't thought to get Maribel's cell number so he could text her from the store. What *size*? He wanted to get eight to fourteen pounds because that made sense, but maybe over fourteen pounds would be best. Better to have a bigger size than too small, right? He knew that much, anyway.

The formula deal was a lot easier to figure out, so he picked up a case. The baby wipes, once he found them, also easy. Did not require a size, only choosing between scented, unscented, with added aloe vera and hypoallergenic. He chose the ones for sensitive skin, just in case.

As Dean was holding the newborn size diapers in one hand and the next larger size in the other, a man came rushing into the aisle and began snatching pacifiers off the rack like there might soon be a shortage of them. Pacifiers! Dean should have thought of that. Before the dude grabbed them all, Dean reached for one.

"Those are the best. Orthodontists recommend them," the man said, noticing Dean.

"Is there a sale going on?"

"Is there? Hope so. We're trying to wean her from these, but it's not working. And no matter what we do, we can never have enough of these on hand. We've lost so many of them under furniture, beds, cars, anywhere. I figure when we move, we're going to find a treasure trove of old and hairy pacifiers. They didn't just *disappear*. Must be hiding somewhere. It's like losing a sock in the dryer. No one has figured out where the other one goes. It's a mystery. Well, pacifiers are like clean socks."

"Uh-huh." Dean cleared his throat and examined the packaging. "How many should I get for my baby?"

"How old is she?"

"Um, she's really...*young*."

The man quirked a brow, thankfully accepting Dean's ignorance as to the age of his pretend child.

"You look familiar. You're that beginning surfer who hangs out at the Salty Dog, aren't you? Cole told me about you."

Dean's hackles went up at being referred to as "beginning" anything, but it was an unfortunately fair assessment.

"I'm Dean Hunter. And you are...?"

He offered his hand in a firm grip. "Adam Cruz. Nice to meet you. I'm one of the Salty Dog owners."

"Pleasure." Dean tipped his hat and reframed his story. "I'm, uh, babysitting? My niece. For my sister, she...she forgot to..."

Tell me how old her baby is?

Adam eyed the diapers Dean held. "Leave enough diapers? They go through those fast. My wife and I have a daughter, too. That's nice of you to babysit. I take people up on that every chance I get. I love my daughter, but holy cow, I need more time with my wife. Ya know?"

"Um, yeah. That's actually why I'm doing this. My sister needed some time with the wife." Dean winced, realizing he'd outed his nonexistent, invisible sister.

"And you're probably wondering what you got yourself into now."

Dean chuckled and rubbed his chin. "Ha, yeah. You could say that."

"Don't worry. I was terrified the first time I held my baby, afraid I'd break her."

"Yeah, that's how I feel."

Since the moment he'd called Maribel's bluff and hauled the baby with him next door, he had no idea what he was doing and if he'd somehow do more harm than good. Add to that the anxiety of wondering if the mother would come back as promised or if his next-door neighbor would get to be right. She would then turn him into the authorities right along with the baby.

He took the baby, she'd point and say. *And then proceeded to watch YouTube videos on how to take care of her. It was a recipe for disaster from the get-go. I tried to stop him!*

He could almost see *Rodeo Today*'s front-page headline:

Four-Time World Champ Quits Rodeo Circuit to Steal Someone's Baby

Dean held up the two different sizes of diapers. "Which one?"

"Easy. Unless your baby was delivered just today or premature, the newborn size is going to be too small. I made the same rookie mistake. She didn't fit into newborn by the time she was three days old. I'd get the next one up, twelve to eighteen pounds."

"Hey, thanks, buddy. I appreciate it."

Adam waved and rushed away, taking ten pacifiers with him.

When Dean arrived back to the cottage a few minutes later, the noises from inside sounded like *ten* angry babies in there, not *one*. Panic roiled inside of him, but he had nowhere to run. He was going to have to go inside and deal with this mess.

Maribel paced the floor with the screaming child. "Oh my God, you're back! Help!"

Her face flushed and pink, her eyes were nearly popping out of their sockets.

"What did you *do*? What's wrong with the baby?"

"You assume I did something to cause this? How about if you don't accuse me, and I won't accuse you?"

Somehow, he expected her to be better at this, though it might be unfair of him to assume so because she had a uterus. In his case, he would have done better at delivering this child than he probably would taking care of it. It couldn't be much different than assisting in the birth of a calf. And as a bonus, baby cows didn't cry.

"Make a bottle! Quick! She could be hungry. I've already changed her. You did buy more bottles, didn't you?"

Bottles. He forgot the bottles. Stupid Adam leading him to the pacifiers like they were made of gold when Dean should have focused on more bottles instead.

"She left one in the basket. Get it! Now!"

"Stop ordering me around."

He grabbed the bottle and a can of formula, grumbling the entire time.

What had she been doing when he'd been sweating in the store aisle over diapers? All she'd had to do was watch the baby. How hard could that be? She was a sweet little angel the whole fifteen minutes she'd been in his dresser drawer. Following the directions, he mixed the powder with water and poured it into the bottle, shook it then carried it over to Maribel.

"Did you warm it?"

"I was supposed to warm it? Here, give it back. I'll use the microwave."

"Not the microwave!" She hissed. "Good lord, you don't know *anything*. Here, you take her. I'll warm the bottle."

Dean took the baby, who didn't look anything like the

angelic little bundle from earlier. Now she was a wriggling mess with a wail that would kill most grown men. Her little hands were curled into fists like she was mad as hell. He swore he could see her tonsils.

"Hey, hey. Listen, I'm trying to help you. Look, I know you're mad your mama left, but that's not my fault. She'll be back. I hope."

She better come back. He was willing to give the mother the benefit of the doubt, but someone who would abandon her baby and never return was lower than dirt. He hoped she had a damn good excuse.

Dean did his best to pace, shuffle-walk and swing, imitating Maribel. Brianna stopped crying for one second when she opened her eyes, as if shocked someone else was holding her. Still clearly not the person she wanted. Her silence was a momentary lapse, as if taking a breath and gaining strength. She went right back to crying with rejuvenated energy.

"Okay." Maribel appeared with the bottle and pointed to his couch. "Already tested for temperature. Just sit down with her."

He'd never been this awkward and bumbling in his life, but did as Maribel ordered, resenting every second of her authority. Balancing Brianna in the crook of his elbow, he eased the rubber tip of the bottle into her open mouth. She sucked away at the bottle with fervor.

Maribel collapsed on the couch next to Dean. "Guess she was just hungry."

"Why didn't you feed her while I was gone?" The mother had left one can of formula and a bottle after all.

"Are you *kidding* me? You don't know how hard this is! I couldn't hold her and make the formula. I only have two hands, and she cried louder every time I put her down."

More and more, Dean worried he couldn't do this on his own. And she obviously couldn't, either.

"Are all babies this *loud*?"

"She has a good set of lungs on her. I thought she'd never stop." She leaned back. "Oh, would you listen to that?"

"What?"

"Silence. I never knew how much I loved it until it was gone."

He eyed Maribel with suspicion. "How long has she been crying? She was fine before I left."

"She just took one look at me and started wailing. It's hard not to take it personally." Maribel leaned forward, watching the baby take the bottle.

This put Maribel at his elbow, dark hair so close to him he could smell the coconut sweet flowery scent. Cute Stuck-up Girl smelled incredible. His irritation with her ebbed.

"Aw, she's so cute. Check out her perfect skin." She caressed the baby's cheek with the back of her hand.

If it could be said they were staring at the baby, which they probably were, she stared right back. Her dark eyes were wide as she took them both in. This was one smart baby, alert and aware *something* had changed.

"Thanks for helping me," Dean finally said. "I'm sorry if I sound grumpy. Obviously, I couldn't have done this without you."

"I saw how strongly you felt about this."

"I'd say we both have equally strong feelings."

She sighed and offered Brianna her finger, and the little hand fisted around it. "It's just… I've seen this kind of thing before too many times, and it doesn't end well."

"Never?"

Dean didn't want to hear this. He wanted to believe

the mother would return. Sometimes all a mother needed was for someone to have a little faith in her.

Sometimes that's all anyone needed.

"Not with abandoned babies. There's generally abuse in the home, a teenager trying to hide the unwanted pregnancy." She shook her head. "You don't want to hear the rest."

Dean swallowed hard. "But did anyone ever leave a note saying they'd be back for her baby?"

To Dean, the note the mother had left was filled with hope. He remembered too well the taste of hope. No one should be denied a second chance.

"Not to my knowledge."

"Then it's possible. You just haven't heard of any instances. Granted, I agree this is unusual."

"I want to believe she'll come back, but there have been too many disappointments along the line for me. Addiction is powerful. It overcomes love."

That was one belief Dean would never accept. Not in his lifetime.

"Sorry, no. Nothing can overcome love."

Maribel turned her gaze from the baby to him, forcing him to realize how close she was. She had a full mouth and deep brown eyes that shimmered with the hint of a smile. Damn, she was…breathtaking. Much better-looking close up. He'd noticed her, of course, on the beach wearing a skimpy red bikini, displaying long legs and a heart-shaped behind. They often passed each other: her sitting under the umbrella reading, him coming back from his surfing day. After their disastrous first meeting, she'd been easier to dismiss from a safe distance with a curt nod. Far easier than to remind himself he didn't need or want any complications like the type a beautiful woman would bring into his life.

Get your act together before you even think to ask someone to tag along.

Her lips quirked in the start of a smile. "That's...certainly not what I expected you to say."

"Why? You think cowboys don't believe in love?"

"Honestly, you'll have to forgive me because I'm not sure most *men* believe in love. Or at least, I'm not meeting them."

"Not sure who you've been dating, but that's a pretty sad statement."

"It is, isn't it?" Maribel leaned back, putting some distance between them, as if only now aware of how close she'd been. "I'm sorry to make such a blanket statement. You're right, there are some men who believe in love."

"But these are not the men you're dating. Why not?"

"Well, it's not like they wear a sign."

He snorted. "They don't wear a sign, but there are *signs*."

She simply stared at him for a moment as if she was still trying to decide whether or not he could be trusted.

"What are we going to do tonight?" She nudged her chin to Brianna. "About her?"

"We? I'll let her sleep in the drawer, or maybe I'll just lay her on the bed next to me."

She narrowed her eyes like she thought maybe this was a bad idea. "Are you a light or heavy sleeper?"

"Light." And lately, he hadn't been sleeping at all. But that was a story for another day. "It's a big bed. I won't roll over on her."

Maribel stood. "Okay. You take the first night, and tomorrow I'll take the second."

"You trust me? What if I'm some weirdo?"

"Some weirdo who wants to take care of a baby so her mother won't lose custody? I guess you're my kind of weirdo."

That wasn't enough for him. He pulled out his wallet and opened it to his driver's license, pointing to the photo. "This is me. Take a photo if you'd like."

She glanced at the ID. "That's you. But I…left my phone next door. I'm actually unplugging this vacation."

Unplugging. What a concept.

"I need your cell number anyway. What if I need you in the middle of the night because I'm in over my head here?"

"Just walk over and knock on my door. But…loudly. *I'm* a heavy sleeper."

"Lucky you." He walked her to the door. "Can we agree not to tell anyone else about the baby?"

"I think that's best. I'll check on you two in the morning."

But between old memories, a helpless baby and a beautiful woman next door, Dean would be lucky to get a wink tonight.

Nothing can overcome love.

He certainly wasn't like the men Maribel met on dating apps.

Maribel mulled those words over as she brushed her teeth and got ready for bed, changing into her 49ers long T-shirt. If she hadn't known any better, she'd have thought those words had come out of her own mother's mouth. Her mother often made such sweeping and general statements, seemingly drawing the world into patches of black and white. No gray.

But Maribel certainly did not expect this Greek Adonis–type man with the chiseled jawline and broad shoulders to utter such words. Or to behave with such tenderness and concern toward a baby. Her heart had squeezed tight watching this big man holding a tiny infant close against his chest, as if he'd single-handedly protect her from the world. He might think he could, but Maribel had news for him. It wasn't going to be easy and almost inevitably result in a pain not easily overcome.

He'd been surly with her since the moment they met, his physical countenance often matching his sharp and pointy words. Narrowed eyes, tight jaw. Rigid shoulders. Until that one sentence, laid out for her like a truth bomb. When he'd said the words, his eyes were soft and warm, his voice rich and smooth as mocha.

Is family reunification a myth?

With those words, he'd poured a metaphorical bucket of ice water over her.

Because she used to believe in families. She once believed parents could be reunited with their children simply because of the deep bonds of unconditional love. Parents were hardwired by biology to love their babies and protect them. She'd believed with all her heart before she came front and center with the gray area: addiction. Mental Illness. Poverty. Now, she still lived in those murky shadows. She wished she could see things differently and, as she had in the beginning, with a hope and belief that she could change the world. She now realized she could not.

And if the mother hadn't returned by tomorrow night, Maribel would call the police. Dean wouldn't take it well, and there was no point in preemptively starting an argument by revealing her plan. For now, she'd agreed to do this his way. It certainly didn't mean he would *always* get his way. By tomorrow night, maybe this wouldn't be an issue. The mother would be back, or the baby would be on her way to a competent foster home with a loving couple prepared to keep and nurture a baby.

She settled on her bed, pulling out her book to read before she went to sleep. Recently, on the advice of a friend who wrote a book and ran a website on avoiding burnout and rediscovering your purpose, Maribel had returned to print. Normally she read everything from her phone app, but according to her friend, she'd inadvertently zapped herself out of the joy of reading. Her goal here was to slow down, take her time, touch the paper pages and flip through them. Reading was an experience for more than one sense. It could be both tactile and visual. She'd somehow lost the joy of taking her time with something she loved.

Last week she'd visited Once Upon a Book with Stacy and loaded up on novels with happy endings. If it had a dog on the cover and a couple lovingly smiling, it got purchased. Some of her friends loved the raunchy and realistic stuff about the agonizing pain of breakups. If a book made them ugly cry, it became a forever favorite. Not Maribel. She'd had enough of real life. When she'd wanted to cry, when she wanted a knot in her stomach that wouldn't go away, all she'd had to do was read her case files.

In the first few days of reading print books again, she became aware of two things: her focus was lacking, and she almost didn't have the patience to slow down enough to *read*. So she continued to work at it one page at a time. This week on the beach under an umbrella. In fact, she'd had a quiet week until the baby showed up.

Outside, the sounds of soothing waves rolled in and out, and Maribel focused on turning the pages of her book. In no time at all, she was in the mountains of Humboldt County, where a handsome farmer had taken in a divorced mother of two looking for a new start. Sleep came easily, enveloping her in warmth.

The next morning, Maribel blinked, stretched and listened through the thin wall connecting both cottages. No baby crying. Hardly any noise at all outside. Only a sense of disturbing awareness pulsing and buzzing through her body that she couldn't ignore. Maribel could almost hear her sister Jordan's voice in her head.

Time to admit a few things.

Okay, yes, I'm attracted to the grumpy man. So what? Who wouldn't be?

He exuded alpha male confidence, and it had always been her lot in life to fall for the difficult men. For the ones with permanent scowls and surly attitudes. She couldn't seem to fall in love with someone sweet and kind like Clark, her nicest ex-boyfriend, who'd told her in no uncertain terms, "I'm sorry, Maribel, but you are sucking the life right out of me."

Ouch.

Maribel wasn't great at dating, having spent most of her childhood studying. It wasn't that she was trying to prove something, but early on, Maribel realized her strengths were in textbooks. Whether it was science, math or history, she slayed it. Testing wasn't an issue for her. Blessed with a nearly photographic memory, academia wasn't difficult. Boyfriends, at the time, were. This meant that essentially, she was a little socially hindered when it came to romantic relationships.

She'd tried online dating, setting up her profile on Tinder and the others. One of the men had turned out to be married, making her paranoid enough to check for wedding ring tan lines from that point on. One man had arrived at their coffee date looking perfectly presentable. Slacks, dark button-down, loafers. A face with good character, if not particularly handsome. No tan line. After ordering, he called himself a naughty boy, said he had to be punished from time to time and wanted a dominant woman.

She left without finishing her coffee, went home and removed her profile from that particular dating app.

Now, she went to the kitchen to make coffee, the quiet of the morning reverberating all around her. Dressing quickly, she walked next door to check on the baby. Dean had left the door unlocked, so she let herself inside. Tiptoeing through the connected rooms to the bedroom, she found the baby sound asleep in the drawer wrapped in blankets, her little fisted hands bracing her face, her sweet mouth softly suckling in her sleep.

Dean lay on his back on top of the blankets, wearing board shorts and—*oh my*—no shirt. He'd thrown one arm over his face like he wanted to block everything out. Suddenly, he sprang up on his elbows, eyes squinting into the brightness.

"What? *What?*"

Maribel startled and took two steps back. She hadn't said a word and, in fact, was barely breathing. He wasn't kidding about being a light sleeper.

"It's just…me," Maribel squeaked and held up both palms, surrender style. "Sorry. I woke up early and wanted to check on you two. Go back to sleep."

He ignored her and instead walked around the bed to check on the baby.

"She's doing fine," Maribel whispered. "You can relax."

"Now she's sleeping better than I did." He ran a hand down his face. It was only then she realized he'd gathered his hair into a short ponytail.

He had a good face, chiseled jaw and irresistible stubble.

Down, girl.

"Rough night?" She swallowed.

"She was up at two in the morning wanting…something. Gave her a bottle, but she just wanted to be… I don't know…held?" He scratched his chin, and the stubble made a low sound.

"So, you didn't get much sleep?"

"No big deal. Haven't slept well in a while. You?"

"Like a baby. A very nice rest, thanks."

It wasn't entirely true. She'd lain awake for an hour thinking about the baby. About Dean. The mother and whether or not she would return. Whether or not Maribel was doing the right thing giving her a chance to return before involving the authorities.

"Got news for you. Apparently, babies don't sleep. Kind of like me. If you slept well, you did *not* sleep like a baby."

"That could be why you're grumpy all the time." She cleared her throat when he gave her the side-eye. "What do you do about it?"

"I don't take medication if that's what you're asking."

"No, there's melatonin, which is natural. Personally, I recommend reading before bedtime. Something light and happy."

He turned to study her then, his amber eyes appearing darker near the irises. Well, if he was going to stare, she would stare right back. She wasn't intimidated by good-looking dudes with hot bodies. If someone looked away first, it wouldn't be *her*.

Let that be him. She met his eyes. With a baby between them and the fact it was morning, she couldn't escape the unnatural intimacy of the moment. She was in his bedroom just as he'd rolled out of bed. He stood at her elbow, arms crossed, so close her bare elbow brushed against his naked and warm skin.

And it seemed that a live wire lay sparking between them.

One half of his mouth tipped up in a smile. "How did I do? Did I pass the health inspection?"

Still meeting his gaze, she cleared her throat. "You did fine, obviously."

The gaze he slid her made bells and whistles go off in her head. Her body buzzed, and her legs tightened in response to the hint of a smile on his lips. Smiling, she'd decided, was overrated. Better than a smile was the start of one. The way it began in the eyes, moving slowly. Like a teaser of "coming attractions."

Damn it!

She looked away first, too unnerved by the blatant invitation in his eyes.

"Okay! I see everything is good in here. I'll make her a bottle for when she wakes up, and I can take her next door."

She thought she heard him mutter, "Chicken," as she quietly walked away.

Don't miss

A Charming Doorstep Baby
by Heatherly Bell,

available September 2023 wherever
Harlequin Special Edition books
and ebooks are sold.

www.Harlequin.com

Get 3 FREE REWARDS!

We'll send you 2 FREE Books <u>plus</u> a FREE Mystery Gift.

FREE
Value Over
$20

Both the **Harlequin® Special Edition** and **Harlequin® Heartwarming™** series feature compelling novels filled with stories of love and strength where the bonds of friendship, family and community unite.

YES! Please send me 2 FREE novels from the Harlequin Special Edition or Harlequin Heartwarming series and my FREE Gift (gift is worth about $10 retail). After receiving them, if I don't wish to receive any more books, I can return the shipping statement marked "cancel." If I don't cancel, I will receive 6 brand-new Harlequin Special Edition books every month and be billed just $5.49 each in the U.S. or $6.24 each in Canada, a savings of at least 12% off the cover price, or 4 brand-new Harlequin Heartwarming Larger-Print books every month and be billed just $6.24 each in the U.S. or $6.74 each in Canada, a savings of at least 19% off the cover price. It's quite a bargain! Shipping and handling is just 50¢ per book in the U.S. and $1.25 per book in Canada.* I understand that accepting the 2 free books and gift places me under no obligation to buy anything. I can always return a shipment and cancel at any time by calling the number below. The free books and gift are mine to keep no matter what I decide.

Choose one: ☐ **Harlequin Special Edition**
(235/335 BPA GRMK)

☐ **Harlequin Heartwarming Larger-Print**
(161/361 BPA GRMK)

☐ **Or Try Both!**
(235/335 & 161/361 BPA GRPZ)

Name (please print)

Address   Apt. #

City   State/Province   Zip/Postal Code

Email: Please check this box ☐ if you would like to receive newsletters and promotional emails from Harlequin Enterprises ULC and its affiliates. You can unsubscribe anytime.

Mail to the **Harlequin Reader Service:**
IN U.S.A.: P.O. Box 1341, Buffalo, NY 14240-8531
IN CANADA: P.O. Box 603, Fort Erie, Ontario L2A 5X3

Want to try 2 free books from another series? Call 1-800-873-8635 or visit www.ReaderService.com.

---

*Terms and prices subject to change without notice. Prices do not include sales taxes, which will be charged (if applicable) based on your state or country of residence. Canadian residents will be charged applicable taxes. Offer not valid in Quebec. This offer is limited to one order per household. Books received may not be as shown. Not valid for current subscribers to the Harlequin Special Edition or Harlequin Heartwarming series. All orders subject to approval. Credit or debit balances in a customer's account(s) may be offset by any other outstanding balance owed by or to the customer. Please allow 4 to 6 weeks for delivery. Offer available while quantities last.

Your Privacy—Your information is being collected by Harlequin Enterprises ULC, operating as Harlequin Reader Service. For a complete summary of the information we collect, how we use this information and to whom it is disclosed, please visit our privacy notice located at corporate.harlequin.com/privacy-notice. From time to time we may also exchange your personal information with reputable third parties. If you wish to opt out of this sharing of your personal information, please visit readerservice.com/consumerschoice or call 1-800-873-8635. **Notice to California Residents**—Under California law, you have specific rights to control and access your data. For more information on these rights and how to exercise them, visit corporate.harlequin.com/california-privacy.

HSEHW23

HARLEQUIN
PLUS

Try the best multimedia subscription service for romance readers like you!

Read, Watch and Play.

Experience the easiest way to get the romance content you crave.

Start your **FREE TRIAL** at
www.harlequinplus.com/freetrial.